CIRCUS CREEPS

SINNER'S SIDESHOW BOOK 1

AIDEN PIERCE

A Word of Warning

CIRCUS CREEPS IS ONE OF MY DARKER WORKS, SO PLEASE READ THIS WARNING CAREFULLY.

The characters within this book make a dark spectacle of themselves. Their story contains situations and themes that might be triggering to some such as gore, violence, murder, mentions of parental loss, horror elements, breath play, fear play, knife play, pain play, degradation, demonic clowns, exhibitionism, voyeurism, primal play/chasing, monster appendages, spitting, light vore, dub-con, consensual non-consent, non-con (not between MCs) and other graphic sexual content.

1
Admit One

MEG

Every monster within a fifty-foot radius either wanted to eat me or fuck me.

Perfect, just fucking *perfect.*

As if I didn't already feel like a fish out of water as the only half-blood that had come to watch the monster circus. It's not like I was food to the full-blooded monsters here, but I smelt enough like a human to turn heads as I made my way through the crowd toward the ticket booth.

As a circus brat, I was used to attention. When I performed in the ring, countless eyes watched me—usually with a twenty-five-inch sword shoved down my throat. So, attending another circus as a guest should have been a cakewalk. But...this wasn't like the human circus I'd grown up in.

This was Sinner's Sideshow, the supernatural circus from Hell.

The crowd that had crawled out of the darkness to witness the show was made up of countless other horrors of the night.

It's not that I was scared of them. What bothered me was how I was standing in line for a ticket, minding my own damn business, yet I was drowning.

Drowning in their bloodlust.

With the succubus blood running through my veins, I could feel the emotions of the people around me. Whenever I performed in the ring, I embraced the ability I'd inherited from my mother. I felt what my audience did.

Their thrill. Their wonder. Their fear.

I tasted it all. I craved it, feasted on it.

But the emotions of these monsters were on the...*intense* side. Even if I had the balls to feed on the thick energy in the air, I didn't dare. Not here.

This wasn't the place to bring attention to myself. I'd been stupid to come at all.

I was so out of my element here.

I hadn't performed in months. I hadn't fed in weeks. There was no way these people would accept me. Just because my mother had starred in Sinner's Sideshow years ago didn't mean *I* belonged.

Too bad I wasn't going to take no for an answer.

When the slow-moving line for the ticket booth finally moved, I shoved the slipping strap of my guitar case higher up my shoulder and shuffled forward.

A voice in my head screamed at me to run as far away from this place as possible. But that voice was easy to smother. Even if my succubus side was good at following instructions—which it certainly fucking *wasn't*—there was no point in running. There had to be hundreds of monsters here who could outrun my mortal ass, and I wasn't interested in being anyone's dinner. Not tonight, anyway.

At the thought of food, my stomach grumbled. Shit. I was starving. Real food wouldn't help. The hunger clawing at my gut couldn't be satiated with a carnival dog or a pretzel.

Whenever I got the urge to feed, I'd either find a public space like a grocery store or something and skim whatever emotions hung in the air. If I was really starving, I'd find some random guy to suck off and drain dry. I preferred the inconspicuous feeding from a crowd. If I didn't have to put some random guy's pathetic dick in my mouth, that would be a plus.

Too bad I couldn't do either here. Too risky, and I'd come too far to fuck this up now.

I'd been searching for Sinner's Sideshow for over two years. It had been a nightmare to find. It's not like I could just Google search the show towns and dates. It left no digital paper trail except for the occasional review on the dark web.

My mother's people still lived in the shadows. They didn't want humans to know about them, and to keep it that way, the circus had powerful magic that hid every tent, truck, animal, and even the attendees within its vicinity from the human eye.

As a half-blood, I'd been worried that I wouldn't be able to see it. But there it was, the infamous black and white big top looming ominously in the distance. The sight of it made my heart ache. I missed the circus I'd grown up in so damn much. I missed my dad. My friends.

All of it was long gone.

Squeezing my eyes shut, I summoned an old memory.

"Focus on your breathing," my father's voice echoed from the past. *"That's it, angel. Just like that. Always focus on your breathing when you're in the ring. And remember, don't—"*

"Lock my knees," a teenage me told him with a huff and a roll of my eyes. *"Yeah, Dad. I know."*

My father lowered his sword to the ground and sat on one of the hay bales in the ring. He'd patted the spot beside him, motioning for me to join him. "Then what's got you in a funk?"

I sat next to him, my knuckles paper white as they tightened around my sword's hilt. "I'm scared."

"Aw, honey. That's okay. If you don't want to do this tonight, we can push off your performance until the next town. Or the next state. Whenever you're ready. Or you can just do the usual sword-eating act. You've done that a thousand times. No need for the bells and whistles tonight."

"That's boring," I pouted. *"Everyone is coming to see a fire-eating sword swallower."*

My father brushed a piece of my soft pink hair from out of my eyes. "Meg, honey. You're so beautiful. People would come from miles around just to watch you twiddle your thumbs. Whatever you put out in that ring, they'll eat up. Now come on."

He rose to his feet and pulled me onto mine, his eyes dancing with pride. "You look so much like your mom. Especially in your new costume."

My father had barely ever mentioned my mom, but when he did, I always sensed a pang of fear beneath all the heartbreak. I'd never understood that.

A sigh wound from me as I pulled myself back to the present. The tight bodice of my old circus costume hugged my body from under my baggy hoodie. I'd had it altered since my days at Walker's Circus, but it was pretty much the same outfit.

Same sword. Same act.

Everything else had changed. My dad was dead, and so was Walker's. All I had now was my mission to find someplace where I didn't feel so lost.

"You're holding up the line, bitch."

My eyes shot open, and I slowly turned to face the asshole in line behind me. I guessed that he was some kind of shifter. Maybe a werewolf, judging by the pungent stench of mongrel.

When he registered my face, his eyes widened, and his anger fizzled into lust. "Damn, baby. I was gonna swing by the concessions before the show, but maybe you can be my snack tonight. What are you, anyway? Some kind of siren?"

My eyes narrowed on the shifter. "I'm someone with a sword that knows how to use it."

He licked his lips as they stretched into a skeevy smile. "A sword, huh? I got one of those."

"Yeah." I snorted. "I promise mine's bigger."

The werewolf opened his mouth, probably to spew some tired-ass pickup line, but the ticket attendant yelled for the next customer.

I stepped up to the wooden booth painted in black and white stripes to match the big top. The man behind the counter had grayish skin, pointed ears, and a hooked nose so long it stretched past his lips. He reminded me of the goblins in the *Harry Potter* movies.

"One adult, please."

The goblin gave me a once-over through slitted eyes. "No humans allowed."

"I'm a demon," I told the attendant, donning my unshakable stage smile. "How else would I have been able to find this place?"

He gave a *hmph*.

I pulled out a wad of crumpled bills from my sweatshirt pocket and threw it down on the counter. "I'm a paying customer just like everyone else."

The goblin's suspicion seemed to ease into guarded intrigue as he noted my soft pink eyes. He pointed a finger tipped with a yellowed claw at the guitar case on my back, covered in brightly covered stickers, then pointed to a sign that read: *No outside weapons, drugs, instruments, explosives, or firearms.*

I blinked as I noted the word *outside*. Damn. Their concessions and merch tables had to be pretty wild.

My smile turned sickly sweet. "I don't have any of that. Just lip gloss. Gum. Some body spray." Plus, a twenty-five-inch serrated sword with a canister of isopropyl alcohol, but he didn't need to know that. "I use the guitar case as a purse. I'm one of those "weird girls" you always see on TV."

"Oh, for fuck's sake, Creature. Just sell the girl a damn ticket. You're holding up the line."

I turned my head in the direction of the sing-song voice to find a woman leaning against the side of the ticket booth, her arms folded over her chest. She was covered in colorful tattoos, a lot of them colorful depictions of candy. She wore a pink tank top, a purple plaid skirt, fishnets, and knee-high boots.

The most notable thing about her was her hair, or rather, her lack of hair. On her head was a nest of snakes. Living snakes!

The snake-haired woman grinned at me. "She's a succubus."

"She doesn't smell like a sex demon," Creature scoffed.

"That's because I buy the good deodorant," I sniped.

The woman rolled her eyes and wrapped her knuckles on the side of the booth. "Pretty sure that ancient nose of yours is out of whack, you old bag of bones. Now give her the stupid ticket before the ringmaster finds out you turned away a paying customer."

Fear flashed behind the monster's eyes. "D—don't tell the ringmaster. Here." He quickly handed me a ticket while flinging a glare at the snake-haired woman. "If she gets eaten, don't come crying to me."

"Ugh," she said when we were out of earshot from the ticket booth. "You think he would have seen a half-blood before. You could have just used your succubus powers on him, you know."

I wasn't used to feeling so comfortable around another person. But then again, it had been a long time since I'd been around anyone who hadn't given me weird vibes. This girl's energy was curious, but kind.

"I don't really like doing it. It feels sketchy," I admitted after a beat. The last time I'd used it was to get out of a speeding ticket, five months ago. So I was rusty as hell.

"Sketchy?" Her brows arched high into her hairline, where a snake draped itself across her brow. "Then this is the perfect place to use it, babe. What's your name?"

"Meg."

"I'm Lollie. I work the concession stands here with my sister."

I couldn't take my eyes off the snakes in her hair as they slithered and hissed, their tongues flicking out to taste the air. "Um, Meg? You're staring."

"Shit." I shook my head. "I'm sorry. I didn't mean to."

She laughed. "That's okay. Gorgons are rare. Most of us don't have legs, so we don't make it to the Upside too often. But this is the circus, girl. Where vampires and other basic bitch monsters of this realm come to gawk at all the monstrosities that crawl up from the Downside."

The gorgon's gaze churned with thought, her attention drifting past my shoulder to the guitar case on my back, with its worn hot pink casing and faded gothic stickers. "But you're not here to stare, are you?"

Her perception caught me off guard. "How did you know?"

She shrugged one shoulder. "Half-bloods don't come here for the show. It's a little high-octane for most."

"High-octane?"

"Uh, yeah," she said with a silent *duh* punctuating her sentence. She flicked her hair in a fashion that would remind me of a preppy girl if it wasn't for all the hissing snakes. "This is a show where Monsters from Upside come to see what all the horrors of the Downside are like. Without actually having to go there. Although some actually do go there."

"Wait, you mean people die at the show?"

"Yup. Usually, only people who want to die. But you know, accidents happen," she added with a half-shrug. "So whatever reason you're here, just keep your head straight and stay safe, 'kay?"

A blood-curdling scream from inside the big top had Lollie nervously tucking a snake behind her ear. "Um. On second thought, maybe I should escort you to your seat inside? The front entrance is a haunted house you have to get through before you make it to the main house."

"A haunted house?" At that, I perked up. I loved spooky shit.

Lollie laughed. "Don't get too excited. It's pretty horrifying. People actually get hurt in there. Some of the goons running the thing might give you some trouble."

I chewed my lip as screams of delight and terror rose up from the tent's entrance, pulsating strobe lights and smoke from the fog machine pouring out from the open flap. "What kind of trouble?"

Lollie didn't answer verbally. She didn't have to. The look she gave me had a flood of fear and excitement shimmering through my veins.

"Come on, let's get this over with." She took hold of my arm, leading me into the mouth of the tent. "Oh, and uh, I hope you're not afraid of clowns."

2

Masochist's Paradise

MEG

The haunted house was rank with the scent of fear and sweat, and beneath that lust—the sour kind that made my stomach churn. It should have been enough to dispel my succubus hunger.

It only made it worse.

When I slowed to take a breath—a failed attempt to clear my lungs—Lollie turned. Her brows popped so high they almost sank into the scaly hairline. "You alright?"

"Oh, peachy." I scrunched my nose and forced a smile. "I just love the smell of monster taint and lust. Not the fun kind, either. *Unwashed* taint, and the kind of lust that comes from people who get turned on by rubber masks and plastic butcher knives."

There was also a sinister energy, but I didn't mention that. It didn't sit right with me for several unnerving reasons.

Sometimes I hated my succubus urges. It was awkward being hungry at the most inopportune times and sometimes over the most innocuous shit. Like fresh clothes out of the dryer at the laundromat. The models with really white teeth in dentist advertisements. That one time I found out tampons were two for one at the cash register, and I was able to buy Taco Bell with the extra five bucks.

This wasn't the first haunted house I'd been in. I'd been to some pretty scary ones, including one where you had to sign a waiver, allowing them to put their hands on you. Each time I'd gone in one, I'd gotten butterflies in my tummy. This time around, they were more like hornets, but the excitement was still there, making every sinew in my belly pull taut.

Yup. Out of all the weird shit that had ever gotten me going, this place took the cake.

There was a female scream from a corner of the haunted house, followed by the heavy pound of male footsteps. A second later came the rattle of a chain and a lustful moan.

Lollie blinked through the murky red lighting that illuminated the tent. Could she see me blushing?

"*Oh.*" A look of realization smoothed the creases of her expression. "You're a succubus. You can feel emotions and eat them, right? Makes sense why you're all hot and bothered. Must suck getting turned on by weird shit and have no control over it." There was no judgment in her voice, only understanding.

"I'm sure it could have its perks if I had anything resembling a sex life."

Lollie's lips flattened as if she found this news deeply troubling. "Don't you feed?"

"Only when I have to. I feed from people's auras, just a little bit from a lot of people at once if I'm in a crowded space. That doesn't work if I'm really thirsty, though."

"What do you do then?"

"I'll find some guy to blow. But human men make me nauseous, so it never gets further than that."

Lollie blinked once, twice, three times at me. "You mean it *never* gets further than that?"

I chewed my bottom lip as Lollie intensely stared me down. The haunted house, with all its fake blood and screams and smoke, wasn't even half as scary as being caught under the gorgon's scrutinous gaze. Still, it was nice having someone to talk about this stuff with. I'd only just met her, but it somehow felt like I'd already known her for years. Her aura was safe and comforting.

"Yeah...I guess my succubus side doesn't want me doing it with human guys. At least not for the first time. And I'm never around monsters, at least ones that don't give me the serious ick."

"Shit." Her voice dropped, and she leaned in, her snakes hissing as if to cover her whisper. "Keep that info on the down-low, girl. Especially around here. There are a lot of creeps that would stoop to some pretty messed up shit if it meant sinking their claws into a virgin succubus."

She looked this way and that, making sure no one heard us before pulling us deeper into the haunted house. "If you're hungry, at least you can feed here. Even if it's just a snack."

"Feed? Here?"

She shrugged. "Safer than out in the yard or the main house. Just don't be too obvious with it."

I couldn't argue with that. This space was enclosed enough, protecting me from the mob of people outside should someone take notice that there was a sex demon leeching on the vibes in the air.

"I don't know. The vibes are off in here," I told Lollie as we were forced to stop, our path temporarily blocked by an animatronic grim reaper, lowering his plastic scythe to block our path.

The entire palace oozed ominous energy.

"People get hurt here, don't they?" I wasn't just talking about the haunted house. The entire circus grounds reeked of death.

"Only all the time, girl. Don't worry, though." With a maniacal laugh, the grim reaper lifted his scythe, and we continued our stroll through a graveyard of Styrofoam tomb markers stained in what I was sure was real blood. "The people who come here know what they're getting into. Most of the ones that get fucked or bitten or the occasional limb lopped off are usually into it." There was a moment of silence, as if in respect for the people that had made her add "usually" to her statement.

"Most like it?"

"Well, yeah. Sinner's Sideshow is a masochist's paradise, Meg."

Every nerve in my body twitched with intrigue, and excitement thrummed through my circulation. "Really?"

"You had to know that."

I'd shock her with the things I didn't know about this place. "I was raised by humans. I know fuck all, Lollie. This is an, erm, educational experience for me."

Lollie stared at me for several more seconds before shaking her head. "Girl. This place is gonna chew you up and swallow you if you're not careful."

I ran my tongue over the inside of my lip. She'd meant that as a warning. Instead, my body throbbed with anticipation.

I had to be careful. There was a part of me that was more than happy at the notion of getting eaten.

With my arm looped through Lollie's, we made our way through the haunted house. It was mostly one large room with different paths and sections, separated by hay bales and gothic fencing made out of foam. Some of the decor was really cheesy, with plastic tombstones and animatronic witches with blinking eyes and mechanical cackling.

Then there was the decor that looked too real, like the iron cages shoved off to the corners of the tent and the skeletons that filled them, their fingers gripped around the bars and their jaws open in an eternal scream.

The decorations were eerie and definitely added to the spooky atmosphere of the place. But the real dick kicker, as far as the vibes went, was the thick layer of fear and lust strangling the oxygen out of the space.

It was the haunt workers. They were perfectly dedicated to their role of scaring the ever-loving shit out of the monsters passing through. And they scared more than the crap out of them by the puddles of vomit and piss we had to step over. Lollie jerked on my arm, making me take a sharp sidestep to avoid yet another mysterious puddle.

"Gross. Clean up on aisle three," she joked, her whimsical laugh blending with the rev of a chainsaw and screams of terror in the background.

The next puddle we came across had a man hunched over it on his hands and knees, sucking up the fluid with growl-laced slurps.

Lollie stopped in front of him and propped a hand on her hip. "Sinclair, you're disgusting. At least suck it out of a person, you pathetic leech."

The man slowly lifted his face. Even through the murky lighting, I could tell the man was as pale as death.

"Hey, Lollie-pop. What are you doing coming in through the entrance all these other worthless cattle come through?"

"We got fresh blood tonight, Sin. Meg. This is my rat bastard boyfriend, Sinclair."

"What are you, some kind of tour guide now, babe?"

"No, I'm making sure no one takes a bite out of her."

He licked his blood-soaked lips, his fangs glinting. "I could go for a lick."

The chunky heel of Lollie's boot pushed down on the top of his head, smashing his face into the puddle of blood he'd just been drinking from. He sputtered, sending ruby-red droplets spraying across my pink Converse.

I looked down at the gore-stained fabric of my already-worn sneakers. They did look cooler this way.

"Try it, and I'll crush your skull in," Lollie giggled, her snakes hissing and writhing around their mistress' head.

Sinclair moaned, and on the next beat, his lust bled into the air. "Damn, baby. What are you doing after the show?"

"You. If you behave. You can show me how many licks it takes to get to my center. But you have to count."

A hearty groan of agreement dropped from his bloody lips.

"That's a good vampire," she snickered as she lifted her boot. The second he was free, he shot up and grabbed a fist full of her snakes, yanking her head back with a vicious tug.

I was so close to shifting. But the sounds of pleasure wrenching from her throat had me taking a step back.

"Bite me," she said, her eyes lighting with challenge.

The vampire picked her up, dumped her on a hay bale and in a blink, he was on top of her, the hay staining red as he fed from her.

"I—I'll just be a minute, Meg," she groaned, most of her body concealed from the cape draped over the vampire's shoulders.

"Ah, you have to give me more credit than that, Lollie-pop," Sinclair the vampire said with a dark chuckle. "It will be at least five."

"Um. That's okay." I slowly backed away with an awkward chuckle. "You guys take all the time you need. I'll just explore." I wandered down a different path, their heaving breathing fading behind me.

I plopped myself down on a fake jack-o-lantern, the lightbulb from inside its mouth painting the inside of my thighs with a wash of gold lighting. I pulled out my cell from my hoodie pocket to check the time.

It was still a while before the show started. Maybe this was the time to feed. Lollie was right. This was probably the safest place for me to sate my ache. I could feed on them, but somehow, that didn't feel right.

A giggling woman ran past at a pace that suggested she wanted to be caught. A man wearing a rubber clown mask charged after her, holding a knife over his head while his other hand cupped his crotch. "When I catch you, girlie, I'll let you pick which weapon I stab you with!"

I stared after the couple, debating if I should follow them and hang back just far enough away that they wouldn't notice me feeding from them. No, that didn't feel right either. Plus, that would only make me more hungry. What I needed was someone all to myself. I could drink in so much more when I had physical touch with someone. The thought of feeding from a supernatural for the first time ever had me pocketing my phone and shoving to my feet.

I wandered aimlessly through the haunted house until a shriek filled the air, freezing me in place. There'd been so many screams, but this one was different. There was no thrill underlying this scream.

I followed the intense trail of fear and loathing coming from the direction of the screams. Rounding a corner, I found myself at a dead end.

I wasn't alone.

A woman was on her back, with a man on top of her. If he could be called that. His flesh was pocked and peeling. He had yellow-puss filled boils around the corners of his eyes and mouth, and he stunk of decay.

He was a ghoul, one that was easily twice the size of the girl he held down with ease, even though she was struggling to free herself. Her clothes were torn, exposing her tiny breasts, and he'd ripped her jeans down to her ankles, exposing herself to him. His pants hung slack around his waist, exposing an asscrack stained with shit and who the hell knew what else.

Holding her thighs open, he fucked her so harshly against the ground her body made a sickening "thumping" sound with every thrust that could be heard over her screams. With one hand on her throat, he moved the other to cover her mouth.

"What's the matter? Can't handle a little poke? Stop your struggling, and it will be over soon."

The blood in my veins turned ice cold.

I'd never killed anyone before. Sure, I was a demon. But my last "victim" was a cop I'd enamored to get out of a parking ticket, for Christ's sake. I wasn't a murderer.

That would change tonight.

3

A Fear of Clowns

MEG

I backed up several steps, far enough so the monster wouldn't hear me, and found an alcove with a cauldron and three animatronic witches gathered around it, laughing with their big spoons as they cooked a fake, screaming child.

Unshouldering the straps of my guitar case, I lowered it to the ground and flipped the lid open. My dad's sword sat nestled inside, wrapped up in one of my old favorite t-shirts—a black baby tee with a big-breasted ghost wailing "booobs" on the front. I pulled the blade from the roll of fabric and, with it in hand, made my way back to the ghoul and his victim.

Taking the hilt in both hands, I raised the sword, keeping the blade vertical to the ground.

The evil blood and flesh lust radiating from this sack of rotting shit should have unnerved me. Instead, I felt invigorated.

Finally, a fucking meal served with a side dish of piping hot revenge.

"Hey, fuck rag," I growled, my voice dripping with poison.

The ghoul stopped his brutal assault for just a moment and turned his head to peer at me through the haunted house's dim lighting. A slow grin curved his disgusting mouth. "Don't worry, baby. You can have a turn next."

Anger possessed me like...well, like a demon.

It wasn't often that I shifted. Growing up as a human, I avoided it as much as possible—except on stage, where I could pretend it was a part of my costume. But I didn't bother suppressing it now.

There was a sharp pressure as my little black horns sprouted from my skull, sharp like traditional devil horns, only positioned closer together over my brow. My tail pushed out of the hole made special for my costume, long and thin, wrapping around one of my thighs. My small wings folded beneath my hoodie, staying tucked out of sight.

Most demons had horns and claws, and only female sex demons had wings.

The ghoul's jaw dropped. His stench of bloodlust was so potent now my stomach flipped. "By Discord's Depths. Look at you. I bet your flesh tastes better than this bitch's." The ghoul pulled out of the girl with a sickening sound. She whimpered and crumpled into a fetal position.

"Discord's Depths is exactly where I'm about to send you. I don't know if I believe in Discord. Or Satan or Lucifer or whatever you want to call him. But for your sake, I hope he's real. And I hope he's as twisted as everyone says."

The ghoul slowly stretched to his full height. His bottomless eyes dropped to the sword in my hand while he fisted his own. "What you gonna do with that little needle?"

I smiled, sweet and wide. My pink eyes glowed, and my succubus charm spread from me like poison. Sensing danger, the ghoul took an awkward step back but didn't turn to run. My magic had already crept inside him, keeping him rooted where he stood.

He smiled, the stretch of his mouth popping a blister. The puss oozed down his chin, and I had to suppress the urge to vomit. "Damn, you're an ugly fuck."

Ripping my attention off the ghoul, I stepped around him and crouched beside the girl. She was sobbing now. "Hey. It's going to be okay." I picked a piece of the ghoul's rotting flesh from her tangled blonde hair.

I wasn't really sure how to comfort her other than giving her what I knew was going to make me feel better. "Here, stand up."

I helped her to her feet, took her hand in mine and guided it to grip my sword with me, my hand over hers. "Hold it up."

The girl's eyes widened as it dawned on her that her attacker was in some sort of trance. "What did you do to him?"

"I charmed him. He'll do anything we say. But we gotta be quick. The spell won't hold forever."

"T–tell him to walk forward." Her voice trembled, unsure but assertive enough to let me know she was going to hold it together long enough to rid the world of this waste of space.

"Come here, big guy. We have something for you," I sing-songed.

The giant ghoul lumbered forward. He was so wrapped up in my magic that strings of drool trickled from his mouth, streaking through the puss coating his face. He walked toward us and didn't slow, even as the point of my sword cut into his stomach.

He pushed himself onto the blade until the weapon shuddered and punched through on the other side. The foulest of odors poured from his torn open stomach, along with an opaque, yellowish fluid and all sorts of other odious goodies.

It was only when the monster was fully impaled on the sword that I let up on the charm spell, just enough for him to understand what was happening to him.

"See that?" I laughed as I gently twisted the girl's hand so the serrated edge of the sword dug in, tearing up his insides. "See the terror in his eyes?"

I drank in the monster's fear and regretted it. It was rancid and sat heavy in my gut.

I stabbed him, jerking the girl's arm along with mine, and followed it up with another few jabs for good measure.

"S–stop," he gurgled. Nasty ghoul's blood bubbled at his lips. "P–please."

"What's the matter? Can't handle a little poke? Stop your struggling, and it will be over soon." I smiled sweetly, repeating the words he had said to the girl as he'd raped her.

The stark horror washing over his boiled face had me smiling. "Have fun in the Downside, trash."

I raised my foot, placing it on his stomach and pushed, sliding him off the blade. He fell to the ground with a deafening *thunk*.

I let the girl's hand go. I didn't need to tell her what to do. She knew ghouls didn't like staying dead. She stood over him, tears of hatred beading in her eyes. She stabbed his neck. Again and again, until it was hanging on by just a few ragged tendons as she grunted with each ruthless thrust.

After a dozen more stabs, she kicked the head, sending it flying across the tent. There was a clattering sound, followed by the delighted screams of a group of monsters.

"It looks so real," a girl gushed, her voice distant.

"It's disgusting," a male's voice said, followed by retching.

I looked at the girl standing next to me, her face sheet white. The sword clattered to the ground. I wasn't sure what to say or if there was anything I could say to take away her pain beyond what I'd already done.

Before I could do anything else, she shifted. She was a girl one moment, and in the blink of an eye, she was a small bunny, her snow-white fur caked in blood. As soon as she was gone, my knees buckled. My legs refused to hold me up.

I gasped for air, but no matter how many gulps I took, my lungs still screamed for more.

What was happening to me?

Was this shock?

I'd been so calm before. Maybe now that the bastard was dead and I didn't have to stay strong for the girl, my nerves were taking over. Or maybe I was having a bad reaction to the fear I'd drained from the ghoul. I shouldn't have done that. I'd never fed on fear before, and my body was rebelling. It was like eating eight greasy cheeseburgers, only this wasn't real food, so I couldn't just throw it up.

It sat heavy in my soul.

Burning me up like a fever. Eating at my insides like a parasite.

I curled up on the ground beside the headless ghoul, my mind a whirlwind of thoughts.

I'd come so far, and I'd fought so hard to be here. I couldn't let a botched feeding ruin everything now.

Was this supposed to be a sign from the universe? That a half-blood like me didn't belong at a circus for monsters? I mean, I couldn't even make it through the fucking entrance.

I began to spiral, giving in to the self-doubt.

Then...footsteps pulled me from my darkness.

Was it Lollie and her vampire boyfriend? Other haunted house goers? Would they help me, or just help themselves like the ghoul had with that bunny shifter?

I reached for my sword, my fingers fumbling with the hilt. Before I could grasp it, a large leather boot covered in mysterious stains stepped on the blade, keeping it pinned to the floor.

My gaze followed the long legs wrapped in tight black pants to find a horrifying clown looming over me. His rubber mask leered down at me with painted lips twisted in a smile filled with shark-like teeth and tufts of white and black hair sticking out on top. The mask was the only unappealing thing about the clown. The rest of him was dark perfection. His pants displayed his thick, muscular thighs and the sizable bulge between them. He had on a tight black shirt and a leather harness layered over it, loaded up with all sorts of knives. The tendons and veins bulged against the black cuffs and chained bracelets on his wrists.

He looked like something straight out of an erotic nightmare, bathed in the haunted house's sensual red lighting.

"That was beautiful, little demon," a deep voice growled from behind the mask.

"We saw what you did to that ghoul." I looked in the direction of the second voice to see a second clown standing at my feet. His outfit was almost identical to the first one, only this one wore a white shirt, and his mask had upside-down hearts over his eyes instead of diamonds.

"Y–you saw?"

"That's right. Hot as fuck. What are you? Our little harbinger of justice? A dark angel sent here to clean up our mess?" the clown with the white shirt asked with a rolling chuckle that had goosebumps exploding over my skin.

My brain fumbled for words as it was still coming to terms with the fact that there were *two* of them.

"Th–thanks for the help, assholes," I finally bit out several seconds later.

The clowns laughed almost in perfect unison. For some reason, their laughter sunk straight through my body to settle like a hot coal in my belly, scorching at first, but the warmth quickly spread.

"We noticed the bunny right around when you did. And it looked like you had it under control. It was impressive for a half-blood succubus," the one wearing a black shirt admitted.

My breath hitched. *They knew.*

The clown with his foot on my sword hunched down, his rubber sneer filling my entire field of vision. "Now that you took out the trash for us, the question is..."

The second clown leaned in, picking up where the other clown left off. "What do we do with *you?*"

4

Don't Feed the Clowns

MEG

My mouth froze into an "o" shape as the clowns crouched down to grab me by the arms and drag me away. It wasn't their blood-soaked clown getups or the off-putting masks that looked like they were straight out of *Killer Klowns from Outer Space*. It was the way they smelled. Beneath the metallic fragrance of blood and grime was a musky testosterone with a hint of something sweeter.

I imagined the kind of faces that would go with their scent and their chiseled bodies. Sharp jawlines. Handsome smiles beneath the goofy rubber ones.

Jesus. What was wrong with me? Here I was, being dragged off by two strange monsters in masks, and all I could think about was how sexy they were.

"W–where are you taking me?"

"Not far. Someplace no one will see us."

I should have been scared. Maybe I was a little. But the small pang of fear only seemed to heighten the excitement flooding my system.

"I think our little toy wants us to play with her, bro. You smell that? Succubus pheromones."

"How long has it been since you've fed, little harbinger?"

The concern in the male's tone caught me off guard. "Um. Weeks."

The one wearing the white shirt made a *tsk*ing sound behind his mask. "Silly girl. Sex demons shouldn't come to crowded spaces starving. That's a good way to have a mass murder."

"It's also a good way to start an orgy."

"I'm not a murderer, and I've got my hunger under control," I snapped.

"Hmm. I wonder what your ghoul friend back there would have to say about that."

"I killed him because he was a rapist piece of trash. His death was too good for him. I should have cut off his dick and made him choke on it."

"He *was* trash. And a beautiful thing like you has no business feeding on crap like that. Now you're sick." Black Shirt dragged me into the alcove where I left my guitar case behind the cackling witch's cauldron. Their cauldron was large enough to conceal us from anyone walking past.

The clown crouched over me, his attention presumably on my guitar case propped against the cauldron by the angle of his head. "That yours?"

"Uh, yeah. I use it to carry my sword."

I lifted my head even though every muscle in my body screamed at me to stay still until the pain subsided. The second clown was nowhere in sight. "Where's Thing Number Two?"

The clown gave a small laugh. Again, the sound coming from behind the mask was nice, a stark contrast to the monster's costume. "If that's a pop culture thing, I'm afraid I don't know the reference. I've been watching a lot of movies to catch up on human lingo, but at the end of the day I'm still just a monster from the Downside."

A Downside monster? Lollie briefly mentioned that she was from the Downside, but she didn't seem like a monster from Hell. With this guy, on the other hand, a thousand possibilities lurked beneath his mask.

"What, no Dr. Seuss in Hell?" I tried to joke but winced. It was like the fear I had taken from the ghoul with solidifying inside me, hardening like cement.

"Afraid not. And my brother probably went to clean up your mess. No one will know what happened."

"What, so I owe you now?"

"You do."

"Fuck off." I slashed my claws at his face—since I was still shifted, my pretty pink manicure was razor sharp. I could split his throat if he came close enough. That would make kill number two for the day. Although the thought of killing this one made me sad for some reason. Probably the vibe I was getting from him. He didn't seem evil or nefarious.

If anything, I could finally breathe again while he was close.

He kept his grip tight on my wrist, and even though I couldn't see through the mesh screens behind the gaping clown eyes, I could feel his gaze burning into me.

Just to throw me for another loop, his thumb rubbed gentle little circles on the inside of my wrist. "Are you okay?"

"Why do you care? Isn't this the part where you eat me?"

I expected him to laugh again. Instead, he canted his head, and I felt his stare intensify. "Do you want me to eat you?"

There was no inflection in his tone to suggest it was a joke. He was asking a serious question.

Yes. No. *Fuck*. Maybe.

I was still laying on my back with him crouched beside me, the fire under the cauldron—made of an orange LED bulb, a fan, and strips of cloth—consuming us in an amber light.

Suddenly, it was as if the ball of tension inside me exploded. I doubled over, curling up on my side. I ground my teeth together so hard it felt like they might crack.

Beads of sweat pebbled my brow. My hair stuck to my temples. I felt disgusting.

This was the part where the clown was supposed to back off. I felt like any minute, I was going to combust from both ends. This was worse than the food poisoning I'd gotten once from a bad shrimp burrito.

But he threw me when he got on his side, looped in around my middle, and pulled me close to him.

Here I was, sick to my stomach, spooning a clown behind a plastic cauldron a few feet away from the headless ghoul I'd just murdered. And who said romance was dead?

"If you feed from somebody else on a stronger emotion, you'll feel better."

"That's what this is? You make yourself look like the hero just to get in my pants?"

He let out a dark laugh. "That's one way of thanking me for cleaning up your mess and offering you a meal."

He leaned over, his hand flat against the ground in front of me, caging me against his hard chest. He was so warm, and his aura was...comforting. It was a stark contrast to his rough, hunger-laced voice filtering through the mask's grinning mouth.

"We both know you want me to touch you, little harbinger," he said, his steely voice wrapped in velvet. "You might be mortal, but you're still a sex demon. Your body knows when it's found a suitable victim."

Victim. Ha. That was hardly the word I'd use for him. But he wasn't wrong. When I came too close to a human man, I always got nauseous. Sometimes if I was really hungry, I'd be able to stomach a blow job. But they were never, ever able to touch me.

Was it a "good" idea to allow this clown to—shit, I didn't even know what he had in mind. I wasn't about to lose my virginity to a guy in a clown mask, even if the idea didn't turn me off.

I wanted to do *something* though. I'd never been with a monster. Curiosity was eating me alive.

I closed my eyes, trying to steady my rioting heart. "What are you going to do to me?"

He trailed the back of his knuckles down my arm, making the little hairs stand up in the wake of his touch. "Nothing you don't want me to."

I would have snorted if even the slightest rumble of my chest wasn't total agony. "Well, aren't you just the proper fucking gentleman."

"Not really. Not usually, anyway. But you just watched a girl get raped, and you brutally murdered the bastard for the trouble. I'm not dumb enough to be the second male monster to get on your shit list tonight, harbinger. Not when I've seen what you can do with that sword."

I twisted around to look at the clown, even though it hurt. For some reason, next to this stranger, the pain wasn't so bad. "I don't have my sword now, so you're safe."

"I don't think so. You have other ways of ripping out my bowels." The clown took my wrist, my pulse launching into light speed as I watched him guide my fingers to his neck and slip them up and under his mask.

A moan caught in my throat when I felt his wet lips close around my manicured claw. His tongue ran over the razor-sharp tip, the wet appendage painting teasing strokes over my flesh.

"This is the part where you start feeding, harbinger."

Why did he keep calling me that? I wasn't the harbinger of anything. I'd come here for...My mind splintered, losing my train of thought. Oh, *God.*

The clown's mouth closed around my finger, the suction on such an innocent part of my body making my thighs tremble and the place between them heat. The lust rolled off of him in waves, the invisible energy filling my mouth and sliding down my throat, smooth and easy.

His lust was the best thing I'd ever tasted. It was rich, velvety and jagged all at the same time. It had weight to it, making me feel...full. Not in a sated way. It was like he was inside me, stretching me, making himself right at home within my heat.

Something inside me came to life, something that had been dormant until now.

"Touch me." The words clawing from my throat barely sounded like my own. "Make this go away."

Whatever was awakening inside me, it didn't give two fucks that I was begging a clown to pleasure me. Right now, all that mattered was the drug that was this monster—whatever he was behind the mask, it didn't matter—and how he felt against me, around me, *inside* me.

Pulling my finger from his mouth, he grabbed my horn and shoved my cheek to the ground. He rolled on top of me, his other hand wedging underneath me to snake under the hem of my hoodie.

"Anytime you want me to stop, you say 'playtime's over,'" he huffed into my ear, the rubber mask's red nose so close the scent of it filled my nostrils. "Got it?"

"The killer clown is giving me a safe word? That's so *cute*."

His grip on my horn tightened. "Big talk coming from a virgin."

The air between us turned molten. Fuck. He knew that, too? How had he known I was a succubus, a half-blood, and a virgin? What *was* he?

"That's right, baby." The pads of his fingers stroked the ridges of my horn. "I can smell your hymen from here."

"That's creepy."

His hand skimmed over my inner thigh to rub over the fabric covering my apex. "Says the demon who's wet with the thought of a stranger in a clown mask railing her in a haunted house."

Strangled noises escaped from my mouth as he smashed my face into the filthy ground, fingers slipping beneath the thin strip of fabric covering my pussy.

"What are you wearing? Is this a costume? And what's with the sword, anyway? You're not supposed to have that in here."

"Are you wanting to play twenty questions, or do you want to play with *me?*"

"Good point. That's fine. I don't need answers from you. All I need is this sweet pussy dripping for me."

Drip, it did.

The stroke of his fingers through my folds turned me to liquid.

"Shaved pussy. I like that," he gritted out, his breath coming out harsher—muffled by his mask.

"I don't give a shit what you like," I groaned into the foam slab I laid on, meant to look like old-fashioned cobblestone.

"Bullshit. I think you do. Otherwise, you wouldn't have much of a meal from me, would you? You've got me so hard, little harbinger. You feel this?"

I did feel it. The lust seeping from him was almost too much for me to take, but I couldn't drink from him. I'd never gorged myself silly on a man before. My body had never let me. I'd had a boyfriend once, one of the jugglers at Walker's Circus. He'd been nice enough. Boring but nice. I could always touch him, but every time it came to him touching me, my body would rebel. I'd always gotten nauseous, which would immediately kill the mood.

That's why I was still a virgin.

I'd always suspected that my succubus blood wasn't opposed to men. It was opposed to human men. So now that I was finally getting a taste of what it felt like to be touched, *really* touched, I couldn't get enough.

"I asked if you *feel* me, girl," the stranger snarled, pressing his hips forward. When something pressed against my ass, I realized he wasn't talking about his incorporeal hunger.

He was talking about his rock-hard cock.

"Fuck. I–I feel you—oh! *God.*" Intense pleasure shot through my body, and he brought his weight down on me, crushing my clit against his fingers.

"While you're here, little half-blood, you make all your prayers out to Discord."

"I— I d–don't worship the devil," I sputtered, barely able to articulate as his fingers stroked circles over my clit.

"Then you can worship us," another voice said.

The stranger behind me jerked on my horn, forcing my head up. My eyes lifted to see the second clown towering over me, my sword—now shiny-clean—gripped in one hand while his other slipped over the serrated edge.

"My brother polished your sword for you," the scary clown behind me rumbled, a smile in his voice. "The least you can do is polish his in return."

5

Harbinger of Lust

MEG

There was a pregnant pause as they gave me a moment to consider their offer.

As freaky as the rubber clown masks were, they elicited a dark arousal from me that sent sparks shooting through my body like fireworks. Plus, the men were built like Greek gods. Lean frames packed with muscle. Corded, masculine perfection.

In the back of my head, that tiny human voice told me to get the hell out of here. As always, my succubus side won.

My lips bowed with a sultry smile. "Put the sword down before you hurt yourself there, Bozo."

"You got quite the little mouth on you," the clown on top of me chuckled. "What a shame we don't have soap to wash it out with, right, bro?"

"Oh yeah. A real shame. Guess we'll have to find something else to fill up that bratty little hole."

To my surprise, he did as I asked and put the sword away, laying it neatly in my guitar case. Then he returned to stand in front of me, his stance wide.

"Kiss my brother's boots."

"W–what?"

"Did I fucking stutter?" he snapped, and on the next beat, he pushed on my horn, forcing my head down. "Kiss the clown's boots. If our little virgin doesn't want to follow our rules, then say 'playtime is over,' and it ends here."

I didn't want it to end.

This was like one of those sexy dreams I always had, only better, and I didn't want to wake up. Plus, if I was going to call the Sinner's Sideshow home, I was going to be around these clowns all the time. I wanted to show them that I could play their twisted games and win.

Relaxing the muscles in my neck and shoulders, I allowed Black Shirt to hold my head down to his brother's boots. I pressed my lips to the dark leather of them.

Why was this so hot?

"I think our virgin has a thing for degradation," the clown standing over me said.

"She's a succubus with freshly awakened hunger. There's going to be a lot of freaky shit she's into. If only we had the time to explore every little kink *personally* with her."

I moaned against the scare worker's boot as his brother pinched my clit between his thumb and forefinger, giving it a gentle tug. My arms and legs started to shake, and the men laughed.

"She's so cute when she trembles. I want to see her wings. Get them out."

The stranger behind me growled. "No. What if someone sees them? Being a succubus is one thing. But a virgin succubus? It won't be safe for her."

My heart squeezed. These two were actually protecting me. I could take care of myself. I had ever since Walker's went bankrupt and my dad died years ago. But it was nice feeling like I wasn't alone. Even if it was just for a few minutes.

"Fine. We'll just have to find her after the show and take her someplace more private." White Shirt slowly sank to his knees in front of me, took hold of my other horn just as his brother relinquished his grip, and tilted my face up to his.

"Would you like that, baby?" His voice was sumptuous, sinful. All sex. It didn't match the creepy grin on his mask at all. I nodded as best I could with his hand still on my horn.

Screams sounded from the haunted house, and the animatronic witches providing us privacy gave a mechanical cackle. But I barely noticed. All I could focus on was how fucking good I knew this male would taste in my mouth.

I licked my lips, my tongue slow and teasing. Inviting him into my mouth.

I didn't have to use my charm on these two. I had them, hook, line, and sinker.

Dropping my attention to the front of the clown's pants, all the breath drained from my lungs as I imagined how large it had to be to create that kind of bulge. It seemed to thicken as he realized I was staring at it. With one hand on my horn, his other lifted the hem of his white shirt. The first thing I noticed was that his fingernails were painted black, and the edges were chipped where he'd bitten them.

The second was that he had a tattoo of a red balloon right below his navel. Its string disappeared beneath the waistline of his pants. I started to laugh, but it turned to a gasp when he hooked a thumb beneath the band of his pants, slowly pulling it down to reveal the rest of the tattoo.

It was of a naked female clown kneeling with her arms tied behind her back. She was bound in Shibari style with a balloon string, the red balloon attached hovering over her head.

It should have been ridiculous. It was, in a way. But seeing the female girl tied up like that had me heating.

"Show me the rest."

"Ask nicely, little harbinger," the clown beside me scolded, pausing his tender ministrations to give my clit another pinch. "Or I'll have you screaming in a minute, and all the monsters in here will come running to see what a little whore you are."

"P—please," I murmured, my tone pathetic and needy. But I didn't care. The only thing that mattered at this exact moment was finding out what the little pearl of pre-cum gathering at his slit would taste like.

He pulled his pants down until his cock sprang free.

Holy. Shit. It wasn't the thickest I'd ever seen, but it was *long*. Nine inches, if I had to guess. And the texture! It was the veiniest cock I'd ever seen. I didn't realize I was drooling until the clown pushed the beads of my spit back into my mouth, his thumb slipping past my lips.

Instinctually, I sucked on the digit. His hand transitioned from my horn to the top of my head, petting my hair in quiet praise. When he pulled his thumb from my mouth, I lifted my head and parted my lips in invitation. I expected him to be slow about it like he had with everything else.

Instead, he punched his hips forward, the tip of his cock hitting the back of my throat, making me choke.

He grabbed both my horns and rammed me onto his length until my mouth touched his tattoo. He eased back, strings of saliva stretching and breaking, then he pushed back inside.

I couldn't breathe.

Lots of people feared getting strangled by a terrifying clown. Turns out, choking to death on clown cock wasn't the worst way to go.

I growled at the clown's cock when I felt his brother's hand pull away from my clit. "She's getting greedy," the one in my mouth snickered.

The one behind me eased off, pulling my hips back and lifting me up. I felt him shift, and then he hooked a finger under the fabric of my costume and tugged it to the side. I went rigid as the cool air licked my entrance.

His fingers spread my folds, getting a good look at my exposed pussy. "Oh, Discord. She smells like home, bro."

Home. I didn't know anything about these two monsters other than that they were from the Downside. Were they saying I smelt like Hell? Like sin? Or damnation? All of the above, probably.

My lungs slammed together when I heard the unique sound of rubber being peeled off wet skin. Black Shirt was taking off his mask! I tried to turn my head, but White Shirt gripped my horns and pulled out just enough for me to speak if I needed to.

"Is playtime over yet?"

I swallowed and shook my head as much as his invasion would allow.

"Good. I was hoping you'd say that. Whatever you do, don't turn around, alright?"

Frustration singed my blood. I wanted to argue. But I ignored the rebuttal burning in the back of my throat. Arguing with these two wouldn't do any good. I gave a bob of my head.

"Good girl," he cooed.

The second he sank himself back into my mouth, hot breath washed over my backside. I groaned around White Shirt's cock as Black Shirt's mouth closed around my pussy.

I'd never experienced anything like it before. It was warm and wet. It was almost too much for my nerves to take and somehow not enough all at once. His tongue slipped through my folds while his nose burrowed dangerously close to my ass. The clown didn't care. He feasted on me like a starving man. No. Like a ravenous animal.

The more he tasted me, the more frantic he became. Like he couldn't get enough of me. I moaned when his tongue found my hole and danced teasingly around the edges before delving inside.

I wanted to stop and take a breath, but there was no resting. These men were starving for me. I'd given them a taste, and now they wanted more. White Shirt's vice-like grip remained tight on my horns, using them as handlebars to fuck my face. His head rolled back on his shoulders, his clown face lifting to the ceiling to release a soul-deep groan that had me shuddering.

The cackling witches covered the sound, thankfully, as the fall of footsteps neared and then faded. We were probably safe from being discovered, but still, the chance that someone could catch us had me hurtling toward completion.

They must've sensed the end was near because their pacing turned ferocious. When Black Shirt's tongue pushed inside me, White Shirt would pull his cock out, and vice versa, pistoning in perfect synchronicity.

Black Shirt took hold of my thighs, his fingers biting into my flesh hard enough to leave bruises. I almost hoped he would. It would be a nice little reminder of our filthy little fuck in the haunted house.

However, it felt so much bigger than that. These two clowns had helped uncover something inside me. It felt pretty damn huge. Like there was no going back to the person I was after this.

I closed my eyes, my entire body quivering with unholy bliss. I was okay with never going back. I'd come to Sinner's Sideshow for a new beginning. A new me. And this new me was filthy as fuck.

White Shirt's hips came to a complete halt while still seated fully inside my throat. His cock twitched against my tongue. He released a breathy moan. Then with a quick motion, he pulled out as he came so as to leave a sloppy trail of cum from my throat to my chin.

He sighed a sweet and satisfied sound. His finger traced my lips, coating my flesh in his thick seed. *"Swallow."*

I came with a fragmented scream as I did as instructed and swallowed his cum. I jerked, trying to pull away from the tongue plunging in and out of me at an unforgiving pace. But Black Shirt's fingers dug deeper into my thighs as he held me firmly in place, forcing me to ride out the orgasm with his tongue deep inside me.

White hot fire consumed me. My succubus hunger had never felt so sated. Yet, I hadn't had nearly enough. They hadn't taken my virginity. They'd been so firm, yet so gentle.

"Who are you?" I whispered, my face tilted up to watch the clown as he rose to his feet and stuffed himself back into his pants. I craned my neck to see the other one already had his mask back in place.

They only laughed, cold and cruel like they had the first time I'd met them. "We'll find you after the show, little harbinger."

6
Circus of Creeps

MEG

After I wiped my face on my ghost boobs t-shirt, I folded it around my sword to protect the blade and placed it back into my case. I then went on a search for Lollie. Would I tell her what happened? Maybe not. That moment with the scare workers had felt intimate—as intimate as getting spit-roasted by two clowns behind a plastic cauldron could.

After several minutes of searching for the gorgon, I checked my phone and realized she'd probably looked for me, and when she couldn't find me, she headed back to her candy cart.

I left the haunted house and stepped into the main tent.

Being inside the black and white big top was like being trapped in a fever dream. The air was sweaty and the noise disorienting, the energy of it all supremely intense.

It was a cesspool of aggressive emotions and auras.

Even though I knew this place was nothing like Walker's, there was a nostalgia to the atmosphere that had me missing my dad. Being at the circus, any circus, kept his memory close.

The question was, could I stand to breathe in the noxious bloodlust thick in the air? Maybe not if I had to sit in the stands every night. It would be better if I was in the ring, where I could pull the audience's strings and make them feel exactly what I wanted them to.

It wouldn't kill me to sit in the audience for one night.

When I found my seat, I was relieved to find each seat on either side of mine vacant. The empty space was just enough to clear my head of the chaos.

The show hadn't even started yet, and the audience was hyped, drunk on the whisps of dark magic blanketing the house. A brutal fight had broken out between two monsters several rows down from mine. No one made a move to stop it. The audience jeered and threw popcorn at the brawling idiots, the bloodlust in the air so intense my head swam.

Propping my guitar case on the seat next to mine, I kept my hand close to the latch, just in case.

The fight settled down, and everyone fell still in their seats when the lighting in the tent dimmed. There were no show lights. No crew. It was all controlled by magic so palpable I could feel it slide over my skin like a caress.

The hairs on my nape stood on end. I squirmed in my seat, my breathing coming out in fast, short pants. It was as if the elevation had changed. The air was colder, thinner.

Whispers and gasps danced across the stands as the tent's flaps blew open and a violent gust of wind shot inside. My eyes strained through the dark, and I realized it wasn't wind. It was something else, something alive. Its energy was so dominating, it had me gagging like thick smoke, forcing its way into my lungs.

Whatever it was, it was something *evil*.

A disembodied laugh fitting of the devil himself rang out overhead, manic and unhinged.

A dark cloud of sparkling violet smoke circled the center pole, and after a few tense beats, the visage of a man appeared.

I strained in my seat to get a good look at him through the dark.

This had to be the ringmaster of Sinner's Sideshow. The mastermind behind all this madness. He definitely looked the part. He was made of magic and shadows, but his visage was dressed to the nines.

Instead of the typical red velvet tailcoat favored by most ringmasters, his was a deep plum color. The tails were longer than the ones I'd seen Walker's ringmaster wear, hitting mid-calf. His top hat was reminiscent of something that would suit a mad-hatter costume, with one side longer than the other and a slightly sloped top. His head was tilted down, the hat's brim concealing his face. His dark hair was long, billowing behind him as if made of shadows. In his gloved hand was a long cane with a grip I couldn't make out the shape of from this distance.

He was slender, tall, and possessed a commanding presence that had every soul in the audience shivering in anticipation.

Whoever this monster was, he held everyone in the palm of his silk-swathed hand.

"Spooks and specters. Creeps and cunts. Crawling out to you straight from the deepest depths of the Downside is the greatest spectacle on Earth. Featuring haunts and horrors known to give the vilest of monsters nightmares."

My breath caught at the ringmaster's voice. It was dark and decadent, smooth and sweet like molten honey.

Slowly, he lifted his head, and my heart damn near gave out. Piercing emerald eyes punched through my chest, puncturing my lungs. But hey, who needed to breathe when I could die and go to the Downside? Maybe there'd be more men like *him.*

The ringmaster was dark magic incarnate, with a face that was all shadows and gem-sharp eyes filled with secrets.

"I welcome you all to Sinner's Sideshow," he continued. "Where you're sure to wet yourself with delight."

A man on a trapeze swung over the ring, cackling madly. "Wet themselves with blood, maybe!"

He was shirtless, wearing nothing but high-waisted diamond-patterned tights that accentuated muscular thighs. His face was painted like a harlequin clown and looked like it had been applied in a hurry. If anything, it gave an edge to his look.

A second man, identical to the first, swung from the opposite end of the tent. "Or cum!"

The two aerialists were so similar, the only difference between them was one had electric blue hair and the other acid green. They had to be twins. Really, *really* hot twins.

When they sailed past one another at the center of the ring, they high-fived with a hyena-like cackle that was as in sync as their act.

The ringmaster gestured toward the twins with his cane, the yellow gems garnishing the hand grip catching in the light. "Presenting your favorite demonic duo, Riff and Raff, the Downside's most mischievous spawn."

They were demons? My chest throbbed as I watched them glide through the air in a fit of mad laughter and crude jokes. I craned my neck to see one of the twins soar overhead.

I could see them now. Sleek black horns sprouted from their temples and curved backward, their tips pointing inward behind their skulls. They didn't have wings—they wouldn't—male demons didn't have those from the little I knew about my kind. But they did have long thin tails that were barbed on the end, coiling through the air behind them.

When one jumped from his trapeze, his tail entwining around his brother's outstretched arm as they went sailing away on the same trapeze, the crowd *ooohed* and *awwed*.

As they passed overhead, my eyes locked with the bottom twin, just for a beat. He blew me a kiss, then cackled at my wide-eyed reaction as he swung away. Everything inside me urged me to get closer.

They were too far away for me to get a read on them, but just looking at them had my chest tightening with emotion. I'd never met another demon before. Demons were strictly Downside monsters. Just looking at them had my body burning.

Those creepy clowns from the haunted house had only put a linchpin in my succubus thirst. Now that my powers had fully awakened, snacking wouldn't cut it anymore. I needed cock. And apparently, my vagina was only in the mood for demon cock.

Sorry, clowns.

Then again, they could have been anything under those masks.

Riff and Raff were mesmerizing to watch—they'd have to be to pull my thoughts away from what had happened in the haunted house.

The way the demons flipped and twirled in the air with seamless precision was impressive enough, but then they brought out the big guns. They weren't just talented aerialists. Riff was a knife thrower, and Raff ate fire. Riff pulled several knives seemingly from nowhere, pinched between his fingers, and flung them at Raff, who dodged each blade while zinging through the air on his trapeze, balls of fire erupting from his mouth as he taunted his twin for having a shitty aim.

They were wickedly gorgeous in their harlequin makeup, their sleek muscles flexing beneath sweat-soaked skin.

I wanted them. I wanted them so bad it hurt.

"Meg! There you are. Geez, you scared the shit out of me." I jerked my head to see Lollie standing behind me, a tray filled with candy and other treats propped on a popped hip. "I was afraid something ate you back in the haunted house."

I bit back a smile. I *did* get eaten, but maybe she didn't need to know that. "I'm fine. Just got lost, is all."

"Still. I'm sorry, girl." The gorgon brushed a snake behind her ear, then, with a blush, pushed it back in place when she saw my attention drop to the fresh fang marks on her neck. "I should have told Sinclair to fuck off. We'd been friends for all of fifteen minutes, and I ditched you."

"It's fine, really, Lollie. Don't stress."

Relief washed over her face. She climbed over the seats and settled into the chair beside me. She set her tray on her lap, picked up a box of chocolate-covered peanuts and ripped it open, popping a handful of candies into her mouth as she stared at me. "Um. You got a bit of drool at the corner of your mouth, girl. Did you want some candy? Or is it the incubi man candy you're salivating over?"

Incubi? My gaze drifted back up to the performers, my jaw dropping. "They're sex demons?"

"Yup. Bet it's been a while since you've seen any males of your kind, huh?"

"A while?" I gave a dry laugh. "Try never."

I felt all of Lollie's serpent eyes drilling into the side of my face. "Never? Holy shit. I bet your succubus thirst or whatever is going crazy. I'm not sure what your intentions are in coming here or how long you plan to stay. Just watch your cooch around those two."

I looked back at her with a frown. "Why?"

"They're total players. Sexy as fuck, sure. But they're supposed to be a nightmare in the sack."

"A nightmare? Like in a good or bad way?"

Lollie's look was so incredulous even her snakes seemed taken aback. "Is there a good kind of nightmare?"

Didn't everyone have nightmares that sat on the cusp of their darkest fantasies? Dreams so malevolently wicked that there was a sensuality to the horror of it all? The kind where you woke up with a scream, your skin soaked with sweat and arousal, breathing heavy, adrenaline coursing through your system like a drug as the memories of the monster who teased you faded with consciousness. Or was that just me?

The gorgon brushed the awkward silence away with a laugh. "And apparently, they are strictly a package deal. They always fuck the same girl together."

My mind went into overdrive. I already knew I had no qualms about being the filling in a sibling sandwich. Not that I knew for sure if the scare actors from the haunted house were actual brothers, but fuck, they could have been.

"Girl, you're drooling again. Here, try to be less obvious about it." She took my wrist and forcibly dumped a small mountain of candy in my palm. "If they notice, they'll have you for an after-show snack."

We munched on the candy together as the twins wrapped up their act.

That's when the show got weird.

The act to follow was a harpy, a giant bird with the largest human breasts I'd ever seen. They were so huge her leaking nipples almost touched the ground. A clown dressed up like a farmer carrying a stool in one hand and a pail in the other walked goofily into the ring. He set the stool down beside the chained-up bird monster, grabbed its nipples, and began to pump the thickest milk I'd ever seen into the bucket. Each drop made a sickening *plunk* into the pail.

The harpy gnashed her beak and rustled her feathers but didn't fight it. She seemed to be grateful for the relief as the clown milked her.

I wrinkled my nose in disgust. "Ugh. People like this?"

Lollie snorted. "No. That's the point. You come to Sinner's Sideshow to be grossed out. The ringmaster always starts with the twins, turns everyone on, then gives us all whiplash by making a clown do something like that."

She jerked her head to the ring, where the clown had taken the bucket, and wandered to the first row of seats. Two muscular clowns, also dressed up like farmers in overalls and straw hats, held a thrashing member of the audience down as the first clown forced him to drink the milk.

I didn't mean to pick up on the poor bastard's emotions, but it was so strong it was impossible not to ping in.

Lust, with a touch of shame that only seemed to heighten his arousal.

At Sinner's Sideshow, it seemed the audience was every bit as freaky as the cast.

"If you think this shit is weird, the next act is going to blow your fucking mind."

I watched as the milking act ended, and the stagehand came out to set up the ring to look like a butcher's shop, complete with a glass display filled with questionable cuts of meat and a huge butcher block table covered in all sorts of mystery stains.

I shifted uncomfortably in my chair and cast Lollie an uneasy look. "Is it gonna blow my mind or make me blow chunks?"

The gorgon giggled as she munched on her peanuts. "Depends on how strong your stomach is."

A moment later, the ringmaster announced the next act. "Creeps and cunts, introducing…" His voice dropped to a hell-deep growl that shook me down to my bones. "The Butcher."

7

The Butcher

MEG

I wasn't prepared for what entered the ring next. It was a man, no, a giant. A naked giant, all except for the blood-stained butcher's apron he wore—a leather apron that I had a sneaking suspicion wasn't made out of animal hide.

The most disgusting thing about this giant—who was easily eight, maybe nine feet tall—wasn't his brawny body covered in crude scars, his ominous apron, or even the crude meat cleaver clutched in his hand. It was the boar's head that sat between his shoulders. Tusks, moistened snout, wiry hair, and all.

The boar-headed giant lumbered up to the butcher's table and slammed the cleaver into the wood, making everyone in the audience jump. But I had a feeling almost everyone here knew exactly what this act was judging by the lust bleeding into the air, heavy and pungent. "Uh. Lollie? What in Discord's Hell am I about to watch?"

"Just whatever you do, don't raise your hand when he asks for audience participation. Not that you would. Larry doesn't strike me as your type."

"Larry?"

"That's his name. He's a fomorian. A rare type of Upside giant. Usually, you only find them in Ireland. Not exactly a looker. Super nice guy, though. You'd never guess he's a vegetarian. Rumor has it that he was brutally beaten by his clan when he refused to eat human meat. The ringmaster found him years back when the show was touring overseas, and he's been with us ever since."

Before I could ask her to elaborate further, 'Larry' trudged into the center aisle in the stands, making the seats rattle with every quaking step. "Looking for meat. Who shall be my prime cut tonight?" he rumbled with the faintest lick of an Irish accent.

To my shock, countless eager hands shot into the air.

The boar-headed giant raised his snout, his round nostrils twitching as he put on a show of breathing the audience in. "I smell juicy meat."

My stomach churned, but curiosity kept me rooted in my seat. As Larry "the Butcher" neared, I wasn't picking up lust from him or anything even remotely ominous. This was just him putting on a show for these people. Showmen came in all shapes and sizes, especially at Sinner's Sideshow.

As I took a second to take in all the people with their hands in the air, hoping to be selected, I noticed they were all in their human form. As monsters, we had the ability to appear as "normal" to blend in with humans. Here at the circus, most people took the opportunity to appear as their true selves, so it was weird seeing people shifting to their human form in mass as the Butcher passed.

"Why is everyone shifting?"

"Because the butcher only wants human meat." Lollie let out a strangled-sounding laugh as she seemed to remember that she was in the company of a half-blood. "The thought of a monster eating another monster is a little too taboo. But the thought of eating human meat..." She trailed off.

"Because humans are actual food to some of these monsters," I whispered, finishing her sentence.

Lollie frowned, trying to look as sympathetic as possible through her mouthful of chocolate peanuts. "Yeah."

I couldn't say I was surprised. A lot of these monsters regarded humans in the same way humans regarded livestock. They had their purpose, but they were in no way equals. I'd been prepared for that when I'd come here.

Even if I'd managed to win myself a place in the troupe, I was a half-blood. I'd always be seen as lesser.

I continued watching in morbid curiosity when the butcher eventually stopped in front of a woman who was quivering with excitement. Her human form was pretty: a curvy female with silvery hair and lots of tattoos.

"Your meat will make for a colorful addition to my display. The question is, little one, are you too fearful for my cleaver? Fear spoils the taste of the meat."

I shot Lollie a confused look, who mouthed, "Asking for consent."

When I looked back at the woman, she was already on her feet, nodding eagerly to everything the giant stopped to whisper in her ear. Probably giving her a quick rundown on what to expect. Then, a gasp rang out through the house as the butcher grabbed the girl's clothes and tore them off her body with one swift move, leaving her completely naked before the crowd.

Sweeping a thick arm around her middle, the boar man hauled her into the air and threw her onto his shoulder. When he turned around to make his way back into the ring, he flashed this section of the house his bare backside, leaving nothing to cover his ass except for the strap of his apron, which tangled with his curly tail.

He stomped back into the ring and laid her out gently on the table. The air buzzed with anticipation as everyone watched in tense silence as the butcher lifted a bottle of oil and began massaging her.

The lust in the air spiked as a series of moans poured from the girl, and she began to squirm beneath the giant's ministrations as he applied large amounts of oil to her breasts. She had pretty sizable tits, but they looked small in the giant's hands. Even though the boar-headed man was a terrifying sight in his bloody apron, it was clear he was being gentle with her.

As his sausage-like fingers worked over her soft curves, he arched over the table and growled low in her ear. A giggle infiltrated her moans, and the lust over the ring was so strong now I could get a read on it even from this distance.

Carefully, he flipped her over so she was on her tummy, her fingers gripping the edge of the butcher block. He slapped her ass once, twice, three times more. An angry red impression of his hand stained the pale flesh of her ass, stretching across both cheeks.

He held the same hand in the air, everyone cheering. After a beat, he grabbed his apron and tore it off, flinging it away. It fluttered into the first row in the audience, where an excited man squealed in delight at having caught the grotesque memento.

Larry might have been one ugly SOB, but he was gifted in other regions. He had the biggest, fattest cock I'd ever seen. Even from my seat, I could make out the thick ropes of pre-cum oozing from the slit of his uncut cock.

"That poor girl."

Lollie scoffed. "She'll be just fine. Larry takes good care of his volunteers."

The butcher spread the girl's thighs and slowly, carefully inserted his finger inside her. She twitched, her own fingers tightening on the table's edge. The more the giant fed her, the wider the "o" of her mouth became.

"Perfectly juicy. I could eat you right up, girl," the giant said on almost a coo, his free hand smoothing over her ass and gently rubbing the mark he'd left—a temporary brand on his prized "meat."

The girl's face was bright red, and so much lust rolled off her that it made it easier to watch, knowing she was reveling in the pleasure and the lewdness of it all.

The butcher looked up, his gaze narrowing as he surveyed his audience. "Shall I make her more tender?"

The audience cheered, their fists pumping the air. One eager onlooker from the other side of the ring shouted, "Split her roast!"

Giving a great snort of a laugh, the butcher withdrew from her and curled his glistening digits around the handle of his cleaver. With one jerk, he wrenched the crude instrument out of the table and held it up for the crowd to explode in vicious, ear-deafening applause.

My breath caught, and I sent Lollie a nervous look. "What's he going to do with that?"

"It's okay. He won't hurt her."

No sooner than the words were out of Lollie's mouth, the giant flipped the cleaver in the air and caught it by the blade, pinched between his fingers. He lined the handle up with the girl's backside and, at a slow pace, pushed it inside her ass.

She screamed, the sound so shrill I had to double-check that lust and pleasure were still the strongest emotions coming from her.

"Oh, God," Lollie shouted to be heard over the girl's wailing as audience members clamped their hands over their ears. "Of all the monsters in the house, Larry had to pick a fucking banshee."

I grinned and settled back in my seat, the tension in my muscles ebbing away as I started to enjoy the sexual absurdity of the entire show. "At least she's having fun, and Larry seems pretty smug that he got himself a screamer."

Eventually, Larry stopped fucking the girl with the cleaver handle and sunk his own meat into her backside. The banshee screamed her pleasure as the crowd whooped and hollered.

This wasn't like anything I'd seen at Walker's or any other circus on the planet.

Sinner's Sideshow was the most depraved, filthy, obscene show to ever disgrace this Earth. That was the dark beauty of it. It embraced the taboo, the macabre, with zero shame or fucks given. It gave those who walked inside the big top space to let their darkest selves free—to breathe, to play, to simply *be*.

The whole place presented itself as a sinister playground for the horrors of the night, and that's exactly what it was. That meant it was providing monsters with a safe, discreet method to alleviate some of their wicked appetites when they might have found a human victim to provide entertainment otherwise.

I knew fuck all about my mom, but I knew she came from this very troupe years before she'd found a place at Walker's with my dad. This circus was in my blood. Everything about it spoke to the deepest parts of my being.

My attention broke from the Butcher and his banshee to settle on the shadowy figure filling out the ringmaster's outfit like a dark dream.

I would do anything to land a job at Sinner's Sideshow.

Anything.

8

Blood and Leather

MEG

A s act after act came on, Lollie filled me in on all the circus performers and their backyard drama. I tried to pay attention, but I couldn't seem to tear my focus off the ringmaster.

He dominated my senses.

"Meg. Hello!"

A snake tapped my shoulder, used in place of a finger. Thankfully, I didn't have any issues with snakes. Otherwise, my newly formed friendship with Lollie wouldn't be so easy.

"S–sorry." I sent the gorgon an apologetic smile while keeping my eyes on the ringmaster. "What were you saying?"

Lollie followed my line of sight, and her snakes hissed in disapproval. "Okay. Simping for the twins is one thing. But you're not hot for Alistair, are you?"

"Alistair?" As I tasted the name in my mouth, there was a strange stirring inside me. "That would be his name. It sounds ancient and mysterious." I popped my elbow on the arm of my chair and chewed my knuckle in thought. I could feel it—his dark allure. It seeped into the house like the smoke billowing around him. There was something deeply sinister about this monster that had my blood turning hot and cold.

"Alistair." I couldn't resist, so I tested his name on my tongue again. It suited him perfectly.

"Forget it, girl. He's off limits."

"So?" I laughed her off. "I don't want to sleep with him."

My vagina heated, calling me a bold-faced liar.

Lollie's brows gnashed together, calling my BS. "You're a succubus."

"Ouch. I haven't said shit about you turning me to stone tonight, have I? Because that would be feeding into a stereotype. I'm a virgin anyway."

"Something tells me you won't be a virgin for long with fuck me eyes like that, babe," Lollie said, the eye-roll she gave me evident in her voice.

I didn't bother telling Lollie I was interested in the ringmaster for another reason that had nothing to do with sex. Though, the longer I stared at him, the more I imagined it—tried to imagine it. He was currently in an incorporeal state. But all monsters had at least two forms, so if he couldn't mate in this smokey state, he must have had a more solid form. Was it humanlike or more bestial? Was he a top or a bottom? Maybe a switch. Was he gentle? Doubtful. He was the puppet master pulling the strings to this demented circus.

He had to be into some weird ass shit.

Color me intrigued.

Lollie let out a long sigh. "Whatever you're planning, don't. He's bad news."

I turned in my seat to face the gorgon with an innocent smile even though it felt all wrong on my face. "Maybe I'm into bad boys."

Lollie's stare turned stony. She jabbed a finger in Alistair's direction. "That's not a 'bad boy,' Meg. That's an ancient, unholy manifestation of darkness itself that has clawed its way out of the deepest bowels of the Downside and taken on the vague form of a man for the sole purpose of harvesting fear from the monsters of the Upside as an offering to his patron..." Her voice dropped to the lowest of whispers, forcing me to lean in to hear until our foreheads nearly touched. "Discord himself."

Wow. That would make for one hell of a dating profile. And to think the last guy I'd swiped right on had been holding a fish.

I waited for my details on the male looming ominous over the house, but none came. The gorgon had talked nonstop about each person who appeared in the ring and even a few backstage hands. But the monster behind all the madness got no such introduction.

If I was going to be friends with Lollie, I'd need to make a conscious effort not to read her emotions. That said, I couldn't help tapping in just this once.

The ringmaster terrified her. I didn't blame her. You didn't have to be an empath to smell the evil radiating off him like a noxious gas.

What had started out as innocent curiosity was now an inferno of blistering intrigue. "Okay, so the ringmaster is darkness incarnate, I get that. But what *is* he?"

Lollie's face shadowed over with a look of exasperation, but she indulged me. "He's a Shade."

"What's that?"

"A powerful shadow demon. He can pass into the Downside with a snap of his fingers. He can even summon other monsters and bind them to his will. He's supposed to have direct ties to Discord. Rumor has it that they're even friends. I know you're a half-blood, but you've heard of Discord, yeah?"

I'd heard of him. Who hadn't? "Humans call him Lucifer or Satan." I swallowed. "But I figured that most of the stories are bullshit."

"Most are," she said with a sniff. "But he's still the devil. And those stories didn't start from nothing. So I'm serious when I say stay away from him. He has a mate, anyway. They aren't bonded, but they seem serious."

It took me a beat to process this information. "Darkness incarnate has a lover?"

"*Mhm.*" Lollie's mouth quirked with a smile. "Yup. Though master and slave might be better labels for them. Alistair doesn't really 'own' anyone here...except for Daemon."

I blinked. "Who's Daemon?"

The gorgon giggled, and her snakes flicked their tongues like they were laughing with her. "Giiirl. He's only the hottest shit in the whole damn show."

"Now, the moment we've all been waiting for." The ringmaster drifted down to stand at the edge of the ring, his wide grin and glinting green eyes shining from the shadows folding around his broad shoulders. His velvet-soft drawl morphed into a grave-deep growl. "Feast your eyes on the Bitch Tamer."

A chill shot down my spine when a loud bark echoed through the tent. Then another. It sounded like a pack of wild dogs was about to be set loose.

The tent's flaps parted, and a large metal cage on wheels was pushed into the ring.

It was filled with half a dozen vicious dogs. These weren't normal dogs. They were the size of ponies, with golden eyes that blazed with fire. They growled at their handlers pushing the cage, thick tendrils of drool dribbling from their jowls.

I sucked in a breath, stiffening in my seat. Unease hooked in my belly.

It was so stupid. I'd grown up in the circus. There'd been tigers and lions that could tear me to shreds. They hadn't so much as phased me. But I couldn't pick up on their emotions either.

These dogs were different. They were giant Hell beasts with a complicated network of thoughts and emotions, more intelligent than a lot of the human men I'd met. Not that the bar was high.

These dogs were more than vicious. They lived for the taste of blood and flesh.

With a loud bang that had everyone flinching in their seats, the cage's door shot open, and to my horror, the dogs hurtled themselves out into the ring and dispersed into the crowd.

Screams ripped across the house, but no one got up to leave. Not even as one of the dogs latched onto an audience member's head and tore it off with a savage shake. It was like a toy it had in its jaws and not a living, breathing person.

Even over the chaos, I heard the sickening tear of muscle and the crack of bone.

Why wasn't anyone getting up to leave? Maybe because they were completely transfixed by the blood painting the ground and the cantankerous melody of screeches as the dogs moved through the crowd.

"Don't worry," Lollie leaned to whisper in my ear. "Daemon has them trained to stick to the first few rows. The people who buy those seats know what they're in for. Alistair even charges extra for them."

I swung my bewildered gaze in Lollie's direction. "You mean people sign up for this shit? Why?"

"Wow. You really don't know a lot about monsters, do you?"

"I was raised by my human dad. I never knew my mom." I didn't mention that my mom used to work at this very circus. That was a story for later.

If I survived long enough to get to later.

Lollie nodded in sympathy, even though she didn't seem to understand. "Well. Demons are monsters that come from the Downside, like your mom. Most of us will do anything to get out. But you can't just leave. You have to be summoned by a witch or a powerful demon lord like Alistair. Some of us who manage to make it up here don't cope well in the human world. The only way to go back is to die, and their wretched souls return to the Downside. Upside monsters don't even see the Downside until they die, and most monsters are immortal. So, killing themselves is the only way to get there. The monsters who buy those seats just want to go home, Meg."

It was hard for me to grasp the whole wanting to get murdered on purpose thing, but I understood doing whatever it took to find your home again.

I watched as another two dogs dragged a man out of his seat, blood spurting from the gaping holes they tore with every tactical bite. These dogs weren't wild. They were very well trained. Trained by a maniac. But they knew their purpose, and they enjoyed it.

"Mollie sells shit to help the ones who don't get off on the pain," Lollie whispered as one of her snakes gestured to a woman walking through the aisle in the lower rows, her tray filled with a variety of narcotics.

Mollie and Lollie had to be twins, just like Riff and Raff, for how similar they looked. Mollie's energy was darker, more closed off. She was also covered in tattoos, but hers had no color, and her snakes were a dusky violet hue where her sister's were green.

A man in one of the "death" seats waved the gorgon over and handed her some cash with a shaky hand. She seemed to comfort him as she placed a colorful tab on his tongue.

"Don't the drugs make it worse?"

"Sometimes." Lollie shrugged. "But hey. Getting torn apart by Hellhounds while tripping on LSD is a more interesting way to go than sticking a shotgun in your mouth."

"Facts," I said, sticking my hand out to Lollie, who loaded me up with another pile of peanuts. It was easier watching the gore unfold, knowing this was what these monsters had signed up for.

I jumped a little in my seat as fire exploded through the ring. A second later, they disappeared, ash hailing down over the crowd like rain.

As the smoke and ash cleared, a male demon with the visage of a dark god appeared.

Several seconds of barbed silence suffocated the entire house. Then, it shattered in an instant when every female in the audience went wild, barking and begging and clamoring for his attention.

"*That's* Daemon," Lollie informed me, her snakes hissing softly in delight. "You can see why his stage name is the Bitch Tamer."

There was nothing tame about these bitches. They were barely staying in their seats, their arms outstretched as he strode past them, desperate to lap up whatever shred of attention he might bestow.

I couldn't blame them. Daemon was stupidly gorgeous.

The guy was smoking. Literally. Smoke poured off his muscled shoulders in plumes. His brawny frame was covered in tattoos, from his sharp jawline down to where his ink slipped inside the waistband of his pants. His flesh was smudged with soot, and the film of sweat made him glisten in the dim lighting.

The shit I'd do for the privilege of licking him clean.

The fact that he had a bullwhip clutched in his hand should have put me off. Instead, the sight of it had my succubus lust in a frenzy again.

I was learning some new things about myself tonight.

My core pulsed hotter the longer I stared at him. He was a dark fantasy in his leather accessories. He wore a black biker cap with a harness strapped over his bare chest, pronouncing the swells of his pectorals. A spiked collar was wrapped around his thick neck, the spikes glinting as he prowled across the ring with the tail of his whip dragging in the dirt behind him.

Dameon whistled. "Lilith, bring it here, girl!"

The Hellhound named Lilith bounded to her master, the monster's head she'd torn off dangling from her jaws by his blood-caked hair.

She sat at the master's feet, her tail thumping excitedly against the ground. He took the head and examined it with a stony expression before tossing it over his shoulder. One of the twins popped into the ring, smoothly caught the head and dipped back outside.

Daemon patted his hound's head. "Good girl."

Good girl.

He didn't say those words like they were meant for the dog. His voice was too guttural. Too hungry. He wasn't even looking at the dog. His gaze swept over the crowd, charged with a sexual energy that had every female, and some males too, melting in their seats.

"So what's his act, exactly?" I asked Lollie while keeping my eyes glued to Daemon. "He's gotta do more than just look hot."

"It's different every show. Sometimes, he'll have the hounds do tricks. On other nights, he'll mess with the audience. Alistair lets him do almost anything he wants."

I directed my attention back to the ringmaster at the side of the ring. His emerald glare glowed from the shadows, tracking the hellhound tamer prowling around the ring. The shade was too far away to get a read on his emotions, but the hunger in his eyes was unmistakable.

"So Daemon really is Alistair's...?"

"Sex slave? Pet? Bodyguard? All of the above, girl."

My eyes pinged between the mysterious ringmaster and his hellhound tamer. There was a flutter low in my belly. I clenched my thighs together, trying to smother my succubus pheromones. Thank fuck I wasn't the star of the show tonight. No one was going to notice unless there was a bloodhound in the audience.

Daemon cracked his whip, and his blood-splattered hounds bounded back into their cage. When he swung the cage door closed, it seemed the act was over.

Then he froze. Tipping his nose into the air, his chest rose with a deep inhale. A dark grin twisted his lips. "It seems we have a virgin in the house tonight."

9

The Virgin

MEG

We have a virgin in the house tonight. Those words set my nerves on fire, and beads of cold sweat studded my skin.

Was I the virgin? What were the odds that I was the only one here?

Squinting through the dark, I frantically scanned the house. It's not like I could just tell by looking at them, but the kinds of monsters that flocked to Sinner's Sideshow weren't exactly the innocent type.

Lollie stiffened in her seat. "Oh shit."

"What?"

"I didn't think he'd do this bit tonight. Otherwise, I would have warned you."

"Warned me about what?" I asked, trying to keep my voice calm.

"Daemon sometimes does this thing where he sniffs virgins out and has a little fun with them in front of the crowd. The last one here, he had her on all fours, with his whip wrapped around her neck and led her around like a dog on a leash. By the end of it, she was begging for him to give it to her in front of everyone."

Daemon left the ring, prowling up and down the aisles in search of the virgin.

For me.

Panic struck me like a lightning bolt. If he did manage to sniff me out, what would I do? Would I let him do what he wanted? Maybe. My vagina screamed, "yes." After what happened with the scary clowns in the haunted house, my succubus side had fully awakened.

My human inhibitions had been torched at the door.

But there was something about the smug bastard and how he held himself that rubbed me the wrong way. The clowns had been courteous in their dominance over me. Ultimately, I still had the control. Something told me I wouldn't get that luxury with this guy.

Whatever he wanted, I'd make him work for it.

"Lollie, the girl, the one he had on all fours. Did he fuck her in front of everyone?"

"No," the gorgon sighed. She almost seemed disappointed. "Daemon holds himself on a pedestal. He thinks he's Discord's gift to the Upside. No one is good enough for him aside from Alistair. Plus, Alistair doesn't seem like the sharing type. Even if he did share, I doubt Daemon would give anyone the time of day."

With a body like that, maybe he was Discord's gift to the Upside.

An audience member reached out and grabbed Daemon by the wrist as he passed.

The house gasped.

Daemon's eyes narrowed into the deadliest slits, his lips curling to reveal sharp canines. "You dare touch me?"

"Please." The monster gave a pathetic whimper. "I want to go home. I want to see my mate and spawn. Give me a good death, Alpha, so they'll be proud of me when I return."

"One of the death seats," Lollie whispered, her eyes and each one of her snakes watching the scene in transfixion.

Daemon's disposition seemed to soften at the monster's request. His arm shot out as fast as his whip, and his hand plunged through the man's chest. With a sickening *squelch*, he withdrew his hand, holding up the still throbbing heart for the audience to examine.

"Give my regards to your mate," Daemon said on a dark purr.

The monster's eyes widened. He managed the slightest of nods before slumping over in his chair dead.

The house went death-still. A beat later, the stands exploded with cheers, barking and whooping in excitement.

The lust that bled into the air was so intense my eyes watered. Daemon flung the heart over his shoulder, and one of the hounds leaped up to snatch it out of the air.

My heart thrummed at the way blood coated his muscular arm.

Christ. This was the shit I had to be into? Clowns and demons and shadow monsters, and now leather whips and blood, too, because why fucking not? I wanted to roll my eyes at the clichés. The only exposure I'd had to that kind of thing was schlocky internet horror porn, and most of it I found barely palatable.

Not because of what it was, as it turns out. It had to be done right. This male did it right. He wore blood and leather like the devil intended.

Daemon lifted his cap from his head and, with his bloody hand, slicked back his shoulder-length, obsidian-hued hair.

That had me *so* fucking wet.

The more distance his long legs consumed, the stronger my pheromones became.

The male paused, closed his eyes and jerked his nose into the air for a deep breath in. When his eyelids snapped back open, my pussy clenched. He was close enough now that I could see his eyes. They were golden yellow, dotted with smoldering flecks of amber. They were as hot and bright as Hell itself.

He took several steps closer to me, coming in proximity enough for me to finally tap into his emotions.

I shouldn't have done it.

My scent was driving him feral, and with that little nugget of info, my succubus pheromones went haywire. There was no way he wouldn't sniff me out now. Not when everything inside me was doing everything to lure the male into my orbit.

His tongue flicked out, painting a lick over his lips.

Fucking hell.

His tongue was ridiculously long, dripping with thick ropes of saliva. "Our little virgin smells delicious," he growled, his attention wrenching to the side of the ring where the ringmaster quietly observed.

Alistair's shadows swelled around him, dark and tumultuous like a storm. "I think our alpha is about to teach our unmated bitch a few new tricks."

For the first time since Daemon entered the big top, Alistair turned his attention back to the crowd. "Do you want to see her pant?"

The crowd went wild, their enthusiasm deafening.

Lollie set her candy tray on the seat next to her and turned to me, her eyes wide with panic. "We still have time to sneak out before he finds you."

Sneak out. As if. Standing up would only draw more attention to myself, and crawling away most certainly wasn't an option. Throw in the leash, and I'd be right where he'd want me.

"Where are you?" Daemon snarled, his voice all gravel now. I swallowed thickly at his tone. It was raw and hungry. Almost like he wasn't putting on a show anymore. He really was hunting me.

What was he going to do?

Running would put a target on my back. There's no way I'd outrun his hounds. All I could do was sit here and... what? Hope he didn't pick me out from the crowd?

"It's fine, Lollie. I'll just tell him I don't want to participate."

Given my strong reaction to him, I wasn't sure I'd have the strength to tell him no. By Lollie's expression, I wondered if he was the kind of guy who even knew the meaning of the word.

Still, my succubus lust wanted him to sniff me out and see exactly how he decided to handle me in front of all these people.

Maybe I wasn't a demon from Downside, but I could still hold my own. I could do more things with my sword than stuff it inside my throat. I was good at putting it in other people, too. I'd proven that when I'd murdered the ghoul for raping the bunny shifter.

The bigger threat to Daemon was my mouth. I was a brat in pretty much every sense of the word. Something told me he wouldn't like that. Which would only make me run my mouth more.

The anticipation to see how this would play out ate me alive.

He was in our row now, his saunter painfully slow as his eyes stabbed through each and every monster he passed. Some of them swooned as he came within the same breathing air as him. Some shrunk away.

Lollie leaned forward, her eyes dancing with excitement. "By Medusa's fury, he smells divine."

If by divine she meant sinful, smoky, with the metallic tang of blood, salt, and sweat, then yeah. Daemon smelt like dark paradise.

When his eyes locked with mine, I felt Lollie's gaze burn a hole through the side of my head.

"Good luck," she mouthed.

The alpha gave a growling laugh as he came to stand in front of my chair. He had a wide stance, so his knees hit the edge of my seat with my thighs hitting the inside V of his legs. He was so hot, literally. He was like a furnace. As his warmth bled into me, I fought the urge to flinch.

I refused to give him the satisfaction of seeing me squirm beneath him.

"Daemon, baby," Lollie said, her tone suddenly sultry as she leaned toward the male. "Your nose must be on the fritz tonight. That ain't your girl."

The gorgon had a world-class poker face. But going by Daemon's scoff, he wasn't buying it.

He held his whip out so the grip rested under my chin. With the slightest bit of pressure, he tilted my face up, his eyes of burning gold stripping me bare. "My nose never lies, Lollie-*pop*." The alpha seethed, his use of Lollie's nickname more mocking than when Sinclair had used it.

"She's a succubus. There's no way she's never had a full feeding before."

I could sense the gorgon's earnest effort to try and save me from whatever wicked spectacle Daemon planned to make of me, but she wasn't helping.

If anything, she was making it worse.

His dark brows arched high on his face, disappearing beneath the visor of his leather cap. "A succubus? Now *that's* interesting."

Showstopper

MEG

The inflection in the alpha's tone sent a shiver down my spine, which did nothing to abate the heat raging low in my core. I tried to snap my legs closed to trap the scent leaking from me, but Daemon's whip dropped, the hard leather grip guiding them back open.

"I know a virgin cunt when I smell one."

"Yeah, I'm a virgin. Big whoop." I shrugged, feigning nonchalance as best I could. As if this male wasn't going to war with all my senses and winning. "Making a big deal out of it gives me the ick."

"Too bad I don't give a shit. You could be male, female, a squirrel shifter, a three-foot-tall imp, or anything in between. If you come to our filthy little fuck show with a hymen intact, you bet your pretty little cheeks that that's going to pique my interest."

My breath hitched at his words.

The energy radiating from the male was so overwhelming I could barely make sense of it. There was lust for sure, lust so thick and heady it sat heavily on my chest, making me inhale and exhale in short stabbing breaths.

"Looks like you're already panting for me. That's cute. Christ, you're so small. So fragile. If I touch you, you'll snap."

With that, his lust grew in intensity, and I gasped at the vile pang of joy leaching from him at the thought of hurting me.

His stony expression finally broke, and a savage smile stretched his perfect lips.

Jealous murmurs broke out among the other women in the crowd. "She's so small. Too short to go on that ride."

"She stinks of human."

"Look at those pathetic little horns. Is that her true form?"

"She must be some filthy half-blood. How could they let her in?"

"Why is he interested in her?"

"Is she even old enough to be here?"

I tempered myself to the cruel chatter while Daemon's head canted like a dog sticking its ears up at the distant noises. His pupils shrunk, the gold around them expanding as he gave me yet another once-over. "You do look young. How old are you?"

"I'm twenty."

He swore under his breath. "You're just a pup. Didn't you see the signs? This is a twenty-one-plus show. No little girls allowed."

I gave a dry laugh. "If being twenty makes me a little girl, you must be one old fuck."

He didn't look like he was a day over thirty. But so did most supernaturals.

"This bitch needs to learn some obedience." His vicious growl was loud enough for everyone in the house to hear.

If he thought he was going to humiliate me without me giving him a taste of his own stupid medicine, he was sadly mistaken.

I was playing with fire here. But hey, I was a circus brat who had dabbled in fire-eating for years. I wasn't afraid of getting burned anymore.

"Alright. Fine." I leaned back in my chair and spread my legs. "You can smell that I need to feed. So I'm game. Touch me, *Bitch Tamer*. Fuck me. Make me yours." I softened my voice, and for the first time in months, I used my succubi powers. "Let's give them a show."

A noxious cocktail of anger, lust, and frustration rolled off the male as he watched me writhe in my seat.

Just as I expected, Daemon turned to glance back at the ring-master, whose expression was masked by the shadows roiling around him. All I could make out was the glinting jewels of his emerald eyes and the tendrils of his hair billowing around his shoulders as he slowly shook his head.

I grinned, straightening in my seat. "Or are you just all bark and no bite? You love making it look like you're in control on the stage, but you can't actually break loose. Because, in reality, your master has you on a very short leash. Making *you* the bitch."

With those few words, I'd express-laned myself into danger-ous territory.

Normally I wasn't one for screwing with someone's act. But this guy got under my skin in all sorts of ways. Where was the fun if I couldn't get under his, too?

Daemon squared his shoulders, then arched down with one hand clenching my chair's armrest and the other—the bloody one—gripping my jaw.

He brought his face so close to mine, his hot breath was tor-ture on my blazing cheeks. His tongue snaked from his mouth, licking his lips.

I imagined the thick muscle slipping inside me, filling me. I bet he knew just how to move it to make me break. How I'd grab his hair and smother his face against me, grind my clit on that perfect nose. I could only imagine the pleasure a body like his would bring.

My succubus pheromones were more potent than ever.

The alpha's spiked collar strained against his throat with his heavy swallow. A bead of sweat slicked a path down his temple.

"I might not be able to tear you open in the way I'd like." His whisper was too hushed for even Lollie to hear. "But I can still flay you alive, Little Pup. I'll strip you to fucking pieces. Lollie and Mollie can sell your meat to the ghouls, and I'll feed your bones to my hounds."

A little flicker of fear licked at my belly, coiled tightly with pleasure. My vagina and what little remained of my self-preservation were at odds.

I'd suspected my succubus side would become stronger after coming to Sinner's Sideshow. What I hadn't counted on was for it to come roaring to life. This new side of me reveled in the danger of poking this bear of a man. It was doubtful that I'd walk away from this without a few scratches. But hey, I was pretty sure I was something of a masochist anyway.

The anger that emitted from him was sudden and sharp, like a slap across my face.

His hand moved from my chin, and his strong fingers fisted my hair. With a savage tug, he wrenched me to my feet. The guitar case tipped over and, from the awkward way it landed, sprung open to reveal its contents.

The alpha male froze, his glare falling to the sword wrapped in my t-shirt. With the way the t-shirt was rolled, the image of the busty ghost was visible, along with the clown's cum stains standing out against the black fabric with all the subtlety of Batman's bat signal.

Daemon's eyes slowly lifted to lock with mine. "What's the sword for, Little Pup?"

I didn't answer at first. I couldn't. I'd come here to be seen. To be accepted for my talent.

I'd come here to find my place in the show, but this was all wrong. It wasn't supposed to happen like this. I'd inherited my father's act and his sword. They were personal. An extension of myself.

This asshole didn't deserve to know about that piece of me. Not like this.

I donned a poison-dipped smile. "It's for stabbing men who ask too many stupid questions."

The anger that bled from his aura was that of a deranged demon. That didn't scare me. What scared me was the way he suddenly seemed so calm, even though his emotions were anything but.

Even though I could see his face, as plain as day, he wore a mask. I realized I'd pegged Daemon all wrong. He wasn't a dark fantasy. He was an intoxicating nightmare.

And he had me in an utter chokehold.

"Aren't you gonna ask me about the cum stains, Daddy Daemon?" I snickered. "Mister Twenty Questions."

I didn't miss the way his dick thickened in his pants at being called daddy.

He gave me a disquieted smile that hooked under my skin, filling me with fire. "That's not exactly a mystery, little pup. You may be a virgin, but you're still a succubus slut."

I decided in that moment that I hated him.

"Go fuck yourself."

Unphased by my response, he leaned closer, his scent filling my throat with all the potency of a chloroform-soaked rag.

"Answer my fucking question. What's with the sword? Who are you? Why are you here?" He spoke with an even tone, but his words were laced with warning. He was looking for the truth.

"I'm looking for a job," I finally admitted. I lifted up my hoodie to reveal the costume beneath. It was a tight-fitting little bodice that exposed my thick thighs. The costume tailor at Walker's had been the best of the best. Last I heard, she was a costume designer for some Netflix show now.

The front of my bodice had several hand-embroidered designs that looked like leaping flames and dozens of black feathers sewn into the seams.

Daemon's reaction hadn't been what I expected. I wasn't sure what I expected, exactly. But I hadn't counted on this soft, floaty feeling invading his aura. Euphoria, maybe? I had to be reading him wrong.

The world started to make sense again when that familiar anger lurked back, dominating the space around him. "You want to be in the show? Fine. I'll put you in the show."

I tried to pull my hair out of his fist, but his fingers flexed tighter around my pink locks, his knuckles cracking. "Let me go!"

"Keep running your mouth and see what happens."

Before I could reach for my sword, he was hauling me into the aisle. Lollie stared after me, a pained expression etching her face.

I felt every eye in the audience hot on my skin. It was their bloodthirsty curiosity that was the worst of it. They wanted to see Daemon tear me apart. I could feed on their energy, but suddenly my body didn't seem hungry for anything other than the caustic lust that emanated from Daemon the moment he'd scented me.

Too bad that would never happen. The magnetic chemistry we shared was nothing but contempt. Toxic, addicting, intimate contempt.

The ringmaster's emerald glare tracked me as Daemon dragged me into the light of the ring. I was close enough now where I should have been able to get a read on him. There was still nothing like the static between radio stations. Goosebumps exploded over my skin as I realized he wasn't going to stop whatever it was his *bitch tamer* was about to do.

So I did the stupidest thing I could.

I fought back.

I'd never win, although it didn't matter. So long as I made him bleed.

I swiped my claws at Daemon's head. I was faster than I expected. My razor-sharp nails sliced into his cheek.

He didn't so much as flinch.

The house fell into complete silence.

I stood before the terrifying male like a sinner awaiting judgment. Beads the deepest shade of sanguine bled from the ribbons I'd slashed into his face.

He should have been angry. Livid.

So why was the strongest emotion I was getting from him *lust?*

"I hope that felt good, pup. It's the first and the last time you'll ever raise a hand to me with no consequences."

His demeanor was so calm. I didn't trust it for a fucking second.

So, like the brat I was, I raised my hand as if to slice his other cheek. I wasn't going to...probably. I hadn't really decided yet.

It didn't matter. He moved so fast, I didn't have time to react. He snatched my arm and wrenched it behind my back. His other hand gripped my horn, twisting me around so my back was flush with his bare chest, the buckles of his harness digging painfully into my wings.

I cried out in pain. His dick twitched against my ass. "Go ahead and scream," he snarled into my ear. "It will only make me harder."

I hated how much I loved the feel of his rough hands on my bare flesh. I didn't want to like anything about this bastard.

"I'll admit," he began, his breath a hot caress against my neck, "you're sexy as fuck. You're also infuriating. I'd say you have balls as big as mine if it wasn't for the fact that I can scent your dripping cunt. Feel what you do to me, pup?"

He canted his hips, his erection fitting so perfectly against my ass.

"You'd be fun to have around—see if I can tame that bratty mouth of yours. But it doesn't matter how succulent that pussy is, and it doesn't matter if you're the most talented bitch to ever walk into this tent. You're not joining our show."

A fist-sized lump formed in my throat. "Why?"

His fingers smoothed over my hair, tender and almost curious in the way they lingered—a stark contrast to the mean way he held my other arm at the small of my back. "You're not getting into this show because you're a half-blood, baby girl. And this place will eat you alive."

He dragged me to the cage, kicked open the door, and tossed me inside with his dogs. My head slammed into one of the bars, then my body slammed into the ground, and darkness carried me away in its cool embrace.

11

The Shade and His Pet

DAEMON

The moment I'd picked out her sweet scent from the tangle of clashing odors in the house, I wanted her. It was like a breath of fresh heaven in the deepest, most stagnant pits of the Downside.

I wanted her so bad it scared me, and nothing scared me, not even Discord himself.

Then I saw her, and my lust morphed into something deeper. Just by fucking looking at her.

But she was perfect in every goddamn way.

The way her rose-colored hair fell around her shoulders in subtle waves, her soft pink eyes that almost matched in hue. She was short—couldn't have been more than five feet. I towered over her. I liked that, and she had, too, going by the way her body had flushed when she'd looked at me.

When she'd lifted her baggy sweatshirt to offer me a peek at her costume, I hadn't been looking at the garment. I'd used that precious second to memorize her shape so I could retrace it in my mind over and over.

She had medium-sized breasts, a soft little belly, and plump, mouth-watering thighs I'd do anything to worship. But what I'd loved most of all was that flame of defiance flickering bright behind her eyes. I knew fire, and she was filled with it.

All my life, I'd never felt the urge to claim a mate. Until now.

Why did she have to be a half-blood? She'd never survive this place. She sure as shit wouldn't survive me. Especially with that mouth on her. It pissed me off. It challenged me. It dared me to muzzle her. I knew I wouldn't. There was no taming that fire behind her eyes. Hell, I didn't *want* to tame her. I just wanted all the fun of trying.

But claiming a mate meant taking her in my true form. She'd never survive it.

Lust turned to a raging obsession all in an instant, and there was fuck all I could do about it.

Death and darkness! Why did she have to be a fucking half-blooded sex demon? Riff and Raff were hell to be around because they seemed to know exactly what everyone was feeling at all times, and those little shits had no problem blabbing about it to everyone if it served them.

Meaning she knew how much I wanted to crawl inside her and mark every inch of her as mine. And she'd just looked at me and *smiled.*

The dark shit I'd do to have those same lips wrapped around my cock.

No. It could never come to that. I'd tried to take a mate long before I'd left the Downside. My hellbeast had killed her, and she'd been a full-blooded demon. After that, I'd sworn to never try to forge a bond with a mate again.

She couldn't work here.

Maybe I could chase her off. No, that wouldn't work. I'd only just met her, and I already knew she was stubborn as Hell. She'd get a kick out of defying me.

If I couldn't scare her away, Alistair definitely could. But asking him to terrify her didn't sit right with me. The fact that I wanted to mate her would give him a natural interest in her. It was like one of my hounds playing with a favorite toy. They'd chew on it, play with it, and completely desecrate it slowly over the course of months until it finally burst at the seams.

At least I wouldn't have to worry about him taking a sexual interest in her. Females rarely caught his interest, and even when they did, he wouldn't act on it.

If I begged, maybe he'd do this one thing and turn her away. And if she refused to take no for an answer, he could give her a reason to never want to come back.

I stood in front of my hound's cage, staring through the bars at the succubus' sleeping form. She looked so peaceful. In her unconsciousness, she'd shifted back into her human form. It made me wonder if this was her most natural state. Since she was a half-blood, it was possible she was raised as a human. Was she seeking out Sinner's Sideshow so she could finally have a place to explore the side she had to hide all those years?

My hounds slept around her in a pile. They sensed she wasn't like the other females I made a show of in the ring.

As I approached the bars, the leader of the pack, Lilith, lifted her head. I reached through the bars and gave her a pet.

"Keep an eye on her, Lil. If the twins come anywhere near her, give them Hell."

At the mention of the incubus twins, she growled.

I laughed, scratching behind her ears. "That's a good girl."

Lilith nuzzled her damp snout into my palm, then turned to the demoness and began to lick the lump forming on her brow.

Self-hatred stabbed at me like a knife being slipped between my ribs. The act I'd put on to try to put the girl off from pursuing a job here had been a bit too convincing. I doubt my brutality would scare her away, anyway. It would only make her hate me. It was probably for the best. She'd keep her distance.

"You look so woefully pensive, pet."

The voice that spoke from behind was as dark as sin and as subtle as arsenic.

I slowly pivoted to face the shade. Now that the show had wrapped up and the monsters left on the lot were just his employees, Alistair appeared in his human form. If it could even be called that. His skin was pale as death because it *was* dead. The shade didn't have his own human form.

Sure, he could have a humanoid form, but he'd still be made out of shadows and dark magic. To achieve a more human look, he inhabited carcasses that I had sourced for him over the years. All from evil humans, to keep his conscience clean. Because Alistair didn't kill innocents.

I liked this body I'd hunted for him. He was tall, almost as tall as me, with a lithe body that looked so goddamn good wrapped up in those fancy velvet suits he wore.

He'd changed out of his plum-colored ringmaster costume into a pair of slick black trousers, a black collared shirt, and a maroon waist jacket with the silver chain of his watch draping from his pocket. The bottom of the waistcoat was embellished with the faces of harlequin clowns with hearts over their eyes and an X over their mouths.

He sauntered toward me, his stride so smooth it was like he was floating. As the distance between us shrunk, the air in the small supply tent grew thinner.

He stopped in front of me, the points of his shiny shoes touching the muddy tips of my combat boots. "Tell me what you're thinking, pet."

I searched for the right words. When it came to this shade, I had to be careful with the shit that came out of my mouth. Alistair was chaos cloaked in the thin veneer of a tolerant man.

"I was thinking about how terrifying you are. You put on a pretty deranged show tonight. There was more fear in the air than usual."

The shade leaned back, his emerald eyes glittering with mirth. "You're one to talk. I'm not the one strutting around half-naked in leather and spikes, torturing all those poor women with the mere sight of you. You drove them half-mad, knowing you'll never be theirs."

"At least I don't pretend to hide what I am. I'm obviously a sadist. You're the one with the mask."

A phantom smile lurked at the corners of his mouth. "They don't need to know such things. I'm not the spectacle. I'm just the man behind the curtain."

As he spoke, his shadow flickered behind him, then it floated past both of us to hover near the cage. Every muscle in my body pulled taut as the shadow slipped between the cage to hover over the sleeping girl.

The tightness in my chest ebbed away when Alistair's shadow stretched a hand out, only to brush a rogue chunk of hair behind the succubus' ear.

"You shouldn't have been so hard on the girl," the shade hummed as his shadow snapped back into place behind its master. "You could have cracked her head open."

My eyes narrowed in suspicion. I'd known the shade for years, and after all this time, I still couldn't read the slick bastard. "Why do you care?"

"You heard her. She's looking for a job. She'll need to be alive for her audition."

"You can't hire her."

The shade's emerald eyes narrowed in warning. "You know I only like you telling me what to do when you're eight inches deep in me, pet."

Dread hooked in my gut. I peeled my lip in mock disgust as I cast a glance at the cage. "She's a half-blood. She's not one of us. Her stench of human will scare away customers."

I was so full of shit.

The female's scent was the most intoxicating thing I'd ever smelt.

"All she's good for is scrap meat for my dogs," I lied, wrinkling my nose to sell the lie.

My hounds would never hurt her. Even if I gave the command, they still probably wouldn't. They'd sense we were compatible mates. If anything, they'd guard her with their lives. Right now, the cage was the safest place for her.

Alistair's long fingers curled around the grip of his cane. It was the head of a snarling hellhound with citrine eyes. He held it up, slipping the tip through the metal loop dangling from my spiked collar.

He jerked on it, dragging me closer until his lips crashed over mine. There was always a delicious sting in the way he kissed me. As his lips moved over mine, his hand brushed my chest, nails tapping at the buckles of my harness. His touch trailed lower, slipping into the waist of my pants.

I clenched my teeth, biting back a groan as his hand found my cock, and *fisted* it.

Alistair's manic smile stretched wide in the faint green light of his glowing eyes. "Does all the food you throw to your dogs usually give you such an erection?"

I gaped at him, stunned by his perception and reeling from the accusation. A beat later, I recovered, brushing him off with a laugh. "*You* make me hard, Master."

Alistair tipped his head, the light illuminating his amused expression. "What game are you playing? You only call me that when you're trying to butter me up."

I bit my smirking lips and dropped my hand to my groin to cup his hand over my pants. "You know exactly what game this is. We play it all the time."

"Tell me the truth," he said, keeping his hand on my crotch and giving it a hard squeeze—another warning.

"Fuck," I hissed between clenched teeth. "I hate how you can read me like a book."

The shade hummed. "I know. I wish you'd just spit out whatever's on your mind."

"You're not exactly the most approachable monster, Master."

Alitair's attention drifted back to the demoness, sound asleep in the cage. "It's about the girl, isn't it?"

"Look. You know I never ask you for anything. Just do this one thing for me. When she wakes up, send her away. Don't give her a job, no matter how good she is. No matter how many tickets you think she'll sell."

Thoughts churned behind the shade's emerald glare. "You hate her that much?"

"She's—" I chose my next words carefully. "A distraction. For everyone."

Alistair cocked a brow. "But especially for you?"

"There's a part of me that wants to test her limits. I'd break her." There was no lie there. "You don't want me breaking your troupe members, Master. They aren't toys."

"What if I hire her just to be your toy and give you my permission to break her, hmm?" His tongue snaked out, licking the corner of his serpentine smirk. "What then?"

This was a test.

I took a breath, careful to keep the emotion out of my voice and off my face. "It would be a waste."

A tense moment passed between us, then his grip over my dick loosened—but he didn't pull away. "You looked so damn delectable tonight."

He was changing the subject.

"I was just as mesmerized as the rest of them." His smooth voice churned with something that had my dick twitching in his hand. "The way you had those whores in the audience wet and panting for you when you ripped out that monster's heart and fed it to your hounds. Covered in his blood, looking like the grim reaper himself."

I grinned at the shade. He really was a twisted bastard underneath all his layers. Not as much as he used to be, but he was still the Lord of Darkness at the end of the day. I liked that. It kept life at Sinner's Sideshow interesting.

My smile slipped some when my mind wandered back to the girl asleep in the cage behind me. My relationship with the monster circus and its strange master was a fragile ecosystem. The last thing I needed was some bitch screwing it up. No matter how much the voice in my head told me she was more important than all of it combined.

The thought of her leaving had a whine curling up from a primal place deep within.

The ringmaster let out a deep chuckle, thinking the sound was for him.

It was...and it wasn't.

I sighed, resisting the urge to look back at her. "Get me the fuck out of here, Alistair."

I didn't have to ask twice. The shade flashed me a dazzling smile as he withdrew his hand from my cock, and spread out his arms, palms turned upward. Dark, viscous magic began to bleed from his hands, the clouds of thick smoke reminding me of ink in water. It spread like a disease, taking over the tent in a matter of seconds.

When the magic faded, we stood in the ringmaster's caravan. The space was tight, especially with the shade's collection of magic baubles and random trinkets. It was like an episode of *Extreme Hoarders* ancient wizard's edition.

Alistair threw his cane to the corner of the caravan, where his shadow caught it before it hit the ground and propped it carefully against the built-in bookshelf packed tight with antique religious texts and occult books on demonology. The shade was obsessed with human depictions of Hell over the centuries.

"Strip me," he ordered.

I planted the flat of my palm against his chest and pushed him. He fell back onto his bed, bouncing with the mattress before falling still, dark reverie shadowing his face.

I loomed over him at the foot of his bed, my whip in my hand. "Your clothes or your skin?"

"Very cute, hound. You know how long it took us to find a human hide with a complexion suiting my eyes. Tear it, and I just might wear yours next."

Tossing my whip to the floor, I crawled onto the bed. "I fucking love your dirty talk."

My fingers slipped between the jeweled buttons of his waist-coat, and with one swift tug, they went flying in every direction. There was no sound of them hitting the floor or the walls. His clothes were just an illusion, so the buttons fizzled in midair like Alka-Seltzer hitting water.

He moaned, his back arching off the mattress and his hips canting up in search of mine.

"Lay the fuck down," I snarled, shoving him back into the bed.

My pulse hammered with excitement as I bowed my spine and snapped his belt with my teeth. I shredded his pants away from his thighs and watched the remains of the tattered illusion slowly fade.

I sat back on my heels, watching the way his cock sprung free. When we'd first started sleeping together, I had insisted that we mate in his true shade form. The shadow-tentacle cock had been my preference over this.

The cock of his human form. The thing was, it wasn't really human at all. The skin I'd harvested for him from one of our victims was pale as death, and it had been sloppily sewn back together with shadow magic. The threads glittered like stardust, and shadows leaked from the stretched seams.

It had freaked me out the first time I saw it. But now that I knew what it felt like, the sight of it made my mouth water and my dick throb.

With my hands keeping his thighs clamped firmly to the mattress, I took him into my mouth. He bucked against me, and I pushed down harder, the pressure making shadows seep from his seams. They licked at the roof of my mouth like little writhing tentacles.

He shivered, and his eyes rolled into his head as I painted a lick along the underside of his shaft. I allowed the points of my teeth to skim over his flesh, hard enough to leave welts.

His hands sunk into my hair, which was still crusted over with blood. His claws extended, biting into my skull and breaking the skin. The smell of fresh blood mixed with the old.

"You feel like heaven," he said with a shudder.

I pulled the shade from my mouth to flash him a smug grin from behind his cock. "And how would a damnation like you know shit about that?"

His mouth slanted with a frown, his expression serious even as I spit onto his dick, pumping my fist over his length. "I was there when they made it, hound."

Alistair and I had a pretty huge chasm of an age gap between us. I allowed my mind to forget that little detail as often as it could. There was something unsettling about rutting a culmination of the Downside's deepest, most unfathomable depths older than time itself.

I must have had my thoughts written all over my face. He pulled his head up, emerald orbs piercing the dark. "Do I frighten you?"

I laughed as I grabbed his hips and flipped him over so he was on his hands and knees. Doggy style. My favorite.

"Not even a little," I answered honestly. He already knew the answer. He'd asked it a hundred times before. "I'm the only one you don't terrify, and that gets you hard. Now shut up and make your shadow fetch me your cane."

I smacked his ass, satisfaction working through me at the way he squirmed. "*Now.*"

With Alistair, my control was a thin veneer. An illusion. I didn't care much. It's not like I was the shade's slave. Not anymore, anyway. He might have taken me from my home once upon a time, but that was years ago. If anything, he'd saved me. I'd been nothing but a murderous, wild beast back then.

Because of that, I'd be his loyal hound for as long as he'd have me.

There'd been a time when I'd been wild. Alistair had tamed me as much as a beast like me could be tamed. Now, all I wanted was to please him. I wouldn't call what I had for him love. At least it wasn't anything like those stupid human movies made it out to be. Whatever we had, it was warped and wicked.

And it was all ours.

He wouldn't want some half-blood sex demon interfering. There was no reality where she could survive me and my relationship with the shade. It was not likely that he'd take an interest in her, but on the rare chance he did, we'd end her.

When the shadow brought me the cane, I took it, and with a hand clenched around either end, I pressed the shaft to the back of his neck, forcing his face into the pillow. I leaned down, allowing all the weight of my muscled form to slowly settle on the cane like a hydraulic press. It was enough force to crush the windpipe of a human lover or a weaker Upside monster.

"Now tell your shadow to either hold the cane for me or take my cock out and get it ready for your ass. Your choice."

He let out a moan muffled by the pillows. His shadow crept onto the bed between us, its translucent hand hooking into my pants.

I smirked. "Good choice—Oh *fuck*." The shadow's fingers curled around my shaft, its digits having to grow for its fingertips to swallow my girth. It stroked me several times, working me up to a steady pant.

When I released a low growl of impatience, it guided my cock's tip to our master's ass.

With Alistair's orifices, no lube was needed. He was naturally slick and smooth. The perfect fleshlight.

Raising a leg, I planted one foot on the bed and nudged my hips forward. I took my time sinking into his tight hole, savoring the way his internal shadows licked over my cock.

The shade craned his neck, one eye glaring up at me through his writhing mane of hair. "Damn you, hound. Your pace is torture."

"Good. I want this to hurt."

Alistair squeezed his eyes shut, his body shaking from the pleasure and the pain of our connection. "Damn you. Damn you. Daaaaamn you."

I smiled to myself as I finally picked up the rhythm. He could curse me all he wanted. From his lips, those words meant something different. They carried more weight than a curse ever could.

I rode him hard, pounding him with more ferocity than usual as I tried to fuck away the thought of her. But even as I came with a cry, intense bliss wracking my body, all I could think about was the girl fast asleep with my hellhounds.

The girl whose name I didn't even know.

12
Double Trouble

MEG

I dreamt I was in the ring again. It was my sanctuary.

I was performing my old act, the one my dad had taught me. Every time I brought out his old sword, I felt him with me.

For this performance, I was going the extra mile and doing the fire-eating bit. Fire eaters didn't literally eat fire. We just made it look like we were swallowing it. The trick was to extinguish the fire quickly by closing your mouth over the flame to smother the oxygen.

Fire eating while sword swallowing was a dangerous stunt. I'd credit my skill at it to my demon blood, but my dad had been the one to teach me. He'd always been daring. After all, he'd managed to reel in the heart of a succubus. Because the thing about female sex demons was they couldn't get pregnant unless they wanted to. My mom had wanted me.

It didn't make sense why she'd left us.

At least she'd chosen a good man to leave her baby with. My father had raised me well, with his circus troupe as his village.

I wish I knew more about her. Until I learned more, the time I had with my dad would have to be enough.

Now that he was gone, every one of my performances kept his memory close. I just wish he could see me now, doing the trick I'd always been afraid of in my days at Walker's.

Taking the bottle of fuel in my hand, I dipped the tip of my sword into the clear liquid. I lit the blade with a lighter, and the flame jumped to life.

Spreading my stance wide, I tilted my head back and slipped the blade inside my mouth. With the tip inside, I clamped my lips tight over the flat ends of the blade. With the flame extinguished, I worked the entire sword down my throat.

The audience gasped and clapped their delight.

I started to carefully extract the blade from my throat when the flames sprung back to life, all on their own.

This is a dream, I reminded myself. *Don't freak out.*

This was one of those nightmares. The kind that terrified me to my core, and yet there was a part of me that didn't want to wake up. I was the girl who wanted monsters under the bed to eat her. It made me feel alive.

I hadn't felt alive since I was at Walker's when my dad was still around. But everything had fallen to shit after he died. I was left alone, and now all I really felt was numb.

Except in my nightmares.

The flames licked higher and higher, the heat making the crowd behind me flicker and blend with the shadows.

The fire consuming my sword morphed into a man made of flames, his engorged muscled consisting of dancing amber light. He had the head of a hound, with eyes as bright as hellfire, billowing smoke cascading from his nose with every breath he took.

Despite the heat, my blood turned ice cold as I realized what part of him was inside my throat.

"Take it, little pup." The hound gripped my head in his great claws, burning up my pink hair. "Take what I give you."

He pistoned his hips back and forth, ramming the sword up and down my throat. I screamed as the jagged blade sliced my esophagus. My hands fumbled for the sword's hilt, but it was consumed by the hound's blazing groin, the fire scorching my skin.

I coughed up thick gobs of blood, the cool liquid the only relief against the boils forming over my lips.

The flaming hellhound gave an evil laugh as he fucked my throat with fierce fervor. In the background, the audience joined in, their shadows swirling together with the hellhound's flame as they pointed and jeered.

I was not only drowning in my own blood—I was drowning in their lust for it.

I woke up soaked, my thighs sticky with a mixture of sweat and arousal.

When my vision adjusted, the first thing I noted was the steel bars.

I was still in the cage, and I wasn't alone.

Six giant hellhounds were all snuggled around me. One of them raised its head and set to diligently licking the lump on my forehead.

With a wince, I rubbed the back of my skull as if that would make the sharp pain go away. "Fuck me..."

"Only if you ask nicely," a dark voice said with a chuckle.

My attention jerked to the tent's entrance, where a blue-haired demon stood, his green-haired brother standing behind his shoulder. It was the twin stunt devils from the show. Riff and Raff. What perfect names for them.

They had trouble written all over their faces.

They were even sexier up close. They weren't built like Daemon, with stacks on stacks of muscles. They were tall and lean, with athletic bodies perfect for sailing through the air on the trapeze. Light, lithe, with surprising strength packed in their arms and legs.

Their bright hair was messy, and the white t-shirts they'd pulled on were wrinkled, along with their black denim jeans. Their white clown makeup was smudged, giving me a glimpse of two twin tattoos over their eyebrows. The name "Riff" was spelled out over the left brow of the blue-haired male and "Raff" over the right brow of the one with green hair. They were in their human form, so I knew their white eyes with black X's as pupils were just contacts.

"Having a naughty dream?" the one with blue hair—Riff—taunted with a snicker. "'Cause you smell fucking yummy."

"Smells more like a nightmare," Raff replied with a mock pout. He tilted his head to look at me through the bars of my cage, his green hair spilling over his creepy X'ed out eyes. "Aw, is someone having the creepy sleepies? Careful not to wet yourself. Riff's into that shit."

I'd been so star-struck with the incubi twins during their act, and now, up close, I was even more flustered. They were the only other sex demons I'd ever met.

Incubi.

There was a part of my body, some biological component, that knew these were the only males of my kind that I'd ever been near. Which had me shoving the hem of my hoodie between my soaked thighs.

"Need a towel?" Raff teased.

"Fuck that." His brother stalked closer to the cage. "I'll crawl in there and lick her clean myself."

My mouth went dry, all the moisture in my body sinking south. "W–where am I?"

"Hell," Riff said with a crooked smirk. "At least the closest thing to it on the Upside."

The blue-haired demon strode deeper inside the tent, with Raff looking over his shoulder before following. Like he knew they shouldn't be in here.

They started circling my enclosure slowly, eyeing me like I was a mouse caught in a trap.

"You two goons gonna answer my question? Where the fuck am I?"

"Oooh, careful, bro. She's getting mad." Raff smirked and leaned against a random crate with his arms folded over his chest. "We know what our little harbinger does to men who piss her off."

Everything inside me turned to ice, then melted on the next beat, searing heat sweeping through my body as I realized who these two were. I felt stupid for not realizing it sooner. "You're the two clowns from the haunted house."

Riff grinned at me through the cage bars. "We told you we'd come looking for you after the show."

"You're in a random storage tent," Raff said, finally answering my question after a beat of silence. "It's where we stick the weird shit that doesn't have another place."

"Apparently, that's you," Riff chimed in a teasing tone. "I told Daemon we could stick you in our trailer, but he didn't like that. He thought you'd be better used as dog food."

"Don't be offended, harbinger. He doesn't understand what you can do with swords. Of all varieties." Raff's grin stretched wide. "It's lucky you haven't been eaten yet."

Riff stuffed his face against the cage, his hands gripping the steel bars. He painted a lick over the cool metal, his delicious purr mixing with a mischievous laugh. "Except she has been eating. She's tasty, too. Too good to be dog chow."

Holy shit. Riff was Black Shirt, the clown that had eaten me out. "Y–you…" My ability to articulate was thrown out the window as I watched his tongue slide up the cage bar. I knew the wicked shit that tongue could do. The pleasure it brought. And how I was currently jealous of a metal bar.

"Aw, she's flustered." Raff chuckled. "That's *so* adorable."

I tried to play it off with a shrug. "Of course, I'm flustered. I don't appreciate being locked in a cage and gawked at like some zoo animal. So how about you two goons let me out?" I crawled across the cage on my hands and knees, pressing my face against the bars so that my lips were a kiss away from Raff's. He smelt so damn good I could barely think straight. "And we can continue where we left off at the haunted house, hmm?"

Raff leaned closer but jumped back when the biggest dog in the pack lunged forward, snapping at him through the bars. Raff pointed at his twin and erupted into a fit of mocking laughter.

"Looks like Daemon put his dogs on guard duty. You ain't getting anywhere close to her, bro."

Riff straightened, his hand smoothing down his blue hair with a few angry swipes. In his surprise, he'd shifted into his half-demon form. His tail lashed the air behind him like an angry cat. "What does that bastard care about her? He's got his hands full with Alistair. She's ours."

My upper lip curled, and I bared my fangs at the blue-haired demon. "I'm not *yours* prick. I don't belong to anyone."

Riff ignored me and began pacing back and forth in front of the cage. The dogs growled at him every time he came too close for their liking.

Why were they protecting me? It didn't make sense.

Maybe Daemon instructed them to keep these two away so he could have the sole pleasure of tearing me apart.

My pussy pulsed hot at the thought.

Jesus. Turns out, I was into some messed up shit. Daemon was a dangerous monster who radiated violence and loathing. Not to mention he was a cocky bastard. Lollie had been right. He thought he was Discord's gift to the Upside.

I didn't want to like him in any fucking capacity. He'd looked at me like I was shit on his boots.

He'd taken pleasure in watching me squirm in front of his audience.

And so had I.

I wasn't sure why he resented me so much, and I wasn't sure why our bodies seemed to be so into that fact. What a good little hate fuck he'd make.

"You smell that, brother?" Raff's voice cut through my thoughts. "It's the sickly-sweet smell of shame? I think our little harbinger of justice has a thing for being in a cage. That or she liked how Daemon manhandled her."

Riff bounced excitedly on the balls of his feet. "The little half-blood is ashamed of being *so* turned on. That's so adorable. There's no use feeling guilty for what you're into, baby girl. You're a succubus. It's in your nature to be *fucked*."

Right. They were sex demons, like me. They could sense everything I felt. I wasn't used to that going both ways. No wonder our moment behind the cauldron had been so perfect.

They'd tapped into my emotions.

They'd also pulled me off the edge of a panic attack, fed me, and awakened my dormant succubus powers.

I worried my bottom lip, and their silly smiles fell away, watching me with intent and almost concerned expressions as they felt what I did.

"Thank you," I whispered. "For what you did for me. It was more than fooling around. You guys really helped me."

The twins swapped a look I couldn't read. What I could parse was something warm and sweet radiating from them. They could joke around all they wanted, but under their laughter and their painted faces was something good. Something I wanted to hold and have and make *mine*.

I curled my tail around one of the cage bars and leaned my head against another, my horn clinking against the metal. "Let me out. Please."

There was no sultry purr to my tone. Just sheer, dumb exhaustion.

Raff ran his thumb over his bottom lip, smudging the black paint of his clown smile. "She's trying to get us in trouble with the boss' pet, bro. Looks like we have a sly one on our hands."

Riff's jaw set in frustration. "I'd rather have her on my cock."

"That could be arranged if you let me out of this cage," I pressed.

"We probably would take you up on that if we had the key." Raff sighed, sounding genuinely sorry.

"Then get it," I demanded, this time with more force.

"Not happening, baby. The boss wants you right where you are for now. You're the one who wants to talk to him, right? Said you're looking for a job."

"I am. But that doesn't mean I should be stuffed in a cage and treated like some sideshow oddity."

"You *are* an oddity, harbinger. Sex demons are Downside monsters. The only reason we're here is because we work for Alistair. He's the one who brought us here. We thought we were the only ones of our kind on the Upside. When we saw you in the haunted house, well..."

Raff's eyes flicked to Riff's, who finished his brother's sentence with a, "It was like seeing a ghost. Plus, you're a virgin. You're like a toy that's never been opened. Yet to be broken in."

"Then there's the little detail that's the most interesting of all. You're a half-blood. Sex demons don't breed unless they want to. Meaning your...?"

"Mom," I said dryly, watching them wearily as they began to circle my cage again like vultures biding their time.

Riff started humming a creepy tune as Raff continued, his inflection that of someone telling a scary story. "So your mom somehow made it to the Upside. How is that? What demon lord's dick did she have to suck for them to open a portal, just for her?"

"From the sounds of it, it's the same dick you sucked. My mom used to work at this circus. That's the only reason why I know about Sinner's Sideshow in the first place."

The twins stopped in their tracks. They exchanged looks through my bars.

"You're Astrid's daughter?"

13

Monstrous Attraction

MEG

My heart slammed against my ribs at the mention of my mom's name. I clutched the cage bars, pressing my cheeks between the steel. "You two knew my mom?"

The clowns' expressions shifted, softening at the hope lifting my tone. "Sorry, little harbinger. But no. She left here more than twenty years ago. But she didn't just work here, babe. She ran the entire show."

My lungs slammed together, and I fell back on my ass like I'd been physically slapped by an invisible hand. "W–what?"

Riff's brows shot so high they almost touched his blue hairline. "She never told you?"

"I–I never knew her. She ran out on my dad right after I was born."

"So you came here to figure out what happened to her?"

"No. Not really." Twin frowns curved the brothers' mouths. It was freaky how in sync they were. Could they sense the ache in my chest, cutting into my heart like a dull knife? If they detected the invisible wound my mom's abandonment had left on my soul, they didn't pick at it.

"I'm not trying to find my mom. If she wanted anything to do with me, she wouldn't have left me in the first place. All I'm looking for is a job. The circus is where I belong, and this is pretty much the last one standing."

While it was true that I wasn't interested in finding my mom, I was curious to know about her time here at Sinner's Sideshow before she'd met my dad. Why had she left? Had she really run the whole show?

I started to ask the twins for more info, but the tent's flap brushed back, and Lollie appeared a second later with my guitar case.

Surprise radiated from her when she saw I wasn't alone. "Hi, boys. Great show tonight."

"Thanks, Loll." Raff smiled at the gorgon. "Nice snake bites. Looks like you're back with Sinclair. Congrats."

Lollie gave a terse smile as her snakes moved to cover Sinclair's fang marks. "What can I say? The bloodsucker knows how to grovel, so we made up."

Riff stuck his hands in his jeans pockets, his tail flicking behind him. "Oh yeah, we know. The entire entrance tent smells like dead dick and gorgon pussy. We're gonna have to let that shit air out on the back of the truck so it doesn't carry to the next town, Loll."

Lollie rolled her eyes. "Oh, please. If the haunted house tent smells like sex, that's on you guys. I have a good nose, too, you know. Which poor girl did you charm this time?"

Raff snickered, his gaze jerking to me, but Lollie didn't seem to notice. "We don't need to use cheap sex demon tricks, Lollie-pop. Our victims crawl to us on their hands and knees, willing sacrifices."

The gorgon's eyes skipped between Riff and Raff before finding me in the cage. "I just came to drop off Meg's things. She left her guitar case behind after Daemon decided to randomly manhandle her during the show." Loll's voice was tight with irritation. "Where is the bastard, anyway?"

Raff shrugged. "Probably balls deep in the boss' cosmic asshole."

Riff's attention settled back on me, his white eyes brand-hot on my flesh. "So her name is Meg?"

The gorgon hissed in disapproval. "You didn't even ask her name? If you're going to harass a girl, you should, at the very least, know her damn name."

"Does it matter? It's not like Alistair is going to let her stick around. I bet Daemon's on his knees right now, *begging* him for the privilege of disposing of her himself. He'll have his fun with her, then skin her and bring her carcass back to his master, who will use her pretty little flesh as new covers for his collection on human demonology books."

"Raff," Riff snapped from the tent's outskirts. "You're scaring her."

"So what? She's into it." The green-haired clown winked at me from across the tent. "You *like* being scared, don't you, harbinger? Makes you wet."

Riff's eyes locked with mine. "We won't let Daemon do any of that shit to you, Meg."

A chill shot down my spine. There was an oath-like weight to his words that sat on my chest like an anvil.

Raff whipped around to face his twin, arms crossed over his chest. He'd shifted now, too, his tail lashing back and forth, hissing through the air. These two reminded me of cats. Everything from their feline-like movements to their fickle and self-serving nature.

Their loyalty wouldn't be easily earned.

"Oh. And what exactly are we gonna do to stop him, Riffy? Suck his dick? Remember how well that worked last time? The boss only likes filthy mongrels."

"No. If Meg's act is the greatest shit since bread—"

"*Sliced* bread," Lolli interrupted. "You two really have to work on your human sayings."

"Whatever," Riff snapped. "Point is, if he thinks her act will sell seats, he'll wanna keep her around." He danced forward, tugging at my tail, which stuck through the bars, then danced away again when the dogs lunged. "Then we can play with her all we like until she falls apart. Because you should know, we always break our toys."

"Aw," Lollie snickered. "You *like* her. I've never known you two to get attached to any of the poor girls who've ever been skewered on your tiny dicks."

"They're not small." Raff sent me another wink, his tongue popping from his black-painted lips and curving to the side. "Meg here can tell you all about it."

Lollie slipped me a look that screamed, "*Really*?"

Raff took the momentary distraction to snag my guitar case from the gorgon's hands, ignoring her protests.

"Let's have a better look at what we've got inside here. Last time we saw this, we were a bit preoccupied." He flicked the metal latch open and whistled at the case's contents. "We got ourselves a sword swallower."

Riff chuckled. "Yeah. We know she sucked your dick, bro."

Lollie's stare was so intense that if I had been a man, I was sure I'd turn to stone.

"No, shit for brains," the green-haired clown snapped at his twin. "She's an actual sword swallower. *And* a fire eater," he added as he pulled out a clear plastic bottle. "Isopropyl alcohol? What is this? Baby's first fuel?"

"That's what my dad taught me to use."

"That's because *Daddy* doesn't want his little girl getting burned. But if you're going to survive here, you're going to get used to a world of hurt." Riff stalked closer to the cage, paying less mind to the growling dogs. "But we already know you like a pinch of pain, don't you?"

Raff placed the alcohol back in the case and snapped the lid shut. "If your act is gonna be worthy of our show, you're going to need to pack more heat than this shit, babe."

"Like what?" I asked, my annoyance morphing into genuine intrigue.

The fire-eater shrugged. "If you can't produce your own flame, methanol could be interesting."

"Methanol? You mean racing fuel?"

"Your skin should handle the temperature. The flame burns clear, so if you add borax, the flame will turn green, which will go nicely with your pink hair."

I blinked at him. "That's actually a really good suggestion."

"I'm a pro, babe." He winked. "In the ring and in the sheets."

I opened my mouth to respond, but the air turned death cold. The breath I took in was like ice. I shuddered and scooted closer to the dogs for warmth.

Alarm pinged from Lollie, her snakes coming to life as they sensed it, too. Something powerful was coming. "I'll catch you later, Meg. Try not to die, 'kay?"

She skittered out of the tent, chased away by the dark energy, while the twins remained. I was grateful they stayed with me. I barely knew them, yet I got the vibe that they weren't as cruel as they liked to come off.

They weren't like Daemon.

"Uh-oh. The boss is coming." Raff chuckled.

"Don't let him kill our new toy." Riff jumped up, flipping expertly through the air and latching onto the extension cord, powering the tent's only light source. The bulb flickered, making shadows stretch and dance over the demon's upside-down clown face. "Maybe Meg should be the one to suck his dick. We know how protective he is when he takes a liking to something." Riff cackled as he swayed on the cord.

My eyes widened as intense lust surged through my body. These demonic clowns were freaking terrifying, with or without their masks. I didn't think it was possible to be more unsettled by my attraction to a monster.

Then Alistair entered the tent.

14

The Ringmaster

MEG

Alistair's demeanor was dark and all-consuming. His shadowy mien dominated the entire space within the small tent. My human instincts told me to shrink back and get as much space between us as possible.

Then there was that other side of me, the darker, depraved, monstrous, exhilarating part that had me leaning forward into his dark orbit. The part of me that got off on sucking clown cock behind the plastic haunted house decorations. The one who got wet at being thrown into a cage. The one who would do *anything* for a job here.

The shade reminded me of a venomous spider. There was no use trying to fight him. I'd already fallen into his web. The big question was, what would he do with me now? Hire me? Send me on my way? Wrap my carcass up in silk and suck out my insides?

Alistair strode toward the cage. His green eyes were as sharp as raw emeralds, slicing my lungs into ribbons. He looked different than he had in the ring. At the show, he'd been this ethereal being that looked more shadow than man.

Now, he could almost pass for a human with the face of a man. But it was just a mask, with about as much authenticity as the rubber ones the twins had worn in the haunted house.

Holy Hell.

It wasn't his skin.

It reminded me of a horror movie I'd seen once, *Texas Chainsaw* or something, where a guy named Leatherface wore the skin of the people he murdered. Only Alistair's flesh was better kept. It almost passed for his own. It was deathly pale. Sinclair had more color to his flesh than the shade. But there were no obvious stitches. It was completely unmarked, and whoever the skin had belonged to before had been a real looker.

As Alistair strode closer, eating up the precious distance between us, the dogs in the cage began to whimper and shrink to the back of the enclosure.

My blood turned cold. These vicious hellhounds were afraid of him.

But what unsettled me the most was that I couldn't get a read on the creature.

The shade stood just a few feet away from my cage. If I reached my arm between the bars, I could touch him. So close. Yet I couldn't detect so much as a crumb of emotion.

That had never happened before.

He seemed to omit some kind of magic that interfered with my succubus powers.

My chest twisted into knots. Great. Just spectacular. I hated using my succubus charm to pull males into my thrall, but it had been my last-ditch escape plan if shit hit the fan.

So much for that.

I couldn't even pick up on Riff or Raff's emotions anymore. Alistair's orbit was a total dead zone. It made me wonder if the shade even processed thoughts and feelings like everyone else. He was a master of shadows, a creature from the deepest darkness in all existence. Hell, he *was* darkness. Everything about him was an illusion. A trick.

He had to be hiding something truly heinous under that dead flesh he wore.

A growl at the shade's feet pulled my attention downward.

I'd been so engrossed with the ringmaster that I hadn't noticed the hellhound at his side, although I wasn't sure how I'd missed it. The beast was even bigger than the others. Unlike the ones in the cage, it wore a spiked collar. Daemon's dogs were all black, but Alistair's hound was colored like a Doberman, black and brown, and...Wait. Was that a piercing in its ear?

I honed in on the metal ring adorning the hound's cropped ear, and my eyes trailed back to Alistair, who watched me with quiet interest. "You pierced your dog's ear?"

The shade's mouth curved with a dazzling smile that would have knocked me on my ass if I wasn't already sitting. He was charming. So macabrely beautiful.

"I'm a creature made entirely out of shadows, wearing human skin safe to assume is not my own. And your first concern is for my hound's accessories?"

I shrugged, unable to resist the invisible tether that seemed to pull me closer to the monster. I gripped the bars, giving both of them another once-over. "It's just weird, is all."

"You'll find there's plenty of 'weird' at Sinner's Sideshow. Though, I suspect you already know that, Miss Meg. Since your mother worked here."

I gaped at him, the silence swaddling us cold and suffocating. "You were eavesdropping on us?"

Amusement had his jeweled eyes twinkling. "Do shadows eavesdrop?"

With a thick swallow, I tamped down on my nerves and tried my best to look unphased. "Great. Since you were spying on my convo with Tweedle Dee and Tweedle Dum over here," I jerked my thumb in the twins' direction, "then you know why I'm here. All I'm looking for is a job."

I paused, waiting for the ringmaster's response.

For two years, I'd been chasing Sinner's Sideshow. It had been as elusive as a shadow and just as catchable. Now that I was finally meeting the mastermind behind it all, it made perfect sense.

Now, everything hinged on his response. If he denied me a job, it would be two years down the drain, and I'd be back to sleeping in my car and performing at the odd ren faire or country carnival.

I'd rather take my chances with the monsters here than go back to that.

I couldn't read Alistair's emotions, but his expression wasn't hard to parse. His wide, Cheshire cat grin said it all. He knew he had me hook, line, and sinker.

I sat in my cage among the animals, waiting for the master to speak like a dog waiting for a bone. He fed off my anxiety, my anticipation, my frustration, and the strange lust he stirred up inside me.

Even the twins seemed nervous, waiting for his reply. They didn't dare breathe a word as we all waited for the ringmaster's verdict. Riff still hung from the extension cord dangling from the ceiling, its slight sway making Alistair's shadows shift around him.

The shade seemed content to let us fester in the silence as he picked a speck of nothing—or nothing I could see with my half-human eyes—off his suit jacket.

"Hmm, what do you think, boy?" He directed his question to the hound at his heel. By the fond look he wore, it was safe to venture that he loved his dog.

That little nugget of info had the muscles in my shoulders relaxing. For all the danger and chaos that seemed to ooze off the male like acid, at least he was a dog person.

The dog, on the other hand, didn't seem to be as nice. His jowls peeled to reveal vicious fangs that were surprisingly white. His low growl sunk through me like a rock, settling low in my belly.

Oh, fucking gross. Demon sex clowns were one thing. A creepy ringmaster made of shadows that wore the skin of his victims was a stretch, but I was warming up to the dark thoughts brewing in my mind.

But this was just a dog. I wasn't into animals.

There had to be something in the air here.

Alistair arched a perfectly shaped brow. "I don't think my hound is very fond of you."

Unable to look at the door, I swung my attention to the twins. Suddenly, I found myself grateful that our powers were deactivated in Alistair's presence.

"I'm more of a cat person anyway," I said, a toxic smile spreading my lips. "So how about it, boss? Gonna let me show you what I can do?"

"You do not belong here."

My heart plummeted. "Where in the hell do I belong then? My old circus is gone. They're all gone. I'm just supposed to go back and pretend I'm a normal human? Fuck that shit. Look at me!"

I rapped my knuckles on my horns. They were small, but they were still there. It was hell holding up my human form day in and day out. "The only time I can be my real self is on stage. But here, I can always just be me. I'm a monster. My mom used to run this whole show, right? Doesn't her daughter deserve an audition?"

He sighed, looking troubled. "You're stubborn. Just like your mother."

He knew my mom. I wasn't sure what I was going to do with that information yet or if I'd do anything at all. Deep down, I wanted to know more about her. But on the surface, I didn't *want* to. I didn't want to know shit about the woman who'd abandoned my sweet father and left him with a newborn monster to raise all on his own. Still, no matter how much I tried to strangle my curiosity, it wouldn't die.

"She wouldn't want you working here," Alistair said, his brows plunging into a disturbing scowl. "But I never cared much for her."

With a winding sigh, his suit jacket opened up...all on its own. My eyes strained through the dimly lit tent, and my hands trembled around my cell bars when I saw it.

His shadow had stepped in front of him—even though the source of light and Alistair himself hadn't moved—and reached into the pocket of his waistcoat to extract a key.

The shadow was much larger than the shade's human form, with gnarly horns sprouting from its head that looped around *twice.* Its eyes were a glinting red, shaped like four-pointed stars.

It was like a Jekyll and Hyde situation.

Who was this monster, really? What kind of nightmares lurked beneath his stolen skin? What horror was the sinister allure he wore like a smoke screen hiding?

Daemon probably knew. Lollie had said those two were sleeping together. My mind went back to the leather and spike-clad hellhound tamer. He was domination incarnate. It would take someone as brutal as him to handle an entity like Alistair. What were those two like together?

I'd pay good money to watch them fuck. Maybe they should stick that in the show.

Heat crept up my spine, to my nape, and spread to my cheeks.

Alistair's shadow floated toward the cage and stuck the key into the lock. With a loud click, the door swung open. The dogs whimpered at the far end of the cage, their golden eyes widening with fear as Alistair's shadow held out its claw.

I hesitated, just for a beat, before placing my hand in his. If it could even be called a hand. It was a claw easily the size of my head, tipped with vicious talons that could easily slice me to shreds.

The shadow-beast was translucent, with its master's form visible on the other side. My hand in his felt solid. It helped me out of the cage and passed behind me, closing the door. I sucked in a breath when its rippling shadows brushed my skin, lingering, its palm sliding over my ass.

Its touch was warm and...comforting.

Before I could process what had just happened, it shot back behind Alistair and morphed into an unassuming shadow.

I searched his face for any indication that he'd made his shadow grope me. The twitch of his lips, a wicked glint in his eye. Nothing. He either had the world's best poker face, or his shadow had a will of its own.

"What's your name?"

I sent him a confused look. "Um. It's Meg, like I already said. It's not like it's changed in the last ten minutes."

"Not your nickname. The proper demonic name your mother gave you."

"Am I supposed to be telling you that? If I tell you, you're not going to own my soul or something?"

The twins erupted into a fit of hyena-like laughter. Riff laughed so hard he slipped from the extension cord and barely managed to land on his feet.

Alistair donned a grin that was a little too wide for comfort.

"That's just a myth. You'll find most human lore on demons and Hell is wrong. If I was interested in owning you, little half-blood, it's not your name I'd be claiming."

"Oh. Um..." I shuffled and pulled my hoodie tighter around my body. "It's Megaera."

"Megaera," he repeated. "Pretty. Named after one of the Greek gods of vengeance."

Something dark brewed behind Alistair's gaze. It hooked deep in my gut like a splinter I'd have to claw to get out.

"So, uh, can I audition for you or what?"

"You have an hour to prepare," he finally said after what felt like an eternity. "We'll be waiting for you in the big top."

Alistair turned to leave, his hound trailing behind. In the tent's opening, he stopped and slowly slid me one last lingering look. His shadow loomed ominously behind him, the horns lining up so they looked like they were sprouting from his top hat.

"Don't disappoint me like your mother, Megaera."

15
Dark Oath

ALISTAIR

My hellhound thought he was clever. No matter how intelligent my hound was, there was no fooling me.

I was too old to be tricked by a dog.

No matter how loyal Daemon was to me or how stubborn, he couldn't defy nature. It didn't happen to all shifters, but it wasn't uncommon—that instinctual urge to forge a mating bond with another. Did he lie because he thought I'd be jealous? He wasn't wrong.

I wasn't accustomed to sharing my toys.

But these days, Daemon was so much more than a plaything. Two monsters like us weren't capable of love. But I cared for him, and he cared for me—as much as his black heart could. Though, I had a creeping feeling that this girl would soften his rough edges. If I allowed her to stay, he'd be different with her.

Something akin to envy flared low in the pits of my being.

I was the one who had found him as the wild hound he'd been all those years ago, murderous and bloodthirsty. I'd taken him from that wild alpha and had turned him into what he was today.

I'd done the work to tame him.

But there was a part of him still closed off that even I couldn't seem to open. After he'd killed the female he'd tried to take as his mate, he refused to take another.

Not even me. No matter how many times I'd commanded it. He'd refused. But this girl, this random little half-blood, was what stoked that fire within my old hound?

He'd kill her, too, and he knew it.

That was why he wanted her gone. If only the bastard trusted me enough to tell me the full truth of it. Then I would tell him there was no point in hurting the girl, not when I'd gone to the lengths I had to protect her when she was still in her mother's belly. Back when all that brutal business with Astrid had unfolded.

Even Daemon didn't know what had fully transpired between Astrid and I the night I'd tracked down the murderous bitch. He knew nothing about the deal we'd struck.

He had no idea Astrid's unborn babe was the only reason I'd let her walk free.

If Meg was any other girl, I might just kill her. I had a rule about not harming innocents, but my possessiveness over Daemon overrode whatever vestiges of humanity I possessed.

I wouldn't care less about her being his "true" mate or whatever Upside monsters like to call it. I was from the deepest bowels of Hell. I had nothing to do with the stars or destiny, and the funny thing about stars was that they would be extinguished.

Where I would last for all eternity.

Killing the half-blood would solve Daemon's little problem just like that. I wouldn't make her suffer, even though the dark, eldritch part of me wanted to make her scream.

To feast and fuck and fester in her fear.

She really was a curious creature. If I broke her open, what would spill out? What color was her soul? If I held it in my hand, would Daemon whine and whimper like a dog waiting for a treat? Her skin was far too pretty to allow it to go to waste. Maybe I'd harvest it without his knowing. Then, months from now, when he'd forgotten all about her, I'd wear it to our bed.

I waived away the dark thought before it could take root in my mind.

In any case, as much as I loathed Astrid, I'd made an oath to her. I wouldn't go back on it.

The entire reason I'd come to the Upside in the first place was to put a stop to the succubus' indiscriminate killing spree. I hadn't planned on taking over the circus, but orchestrating the offerings, wringing the fear from our patrons personally, it had been all too fun. I became addicted.

I didn't intend to go back.

It was a funny twist of fate that Astrid's daughter had shown up out of nowhere. Did she know the full extent of what happened with her mother all those years ago? Was she here to avenge her mother under the guise of looking for employment? Astrid had named her after a goddess of vengeance, after all. Had that been intentional, or did fate really have such a sick sense of humor?

But Meg didn't seem privy to her mother's deeds. Good. We'd keep it that way.

After her audition—because I wasn't going to miss the opportunity to watch Daemon sweat—I'd send her on her way.

I almost felt sorry for the girl. She was probably just looking for a place to call home. I couldn't imagine she felt like she belonged among the humans. Oh well. Her fate here would be far worse in the end. If anything, I was saving her.

Daemon would kill her if she stayed, and he'd hate himself for it in the end.

A serene smile split the lips of the human mask I wore. I was saving them both from one another. If anything, I was their *savior.*

"Shift back," I told the hound at my heel as I glided toward the big tent. "I don't believe she knows you're a hellhound shifter. I want her to know you're there, watching her."

A moment later, Daemon walked swiftly behind me, naked, his inked flesh washed in the faint moonlight. Several of the stagehands, especially the females, stopped to stare. I'd once ripped a clown's eyes out for staring too long. Now, it barely fazed me. All this exposure to the human world really had changed me.

He stopped, his glare cutting into the back of my head as I kept walking toward the big top. "Why?" the hellhound demanded in his guttural timbre.

I slowly turned to face him, planting my cane between my feet with my hands on the grip. "You make her nervous. If she's going to perform in front of our clientele, she'll have to get used to being uncomfortable."

His lip curled back. "No, why are you bothering with all this bullshit? I already asked you not to hire her."

"You did, and I'm choosing to ignore your request because you're still not telling me the truth." I got in his face, rage making my eyes flash red. Any other monster might have died from fear.

Not Daemon.

"Fine," he snarled. "You want the truth? I want her. I want her so bad it fucking scares me, Alistair. I want to shove myself so deep inside her until she tastes me. I want to cover her in my marks so monsters from miles away know she belongs to me. I want to extinguish the flame behind her eyes only so I can light it again. My hellbeast wants to consume her, Alistair. If the fire doesn't ruin her, my three heads will."

His voice fell painfully hushed as my employees watched in fascination. "Back to work, you imps. *Now!*" At the demonic bellowing of my disembodied voice and the stretch of my shadow, as it swelled to ten times my size, they scattered like frightened children.

Their fear laced the air, and I tasted it and sighed as it slithered inside me like satisfying pipe smoke. I rarely fed on my staff's fear, but I knew it well. So when there was a new flavor to it, I whipped back around to face Daemon.

"*By death and darkness.* You're afraid. The idea of killing that girl actually scares you."

The hellhound's golden eyes shone brightly through the dark night. "I don't want to repeat what happened the last time I was selfish and tried to claim a mate. Please, Master. I perform in your demented show. I kill your enemies. I've given you my body almost every night for the last two decades. I've asked for nothing in return."

I tapped the end of my cane against my shoe in thought. I hated when he gave me those puppy eyes. They were impossible to resist. Little did he know, I was already going to honor his request, even if he was a lying bastard.

"What would you have me do?"

"Tell her to leave, forever. Threaten her if you have to."

I shook my head with a sigh. "And if she doesn't take no for an answer? She's Astrid's daughter. She's inherited more than her pretty looks. She reeks of her stubbornness."

"Then scare her. It's what you do best, right? You instill fear, and you feast on it. Make her wet herself with terror."

"And what do I get in return for this favor to you? Will you claim me as your mate?"

My nerves lurched into overdrive as I waited for him to speak, even though I already knew his answer.

The hound gave an aggressive exhale. "We've been over this. I won't shift into my hellbeast form ever again. Not for anyone, not even you."

He stepped closer, took my hand, and guided it to his cock. It hardened in my grasp the moment my fingers curled around its girth. He was so warm, like a furnace. He'd been such a comfort in the Downside's cold darkness.

"You know I'll be grateful." Hunger bled into his molten irises, giving them a brilliant white glow like freshly smelted gold. How I *craved* this hound's light. He was the only thing that kept my darkness at bay.

He brought his mouth to my cheeks, his hot breath washing over my dead flesh. His tongue traced the edge of my jaw, purposefully slow, demonstrating the strength of the wet muscle. My eyes shuttered closed, and I took in a shaky breath as his cock began to leak, pearls of pre-cum seeping into the fabric covering my hand, making me wish I wasn't wearing gloves.

"And you seem to be pretty fond of the ways I express my gratitude to you, Master," he finally said, his lips moving to claim mine in a fierce kiss full of ache.

I broke away with a conceding sigh, my hand lifting from his cock to affectionately tug on the ring adorning his earlobe. "Fine. I'll scare the ever-loving soul out of your little 'pup.' But you must swear to not interfere, no matter what. I will terrify her however I see fit."

The hellhound tensed, the tendons in his neck pulling the collar around his neck taut. He had reason to be concerned. If he wanted me to terrify this girl, that's exactly what I was going to do. I'd make her see things she could never possibly fathom, even in her darkest and most depraved nightmares.

"What are you going to do?" he hedged.

"Does it matter? Everything will be an illusion. She'll only think it's happening to her."

Daemon's face went stony. He was probably imagining the worst—that I'd make her believe she was being raped or grotesquely tortured. Possibly both.

Those things weren't usually my style, but it was a valid concern. My only rule was to never physically harm an innocent. Shattering their soul and driving them to utter madness, however, was on the table.

"I swear, in your own name, that I won't interfere," he said after a beat. "Just do whatever you have to to make her leave Sinner's Sideshow forever."

"Break that oath to me, and I'll muzzle you again. Just like old times."

16
New Toy

Riff

It had been five years since Raff and I had seen a succubus. Five fucking years. She'd appeared out of nowhere, holding a bloody sword, standing over the body of the rapist she'd murdered like a dark angel.

Our little harbinger of vengeance.

I would have feasted on any emotion I could draw from her aura, but the bitter satisfaction rolling off her had been so sweet. Almost as good as the nectar I'd licked off her virginal pussy.

The best part of it all? *She wanted to stay.*

My brain just about broke with the thought of having her around all the time. Raff wouldn't get his hopes up. He was a pessimist, and I was a dreamer. I wouldn't stop daydreaming about how her pussy had clamped down on my tongue like a vice when she'd screamed her release with Raff's cock stuffed down her throat.

I needed more. I wanted to sample all of her. It was a dangerous game we were playing. Raff and I had shared women before, even one dude once, but it had been mindless, animal sex.

With Megaera, it could be mindless animal sex too—the best we've ever had if earlier today was any clue—and for some reason, I knew it would be more than that. It was like the shit Mollie pushed at the shows. With just one hit, you'd be flying, then when you came down, you'd be left already wanting more. Until it consumed you. The kind you used until there was nothing left.

Alistair had never hired a half-blood before, but that could easily be because they never came around. All she had to do was interest him. She was the estranged daughter of the old ringmaster, so that made her peculiar. I didn't know the full story, but I did know Alistair had some kind of strained history with Astrid. Now her daughter comes crawling back, desperate for a job, with no knowledge of her mother or how she ran shit before? He never could resist taking in a wayward monster.

The only problem was Daemon. The hellhound had reeked of lust when he'd been around her, and the only emotion stronger than that was his resentment for it. Alistair might not keep her around if it meant it would stir drama with his precious pet.

Megaera would have to seriously wow him for that not to be a factor.

We'd help her nail this audition in any way we could. We might be obnoxious, horny little troublemakers, but we could blow anyone's mind in the ring, even Alistair's.

I didn't help anyone, and here I was, ready to bend over backward for her.

Something told me she'd be worth it.

"Um." Meg's awkward laugh cut through my thoughts. "So, is anyone going to explain what Alistair meant by not disappointing him like my mom?" She let out another nervous giggle that did nothing to dispel the rising tension smothering the supply tent. "How did my mom disappoint him?"

"It's not something we have the full picture on, babe. No one does but Daemon, and good luck getting it out of him."

Meg stared at me from across the tent, the disappointment on her face making me wish I'd had a different answer.

"So, uh, what happens if I do disappoint him?"

"That's kind of a loaded question. Everything from telling you that you haven't got the job and to never come back to Sinner's Sideshow again, to being in the show every night...as his new favorite skin suit."

The fear wafting off her was unmistakable, but it tasted different than anything else I'd fed on before. I hadn't been sure of it in the haunt, but I pinpointed it now. Fear and lust.

Death by Discord. Our little harbinger got off on fear, *her* fear.

Why did she have to be so damn perfect? Everything about her drove me bat shit crazy. I was going insane just from my overwhelming need to make her ours.

"Are you going to give me tips to impress Alistair with my audition, or are you just going to stare at me like your jaw is going to unhinge any minute and swallow me whole?"

I smirked at her. "Oh, I'm planning on eating you, alright. But I'm going to make you last. One lick at a time."

She tried to brush off my words with a scoff, but her heart beat so loud I could practically feel her pulse in my mouth.

With an exasperated sigh, Raff pushed off the crate he'd been lounging against and prowled toward her. She stiffened but didn't make a move to draw away. She held her ground as he stopped in front of her, his arms folded over his chest as he looked down at her with a peeled lip, pretending she was an annoyance. As if all three of us couldn't glean how much we wanted to fuck her from the carnal hunger hanging in the air like smoke.

"Why should we help you? My brother took pity on you in the haunt. Why should we save your ass again?"

His tone was sharp and cutting, but there was no hiding the grin lurking at the edge of his mouth. He was teasing her, stirring her anger. She had tasted so damn good earlier when she'd still been riled up after murdering the ghoul. Anger added flavor to the meal, like a splash of hot sauce.

Only the zing of it shot straight to the dick instead of your taste buds.

She clearly hadn't spent any time around other sex demons because she fell right into his trap without a clue of what he was doing.

"*Excuse* me?" she snarled, the slits of her eyes glowing with rage. "I might be a half-blood, but I can sense emotions just like you two clowns. There was no pity—just pigheaded lust. Yeah, I needed to feed to drown out whatever disgusting shit I drank from that rapist. But I don't remember asking for your help, assholes."

"Even if you didn't want help, let's face it…" I approached her from behind, coming to stand directly behind her so she was sandwiched between Raff and me. "You did." I took a piece of her pink hair and slowly wound it around my finger. "You fed from us. It's only fair that we get a meal out of you, right?"

She heated at my words, her gulp so loud there was no missing it. "So, what? If you agree to help me, you want to feed on me?"

"That seems like a fair trade. Don't you think, bro?" I lifted my gaze to find Raff glaring down at our little demon, the lustful red shadows so bright I could see them through his contacts.

"I don't know. As tempting as that is, say she gets in? Who's to say she'd survive working here? I don't want to get hooked on something that isn't going to last."

"Come on, Rafferty," I said with a lopsided grin. "She's tough and has a strong stomach too. Any other half-blood would have dipped out the second Larry brought out that monster pork roll of his."

Raff didn't laugh or even smile. "So what? She's a succubus. Just because she can stomach the weird as fuck sex acts Alistair puts in the show doesn't mean she's going to survive *us*. This also means we gotta protect her from everyone else."

A frown thinned my lips. "No one in the troupe would dare."

"I'm not talking about the troupe. She's a succubus, bro. And a half-blood at that. We put her in the ring, in front of bloodthirsty monsters, and there's gonna be the occasional scumbag who takes a little too much of a liking to her. Know what I mean? Someone will try to steal her."

I knew what he was saying. She was a virgin sex demon. Around here, there were plenty of monsters that would go to fucked-up lengths to make her theirs.

Not that she'd be a virgin for long if we had anything to say about it.

I squared my shoulders, my fist clenching with her lock of hair still in my hand. "We won't let them."

"I *know*. And it's gonna be a big pain in the ass. You ready for that?"

"First off," Meg huffed. "I'm right fucking here. So can we stop talking like I'm not? Also, don't forget how you two goons met me. I can take care of myself."

"I'm not saying you can't hold your own, little harbinger. What I'm saying is that you're going to be a pain in the ass. It's just my brother and I are used to only looking out for ourselves. If you join the show—" Finally, a grin—apart from the painted one he wore—broke out on Raff's face "—we're gonna want to make you our mate."

The silence that folded around us was hot and sticky, like that awkward stretch of time right after sex.

Obviously, the goal was to make her our mate. It had nothing to do with her being the only succubus we'd met on the Upside and everything to do with how much she called to us, on a deep and primal level I doubt she was even aware of.

Which was why it was stupid for Raff to drop that bomb out of nowhere.

"That means you'll be ours to take care of," Raff continued, his sly smile unwavering. "Even if you don't technically 'need' our protection, you're going to get it."

"M–m–mate? Hold up a second." She tried to back up, but she had nowhere to go. She bumped into my chest and whirled around, only to back up into Raff. Raff's arms enclosed around her, his cheek pressing against her temple, leaving a smear of his white face paint.

"We're the only incubi on the Upside. We'd be perfect mates for you. Unless you think you can't handle us." He let out an unhinged laugh that he usually saved for our shows. "Maybe you can't. Riff isn't just a talented knife thrower. He loves knives. He's addicted to the pain they bring."

It suddenly clicked. I knew what he was up to.

He was trying to scare her off.

Guess he hadn't figured out she was into that shit. I grinned, deciding to play along. Only because I didn't think it would work. It would take a lot more to scare off our little harbinger.

"Oh yes. I love the feel of my knife cutting into flesh and sinew. The twitch of muscle against my blade as my victims scream in unholy pain. You caught our tamer show tonight. But just wait until we get a night where Alistair charges us with cleaning out the death seats. You haven't seen anything yet."

I leaned down, a crazed smile bowing my lips as I got in her face. She squirmed in Raff's arms but not hard enough to indicate that she really wanted to get away.

"Knife play is one thing. But what about fireplay, baby? Raff loves to play with fire. If you're not careful, you'll end up burned."

Her succubus pheromones began to leak from between her legs, pungent and intoxicating. It mixed with her lust, taunting us. Daring us not to use the hour Alistair had given us to throw her here on the ground and claim her as ours.

A grain slipped from my throat. "To work here, you're going to have to be jaded to deal with all the bloodshed. But to be with us?" I closed the last bit of distance between us, my mouth brushing over hers. "You're gonna have to get off on it."

Her eyes squeezed shut, and she sighed against the heat of my lips. "I wouldn't mind being your mate. I think."

For a moment that felt like it lasted an eternity, time stood still. Had we heard her right?

My eyes landed back on my brother, who wore the same thunderstruck expression I did.

She wanted us. She wanted us for more than just the pleasure we offered her. It was possible she was saying whatever she had to in order to ensure her help. But this didn't feel like a lie.

My dick hardened. So did Raff's by the way she ground against him, her eyelashes in a flutter. "For now, the deal is that you help me with my audition. Tell me what Alistair wants. Turn me into his perfect act, and I'll let you feed from me. If I actually end up making it into the show, we'll go from there. 'Kay?"

A battle broke out inside me, waged and won all in a breath. Ancient instincts didn't give a damn about this audition. They screamed at me to charm her, to take her virginity, and mark her as ours. The other, sane side—as minuscule as it was—won out.

We needed to focus on helping her win Alistair's interests, or there wouldn't be an opportunity for there to be more than a quick feed and fuck between us.

Reluctantly, I broke away from her and moved to one of the crates where her guitar case lay, popped the lid, and frowned at its contents. "The sword's a twenty-five-incher," I said, more to myself than anything. I didn't have to measure it to know. I knew my blades. "It's impressive for someone so short."

Meg made an adorable little huff at being called short, but at five feet, there was no other way to put it. "It's huge even for a full-grown man. And it's serrated."

I shrugged. "Doesn't matter. Unless it can turn into a twenty-five-inch flesh sword, it's not going to impress the boss by simply stuffing it down your throat."

She smiled sweetly. "Maybe there's a hole of yours I can stuff it inside. Your ass, maybe?" She batted her eyelashes. "Or I can make a new one."

"We don't have time for foreplay, baby." I chuckled, sending her a wink. "What else are you planning on doing?"

"I'm going to light it on fire."

"That's not going to cut it."

Her lips slanted with frustration. "But that's my act."

Raff stuck his hands in his pockets and leaned against a random stack of crates. "You hard of hearing? It's not going to be good enough. You can still do your act, but there's gonna have to be more to it."

"It has to be depraved." I tweaked a brow at her with a suggestive smirk. "This isn't your old family circus, babe. Kiddies aren't in the audience anymore, and your daddy ain't watching."

"Stab someone in the audience, then swallow the sword with his blood still dripping from it," Raff tossed in.

"Fuck the hilt."

He laughed. "Or the blade if you're feeling spicy."

"All the blood will make for nice lube."

"I think that defeats the point of lube, dude," Raff said, his expression darkening.

I rolled my eyes. "It doesn't have to be her blood."

"Stop," she said, getting us both to shut up and turn toward her. "I can't do any of that. That's not my style."

"Then what is your style?"

"Something..." Her voice trailed off, and she chewed her lower lip in thought. "It's something I've done before but only once, after I stopped working at the circus. I was hired out for a bachelor party once."

I swapped a look with my brother. We liked where this was going.

"What do you need from us?"

"More clothes," she hedged.

Well, that was not the answer I was expecting. Raff gave a nod.

"You can dig through our wardrobe," Raff offered. "There's tons of crap to choose from."

She gave a slow nod as the most delicious blush stained her cheeks. "Is it in your trailer?"

"Yup." Raff casually turned around, strolling toward the tent's exit. "Follow us, babe. We'll dress you up like our little doll. Make you all pretty for the ring." The rasp in my brother's voice had our little demon's pulse pounding hard.

We'd dress up our new toy, alright. But not before playing with her first.

17

Monster Twins

MEG

When I followed the twins outside, through the circus grounds, I couldn't shake the feeling that I was being led to my murder. So why was I so...*excited?*

I needed their help. Access to their wardrobe was essential if I was going to pull off what I had planned for my act. But I was a damn liar if I was going to pretend that's all I wanted from them.

They'd said they wanted to make me their mate.

I smiled to myself. It was an appealing notion. How was it not? After the last few years of being nauseated by every man, I'd found not only one male who could touch me but two? And twins? And they wanted me as their mate? If Lollie was right, they'd had their fair share of females. But they were ready to claim me as their mate after just a taste.

Had it been a serious offer? They could have just been teasing. Still, the thought of it had blood spreading to my pussy, making it tingle and ache. I barely knew them.

My vagina didn't care.

They could touch me.

Daemon turned me on, too, but that would never happen in a million years. The guy was a complete ass.

Then there was Alistair.

The weird, confusing chemistry I shared with the enigmatic shade had the little hairs on my nape standing straight up. It was like watching a horror movie and being turned on by the psychotic killer. You knew you shouldn't want the murderer. But the forbidden nature of it was alluring in itself.

The thing with Alistair was that he seemed worse than a horror movie villain. He seemed to poise himself as the good guy. He wasn't.

If his face was stolen from some dead guy, I'd bet money that his cock wasn't his, either. Then, there was his creepy shadow that seemed to have a mind of its own. It was easily twice as large as Alistair's "human" form. For some reason, the shadow didn't put me on edge in the same way Alistair did.

This fucked up circus was just another shadow, reflecting its twisted master. His stare had crept into my skin and sunk down to my marrow. Now that I'd met him, it was easy to believe that he knew Discord personally. He seemed like company the devil would keep.

I shivered, shuffling closer to Riff as he led me by the hand across the grounds with Raff just a step behind us.

It was raining now—had been for a while, judging by the sloshed-up ground. Mud coated the bottoms of my Chuck Taylor's, suctioning my feet to the sodden earth with every step. When I slipped, Raff caught me and hauled me into his arms.

I blinked up at the demon, my heart stalling in my chest as I watched his clown paint start to melt from the rainfall. His acid-green hair lay flatter against his skull, making his curved horns look so much bigger.

His black-painted lips stretched with an ear-to-ear grin. "What's that human saying? Something about taking a picture?"

"Be–because it lasts longer, yeah," I said in a breathless whisper.

Growing up in the circus, I'd been around clowns my entire life. They'd never really "done" it for me. Demonic sex clowns, on the other hand, were more my speed.

Suddenly, Raff hiked me up higher to his chest and pressed a kiss to my brow. Stunned, my lips parted, and a silly little "*Oh*" left me.

"Good girl," he said with a chuckle.

I blinked up at him, too stunned to speak for several beats. "What did I do?"

"I'm not picking up any more shame from you. That's good. Shame is a useless human emotion and has no place at Sinner's Sideshow, babe. Like what you want to like. Fuck what you want to fuck. Be messy. Be obscene. Be yourself. No apologies. No fucks given. That's how we do it here."

I nodded. No apologies, no fucks given. It sounded like dark paradise.

Movement in my periphery drew my attention to a fire in the distance. My eyes strained to make sense of the murky silhouettes of people blotted out by the dreary night.

"What are they doing?" I asked in a tremulous whisper.

Riff turned, following my line of sight to the procession of blurred bodies leading up to the bonfire. His expression darkened through the rain. "Leaving no trace that they were ever here."

That's when it clicked. What they were doing. Clowns and the odd stagehands were dragging bodies through the mud and throwing them into the fire. They were disposing of the corpses of the people who'd purchased Alistair's "death seats."

My eyes widened as two clowns picked up a particularly large body—probably a troll or something—and swung it back and forth by its arms and legs, building momentum. On the fourth swing, they tossed the corpse into the flames in a gust of smoke and embers.

There one moment and gone the next.

Raff must have sensed me tensing in his arms because he kissed me, his lips catching the corner of my mouth. "Don't worry. They're just going home, Megaera."

This soft side of the demon caught me off guard—more than the burning bodies—but I accepted the comfort he offered with a nod.

If I was going to call this place my home, I'd have to get used to the bloodshed and murder. Here, those things were normal. It wasn't like innocents were dying. All those people bought those seats with the intention of going to Hell.

Riff and Raff took me to their trailer on the very edge of the lot, far from the other tents and the rest of the troupe's vehicles. I wasn't sure if the magic concealing the circus stretched to the parking lot, but everything here seemed normal—unassuming vans and trailers. You'd never know they were owned by monsters.

The twins' residence was an unmarked black beast of a trailer. Fancier than any of the ones that had been at Walker's.

Riff opened the door and stepped inside, sweeping an appraising look before tossing an apologetic look down at me. "Whoopsie. Didn't know we'd have company."

Raff carried me inside, setting me down once we crossed the threshold. The place was a mess with clothes and random items strewn everywhere, but it didn't faze me in the slightest. I'd been living in my car for almost two years, and one glance inside was pretty damning of that fact. And the twins' space was way more upscale than my piece of shit Volkswagen Bug, or the "clown car," as my dad had called it. The finishes here were sleek, black, and modern. The kitchenette had stainless steel appliances and marble tiling. Riff flipped on the LED lights affixed to the ceiling, their red coloring washing everything in a sensual glow.

They were horror and sci-fi fans. Every inch of spare wall space was covered in movie posters—including ones for *Killer Klowns from Outer Space* and *Mars Attacks!*—and paraphernalia. Displays held dozens of masks, from horror movie icons to terrifying rubber clown masks with tuffs of bright-colored hair and twisted smiles.

There were also collections of throwing knives, containers of fuel for fire eating, and all sorts of things you'd expect for two demonic circus performers.

I felt their eyes burn into my skin as I took everything in. "So I'm confused. Are you guys scare actors, clowns, aerialists, sideshow freaks?"

"All of the above, baby," Riff said with a low snicker. "We're whatever the boss wants us to be. We can do it all."

I nodded as I moved deeper into the trailer. Their vast collection of masks and slutty stage costumes was intimidating. "What, no giant clown shoes or goofy red noses?" I laughed, trying to disperse some of the building tension.

"No." Raff chuckled. "You need to train up on your clown knowledge. That shit is associated with character clowns. If you have to put a label on it, we're harlequins."

"Harlequins. The sexiest of clowns." I smirked as my mind wandered to the part of my brain where I kept all my circus lore. "The word harlequin is derived from the old French word for the leader of a *la maisnie Hellequin*, which is said to be a gang of demons who flew through the night on horseback."

The twins glanced at one another before looking at me with impressed expressions. "Very good, harbinger," Raff praised. "The first clowns of Sinner's Sideshow basically invented the harlequin, back when the circus first came to the Upside in the 16th century."

"These days we put a new spin on it," Riff said, pointing to the far end of the room.

I followed his gesture to an alcove—a closet with the doors removed—stuffed with custom pieces.

"Whoa," I mumbled as I drifted toward the closet, where a dresser, several hooks, and a couple of mannequins displayed their collection of leather, PVC, and fetish gear. "It's like a Spirit Halloween store had a baby with a gay porn studio's costuming department."

"We'll take that as a compliment."

I froze when my gaze landed on a mannequin pushed against the corner of the closet, somewhat tucked away. It was a slutty nun costume complete with a freaky clown mask, topped with a floppy harlequin cap made to look like a nun's veil.

"You guys are serious creeps," I said with a laugh. The slutty clown nun costume was hot as shit, but a stab of jealousy struck me between the ribs knowing another woman had worn it. Someone they'd been involved with, probably.

Raff gave a dark cackle. "Discord's darkness, Riff. Have you ever smelled lust so potent? She likes your costume from your slutty sister gag."

"Wait." I whipped around to face Riff, who was scrubbing the back of his skull with the flat of his hand, looking abashed. "*Your* act? You wore this."

"Yeah. It was just a one-night act, but it was kind of awesome. It was on a night when I was in charge of the death seats. It had all been demons that booked those seats, so I got this and some crucifix-shaped knives."

My imagination went wild with thoughts of the blue-haired demon dressed as a nun—with the chunky-heeled goth boots and fishnets on the floor next to the mannequin—slaying demons with a bladed crucifix.

"That's pretty fucking kickass, Riff."

"Yeah?" He perked up, a crooked grin taking over his face. By now, his creepy clown paint had almost completely faded, revealing his natural smile beneath. He came to stand beside me, his gaze slipping down the length of my body. "It would look better on you."

"This could work for what I have in mind."

"Are you gonna let us in on the secret?"

"Nope." I tugged my hoodie over my head and let it drop to the ground. "You're going to have to sit in on my audition if you want to see."

"Like we'd miss it," Raff whispered as he came to stand beside his brother. "Fuck, you're gorgeous, harbinger."

Heat crept up the back of my neck and spread to the rest of my face. It was a weird little pet name they'd stuck me with, but I loved it. It made me feel powerful. Every time they said it, I heard a dark sort of reverence in their tone.

"Is that the costume you wore for your old act?"

"Mmm." I nodded with a smile, looking down fondly at the bodice.

Raff's hands ran down my bodice, and my breath hitched when his fingers traced the embroidered flames decorating my breasts. "It's pretty. It's meant to make you look like a dark angel, right? I'm guessing it was the only time in the human realm where you could shift without raising suspicion, where it passes as part of your costume."

I swallowed, emotion thick in my throat. "Yeah. So it's nice being here where I can let it out all the time. It's like..."

"Like letting your feet out of too-tight shoes."

I blinked at Riff, taken aback by the surprisingly accurate description. "I'm not trying to be rude, but how would you know what it's like to hide your true form?"

If he was offended, he didn't show it, and the only trace of emotion from his aura was amusement. "Sure, we have never been forced into our human forms before, at least not for long. We've made snack runs and caught the occasional movie. It's only for a few hours at a time at most. Still, we've been suppressing our full demonic forms for years."

"You two have full demon forms?" It was hard to imagine them more than with horns and a tail. It was the only other form I had. It was probably for the best that I didn't have a huge, beastly monster to shift into. It would have been harder to hide when I'd gone through puberty, and shifts had happened by accident.

"Yup. We're *huge*," Raff explained through a fang-filled smirk.

"Massive."

"Big horns." Riff motioned in the air, his hands shaping horns much bigger than the sleek ones that curled back with his rain-slicked hair. "Big cocks."

"And big egos," I interrupted with an eye roll and a bridled smile. "So why can't you let your full forms out?"

"Alistair doesn't like it."

"What, so is everyone here his bitch?"

"Pretty much." Raff let out a laugh as he hopped up on the kitchen counter, which, thanks to the trailer's close quarters, was just a few steps from the closet. He lounged back on his elbows, his tail coiling around his leg. "And Daemon is our leader. He takes one for the team by being the only one who fucks him."

Riff shook his head. "I don't know, bro. He's kind of hot. He's got this Willy Wonka meets Leatherface from *Texas Chainsaw Massacre* sort of thing going on. I can get into it."

My lips quirked at the references. They must have watched a lot of movies. Made sense for demons wanting to blend in with the Upside whenever they wandered off circus grounds.

"Everyone in the troupe is full of shit when they say they wouldn't fuck him if he gave them the chance," Riff continued. "They're just trying to save face because no one else here is good enough for him except for Daemon."

"*Tch.* Yeah, not good enough just because no one else in the troupe has three dicks."

It took me a moment to process this new direction of the conversation. I couldn't tell if they were bullshitting me or not. "Wait. Backup, Daemon has three dicks?"

"In his true form, yeah." Riff shot his brother a glare, silently scolding him for saying something he shouldn't have. "But he never shifts into his hellish form. None of us do."

"Why doesn't Alistair let you fully shift?"

"Well, he would let Daemon, but Daemon doesn't want to. Something about hurting an old mate years back."

He had a mate. Why did my heart ache at this news? Why did I care?

I became aware of the way the twins stared at me with surprise at first, then sympathy. "You don't have to be jealous, Meg," Raff said in a soft voice. "She's dead."

Whatever envy I felt was immediately replaced with regret, which sat on my chest like an anvil. "It's not like I want to be his mate. I didn't come here looking for lovers. I came here for a job."

"Still, there's no denying that your powers are awakening. Naturally, you're going to want to explore your nature. We're not here to force you into doing that."

"It's not like we're going to discourage you either."

"Maybe you didn't come here to learn about your mom. But you came here to learn about yourself. Right? To finally let your monstrous side, along with all its instincts, out to play."

"So. We have a little less than an hour to get you to your audition. It won't take that long to get you dressed and painted."

"And you do owe us a meal for helping you. That's the deal," Riff said with a gleam in his eyes.

"So, how about it? Wanna play?"

"Yes. But I have a request. I want you two to feed from me in your true forms. I want to see you. The real versions of you."

18

Kryptonite

RAFF

She wanted to see our full demonic forms.

No, she didn't want to just see them. She wanted us to touch her in our most monstrous state.

Was I dreaming?

Who was this wicked angel, and what had we done to deserve her?

"We—we're not supposed to," Riff said in a rasp.

"We can stay right here." She sucked her bottom lip between her teeth as the blush over her cheeks deepened to a delicious hue of red. My dick went hard at the thought of covering her whole body in that color. "No one will see."

Fuck. This girl was our...What was that human saying? Kryptonite.

I never wanted a mate for myself. The occasional pump and dump, sure. But I didn't want to get attached. The only person I ever wanted to have to look out for was my little brother.

Yes, we were twins. But I was technically a few minutes older, even though Daemon liked to claim that our mother's tired-out pussy was so stretched out, we both probably crawled out at once.

In any case, Riff acted like the younger one out of us two. He was the goofier one. The less jaded one. He was almost bolder with his acts, like the nun side dish he'd come up with. He was absolutely unhinged.

A great performer. A good brother. But sometimes he did stupid ass shit.

Like falling for this half-blood the moment he'd laid eyes on her.

I didn't want to see him get hurt. The odds seemed pretty slim that Alistair would let Meg into the troupe. She was a half-blood, which meant she was more fragile than the rest of us. She'd also been raised as a human. Meaning she wasn't desensitized to all the shit that went down at our shows, like all the drugs, the brawls, the murder.

It's not like humans were involved, so there was that. But still. Sinner's Sideshow wasn't a place for the faint-hearted. Then she fooled around with us. And I knew she'd fit right in.

Now, I wanted her as much as Riff did.

Even if she could keep up with the brutality, it didn't change the fact that she was Astrid's daughter. I'd never worked for the demoness. Riff and I had been younglings in the Downside at the time. But we'd been around long enough to know the gist of what went down.

The entire point of Sinner's Sideshow was to spill blood, all in the name of Satan. Blood sacrifices. Souls for his realm. But Astrid had gone rogue, spilling mortal and monster blood without so much as a drop of discretion.

Satan had sent one of the strongest of demons in all of the Downside to dispose of her. She fled. Found another circus to take her in. Fell in love. No one knew what Alistair had done to her. Or if he'd even found her at all.

Whatever happened, she'd lived long enough to have her baby.

Alistair took over the circus, murdered every member of her troupe, sent their souls back to the Underside, then hand-selected a new troupe. My brother and I had come along five years ago. The Upside wasn't paradise, but it was a Hell of a lot closer than the Downside.

Alistair had saved us from that place. He was good, at least to us.

But it was hard to tell how he felt about the daughter of the woman he'd been sent to kill. I couldn't get a read on the monster, but I'd spent enough time around him to know when something crawled under that stolen skin of his.

Something bad was about to happen. Riff didn't sense it, but I did.

If I had any fucking sense, I wouldn't let us get involved with her. We couldn't get too attached.

Eh, who was I kidding? That ship had already sailed the Styx.

From the moment she'd wrapped her perfect lips around my dick in the haunt, it had been too late. So might as well enjoy her while we could and revel in the fantasy that one day she'd be our mate.

Before Alistair inevitably took her away.

"Fine," I said after several moments of pregnant silence. "You want to see a monster? You'll get one. Just one, though. There isn't enough room for both of us to shift here. Besides, you're still a virgin. I'll stay in this form to keep Riff in check and make sure he doesn't get carried away."

Her brows formed an angry *V*. "I don't need a chaperone."

"If you need to be able to walk for your audition in an hour, then yes, you do. We weren't shitting you when we said we get carried away in our true forms. Instincts take over. Besides, if we're going to get the opportunity to pluck that cherry of yours, we're going to need a lot more than an hour."

The thick cloud of succubus pheromones shrouding her spiked in potency. "I want you to take it tonight."

"No," I said firmly, fighting the urge to give in. There was a chance we'd never get to be with her again after tonight, but it wasn't worth rushing this. "We're gonna want to take our time. Make it good for you. You deserve that."

"So...what are you going to do to me then?" she asked, her breath hitching audibly in her throat. I took her by the hand and led her down the hall to the bedroom at the end of the trailer, Riff tailing close behind.

When we stepped through the door, her heart hammered so hard I could feel it in her fingertips. Her eyes scanned the room, taking in the makeup vanity in the corner, then the random assortment of shit on the dresser, like my blow torch, a bong to smoke my favorite Upside plant, and one of Riff's knives sticking out of the wood. Propped up against the dresser were Riff's stilts, and hanging off the end of it was a ball gag.

Next, her eyes went to the collection of BDSM gear mounted over our headboard. Floggers. Paddles. Cuffs. More masks—Ghostface, Jason, and a few other horror movie classics.

She pulled her hand from mine to prop a hand on her hip, feigning disapproval. She was so adorable when she tried to hide how flustered she was. "You guys share the same bed? With all this freaky stuff just lying around?"

I turned to Riff, who leaned against the bedroom door frame, a dark smirk perched on his lips. "Nervous?"

"No," she added too quickly. "You guys are just really close, is all. What, do you fuck each other if you can't trick some girl into your bed?"

This little half-blood was inexperienced and nervous. Too green for Sinner's Sideshow, that was for damn sure. But underneath that, she was brave, intelligent, and bratty as hell.

She was absolutely perfect. I couldn't wait to ruin her.

"Wow, a twincest joke. *Original.*" I pushed on her chest so she fell back into our bed. She fell with a surprised look, but lust-pink shadows danced behind her eyes a moment later as she gave in.

"We're just close, is all," I said with a grin, standing over her at the foot of the bed. "We share the same interests. The same bed. The same meals."

Riff shoved off against the door frame, prowling closer. "The same pussy."

"Which is exactly what all these toys are for. We like to entertain. We're—what do you call it? Hospitable."

Riff chuckled behind me. "Yeah. We're hospitable."

"You sure about that? Because I've been here for five minutes, and I haven't gotten so much as a kiss yet. I thought you two were supposed to be sex demons."

"You're going to be getting a lot more than a kiss, little harbinger."

She flushed at the nickname—she liked it. As she should. She helped that bunny shifter when most monsters would have turned a blind eye. She was righteous and good. That was rare for our kind.

I wanted to suck out everything good and pure about her like a goddamn vampire.

I pulled my shirt over my head and moved slowly as I felt her eyes on me, drinking in every flexing muscle. Tossing the shirt to the corner of the room, I looked back down at her to find her eyes on the balloon tattoo peeking out over my belt.

Her lips pulled into a heated smirk as she was probably re-calling the entire tattoo. "So, do all the ladies go crazy for the Shibari clown tattoo?"

"It's popular. I don't think anyone's liked it as much as you, though."

"I never said shit about liking it."

"You don't have to. Emotion reading sex demon, remember? Or maybe the lust I was picking up from you back in the haunt was because you had a throat full of demon dick. Either way, you were fucking dripping for me, girl."

She gave a mock yawn. "Do you always talk so much when you have a girl in your bed?"

This little demon was taunting me. No other female had ever dared. I guess she liked playing with fire—something we had in common.

"I know your old costume is important to you. So I'm giving you ten seconds to get out of it before I fucking tear it off your body."

Her eyes widened. On the next beat, she was tugging her hoodie over her head and peeling the black bodysuit down her legs. She threw the clothes to the floor, leaving herself naked in our bed.

It took everything in me not to come right there from the mere sight of her.

Death by Discord. She really was a dark angel. Every supple curve and stretch of perfect ivory skin was unholy perfection. She had plump thighs with medium-sized breasts to create a subtle pear shape that had my mouth watering. Each rosy nipple was accented with a metal barbell.

Fuck me. She had pierced nipples.

She had a tattoo of a flaming circus tent on her right thigh. Her hand smoothed over the inked flesh when she caught me staring at it. "I got it not long after Walker's went under. The tattoo was my alternative to therapy."

Grief started to leak from her like a dam about to break.

"Meg—" Riff started, probably feeling the need to comfort her.

"Don't," she said, with enough force behind her tone to silence the blue-haired demon before he could get out another word. "I don't want to talk about it."

I looked at Riff, whose gaze had hardened, but I could read it all the same. She didn't need to be comforted. What she needed was a distraction from whatever thoughts of her past plagued her.

I lowered myself onto the bed and crawled over her, caging her head between my hands. "I'm going to kiss you now."

Her plush lips parted for her tongue to slip out, wetting them in invitation. "Finally."

My mouth crashed into hers hard enough to knock out a gasp. I devoured it, pushing my tongue into her mouth, our teeth knocking together, the points of my canines cutting her deep enough to draw a bead of blood.

I wasn't usually this brutal with my kisses. But being what I was, I had the ability to sense what my partner wanted. And

Meg liked a little pain, even if she hadn't been with anyone that she trusted or liked enough to give it to her. I'd be rougher with her now because when Riff shifted, I'd have to be the gentle one to make sure we didn't spoil our little virgin too quickly.

As my lips suctioned firmly around hers, I pinched her nose. Her eyes flew open, and she let out a muffled little "*Mmph!*"

When she started to thrash beneath me, I bore down on her, making sure she knew exactly how hard her struggling made me.

"Let up, Rafferty." My twin's command came out dark and full of warning. "If we give her a safeword, she's gotta be able to fucking use it."

I pulled back, tucking a wild lock of hair behind her ear as she gaped up at me, her chest heaving. "Y–you bastard."

She could curse me all she wanted. There was no hiding the feral excitement dancing behind her eyes. "If you want me to stop, you know the magic words. 'Playtime is over.' Say them, and we'll skip this shit and go right to getting you dressed for your audition."

"Go to Hell."

I grinned and reached over her for a set of handcuffs mounted on the wall. "That's what I thought. Now be a good girl and put your hands over your head."

19

Knives, Cuffs and Tongues

MEG

I gulped down several broken gasps of air. No matter how much oxygen I managed to swallow down, I couldn't seem to replace what Raff had stolen. My lungs screamed. My whole chest burned.

And it had felt *good*.

I did as I was told—which was something I never did, but hey. Exceptions had to be made when incubi twins were involved.

Placing my arms over my head, Raff fastened the cuffs over my wrists. When he leaned back to admire the scene, I discovered that he'd secured the chain connecting the cuffs to the headboard.

He brushed the back of his knuckles over one of my horns. They were small compared to his, no longer than two-inch points sitting over my brow in the stereotypical place while their horns emerged over their ears and curved back, tips pointed inward at the back of their skulls.

"Spread your wings," he told me in a tender voice that had my blush spreading down my chest to my nipples. "I have to see them."

Even though I had been in my demon form most of the night, my wings had been hidden under my hoodie. At this point, I had them tucked between my shoulder blades. Since I was raised as a human, it's not like I was an expert on sex demons. But I did know that only succubi had wings. They were like male peacock tails. Meant for seduction. Which was why Riff and Raff stared at me, practically drooling at the mouths as they waited for me to unfurl my wings.

If Raff hadn't asked, I would have kept them tucked against my back. Since I was a half-blood, they were so small. Compared to the full-blooded succubi in the Downside, they had to be pretty wimpy.

With a tentative breath, I arched off the bed enough to unfold them and stretch them out. Each wing was two feet on either side and not an inch more. Raff's chest hitched, and I thought he was about to laugh, but instead, his hand spread over the black leather skin of my wing. His hand was so huge it covered much of my wing. "You look so damn sexy, harbinger."

I blinked up at him as my heart twisted into knots.

This. What was this feeling? As a creature who fed on emotions, I'd thought there wasn't anything I hadn't felt before. This strange sensation wrapping around my heart like barbed wire was new. It freaking hurt, but...It was warm and comforting, like standing too close to a fire on a cold night.

"Let me shift," Riff said, shuffling with impatience at the foot of the bed. "You heard her. She wants a monster between her legs."

"We have to ease her into that. Get the box of toys under the bed."

My mind began to splinter under the wake of lust radiating from them as Riff crouched and pulled out a black shoe box from the bed.

I laughed. "You keep your sex toys in a shoe box?"

The twins swapped a look, a rabid smirk slowly stretching their mouths. Riff glanced back at me as he reached into the box and brandished a butterfly knife. "Who said anything about 'sex' toys?"

I gasped and jerked on my cuffs. "You hurt me, and I'll kill you both."

"Oh, we have no doubt about that, harbinger. I almost wanna see that. I bet you'd look so pretty covered in our blood." Riff set the box down on the dresser and handed the knife to his brother.

With a flourish, the blade flashed in the dim red lighting of their room, and the knife handles fell open. He held the knife by the blade, and one of the handles, the other half of the handle, pointed toward me.

Whatever he was going to do to me, it wasn't going to be with the blade.

How twisted was I that I was almost disappointed?

"Playtime can end anytime, baby," he reminded me.

I didn't want it to end. "Whatever you're going to do, just do it. We don't have much time."

Instead, his eyes shone bright with his wide grin. "Open your legs."

Before his command had fully left his tongue, my thighs were instinctually parting. An audible breath latched in his chest as my pheromones bled into the air. "Discord's Depths, you smell infernally good, little harbinger."

It was nice. Being desired like this. Being comfortable. This went deeper than lust. There was something bigger, something invisible, drawing us together.

It was stupid, but I already felt like I knew them. They understood me.

There was no hiding my lust and my weird inclination for the macabre and the weird. It was...cathartic. And these two demon clowns encouraged it.

With them, I felt perfectly at home.

Even as he nudged half of the butterfly knife's hilt against my opening.

"Wait... Will this...break my hymen? If I'm going to bleed, I want it to be around your cock."

Riff swore under his breath, then brought his knuckles to his mouth and bit down.

Whatever embarrassment I felt was pushed away with the kindness shining bright in Raff's eyes despite his manic clown smile. "Have you played with toys before?"

"Small ones," I admitted. "Like a bullet. Anything bigger, and I'd get nauseous."

He nodded, unfazed by that news. "Your concubus urges demand you lie with a suitable partner for your first time. So you can probably feed and nourish your powers. You won't fully awaken your abilities until you do. But don't worry. Things like tampons or fingers, or this—" He held up the butterfly hilt, which was no bigger than a finger "—won't affect your hymen tissue. There might be a bit of discomfort, but you shouldn't bleed—if you bleed at all—until you're properly fucked."

My mind stalled out for a beat. The fact that this green-haired clown knew so much about my body was making me so wet, and it didn't go unnoticed. Raff slid the hilt of the knife through my folds, cursing in Infernal tongue. "Look at all this pussy, Rifton. Have you ever seen one so pink and plush and dripping? I've never seen a female cream so much before we've even touched her."

"I know. I can still taste her from earlier," Riff said on a low growl. "Have a lick. It will blow your fucking mind."

Raff sunk the first inch of the hilt inside me as I arched my hips off the bed to welcome the invasion, then he arched down and covered my clit with his mouth.

The chain of my cuffs rattled as the pleasure of his tongue sliding through my folds had me twitching beneath him. He groaned against me, the vibrations tickling my aching clit.

Riff's eyes burned into me from the foot of the bed. "You like having my brother's tongue on you while he fucks you with my favorite knife?"

I gave a lust-drunk nod, my eyes pleading with Riff as Raff settled down between the cradle of my legs. "Yes. Fuck, yes."

Raff suckled on my clit, the pleasure offsetting any discomfort as he pushed the knife's hilt deeper inside me. "You taste *so good*, Megaera," he moaned against my folds.

The little hairs on my nape stood up when I realized he wasn't talking about my pussy. He had started to feed from me, and what he tasted was the lust of a sex-starved succubus.

His tongue slid a path over my slit, the hot appendage surprisingly strong. He was slow at first, the wet muscle taking its time tasting me. Tracing circles around my clit.

Then, whatever tether had been holding him back snapped.

He feasted on me, the lap and lick of his tongue making my nerves light up with pleasure.

Hot, blistering pleasure. A part of me I'd only been vaguely aware of and hadn't fully understood came roaring to life. "*Oh.*"

"How's my brother's tongue?" Riff's voice cut through the dense fog of lust swaddling my mind.

"G–good."

"Think you can handle a bigger one?"

He was going to shift! "Y–yes!"

Raff sat back on his heels and repositioned himself so he was sitting beside my head. He held the knife's hilt to my lips. It glistened with my juices in the red lighting. "Open up, and suck it."

When my lips parted on his command, he pushed the metal into my mouth, and I licked it clean as I watched Riff strip naked at the foot of the bed.

His shirt came off first, then he ripped off his belt and shoved his jeans and black boxers to the floor.

I gasped around his knife as his cock sprang free. I'd wondered what the demon was packing after I'd given his brother head in the haunted house. Would it be pierced? Tattooed?

The answer was both.

They really were identical in almost every way, including length and girth. Eight to nine-inch territory. When the time came, I wasn't sure how that would work, considering the split butterfly knife hilt had felt like a lot. And it was safe to say they'd both be bigger when fully shifted.

Riff had a Jacob's Ladder piercing, with five barbells running along the underside of his shaft. On top was a tattoo of a sword, its tip pointed toward yet another piercing, a Prince Albert.

He was pierced and inked to sinful perfection.

Then he started to shift. His muscles spasmed as they swelled in size. The terrible sound of cracking bones filled the tiny room as his body expanded to easily twice, three times his original size. His horns were thicker now and shaped more like a ram's. If I thought his cock was big before, it was ridiculously huge now. His piercings seemed so small in comparison.

But for all its obscene glory, I was barely looking at his cock.

I couldn't look away from his head. In the place of his human head was now a skinless skull in the shape of some kind of animal head. An animal that didn't exist on the Upside. His teeth were long and serrated, and his gaping eye holes were filled with a glowing blue light that matched his hair color.

The bone of his head had been painted like a harlequin clown, with diamonds over the eyes and a black triangle over the slits of his nose. The paint had long faded, but it had dyed the bone, making him more terrifying than ever.

"Your turn's over," the skull-headed beast rumbled to Raff, his long tongue painting a lick over his teeth. "Uncuff her. I want to feel her hands on my horns when I split her apart on my tongue."

20

The Virgin and the Monster

MEG

How? How in the actual fuck was I supposed to fit Riff's tongue in his true demonic form?

He had a huge monster skull for a head. Would the fire in his eyes burn? Would his teeth cut me?

Not to be dramatic, but a girl could literally die trying to fit a monster tongue like that. But fuck—what a way to go.

Raff sat back, pulling the knife from my mouth, then brought it to his lips, sucking the last juices up before tossing it onto the dresser. He uncuffed me, his fingertips smoothing over the impressions the leather straps had left. His lips kicked up into a heated smile. "How would you like to go for a ride on the tongue of a fully shifted incubus?"

"You keep asking for my permission. What is this?"

"Because consent is sexy, *brat.*" He let out another one of those crazed laughs, what remained of his painted smile cracking at the corners. "Besides, how good of a meal could we get from you if you're not enjoying yourself? And are you not enjoying yourself? I mean, look what you've done to our sheets."

I followed his line of sight to a wet spot on the bed between my legs. The mattress groaned as Riff pawed up on the bed and pressed his nose to the wet spot, the smooth bone brushing my center as he inhaled.

"I vote that we never wash these sheets again. Then our bed will smell like her forever," he growled.

He looked up at me, his nose moving to my apex as he took another deep breath in.

The blue flames in his eyes rolled through me, filling my veins with fire. I lost myself in their white-hot glow, remaining frozen in place even as he slid his tongue over my thigh.

"Feel that, Riff?" Raff asked his twin. "She's so scared. And oh *so* turned on."

"Our little harbinger gets off on terror," Riff rumbled in his hellish cadence. "What luck. So do we."

Raff lifted me up with ease, temporarily pulling me off the bed while Riff positioned himself so he was lying on his back, his legs hanging off the edge. Once he was settled, Raff set me on my feet.

"Spread your legs wide," he said against the shell of my ear.

With my heart in my mouth and curiosity and excitement eating me alive, I did as I was told. On the next breath, his arms swooped beneath me, and he lifted me up, my thighs spread wide on the shelf his arms created. My hands flew behind his head and locked at his nape to keep my back flush with his chest while he guided us back to the bed.

He knelt between the headboard and his brother's giant skull so my spread opening hovered directly over Riff's skull.

I stared down in awe as his jaw opened wide, his gaping maw of teeth gleaming in the room's dim red glow. If Raff dropped me, my pussy would be cut to ribbons. I knew he wouldn't. His arms held me fast, and even his tail wrapped around my waist for extra security.

So the threat of it, the tiny niggling fear that it could happen, pushed my lust to new heights.

Riff's tongue was huge, a monstrous appendage slick with copious amounts of saliva.

I was so turned on by the sight of it wriggling beneath me that a drop of my arousal pebbled his tongue. He fell still as it absorbed into his taste buds. Then, his cock twitched and thickened.

The monster groaned. "Lower her. Let me eat her."

"Be gentle," Raff told his brother, his voice firm and laced with warning. "Don't break our new toy before we've barely had a chance to play with her."

When he hummed in agreement, Raff lowered me. "This reminds me of the classic trope in old sword and sorcery movies where the virgin is tossed to the monster as a sacrifice."

"Y–you guys watch a lot of movies, don't you?"

"We've had to. It's how we learned English."

"And how do those scenes end?" I panted, pearls of sweat sliding down my temples as Riff's tongue painted a teasing lick up my inner thigh.

Raff pressed his mouth to my ear, his dark chuckle sending a shiver through me. "She gets eaten."

Just as the last word left the incubus' mouth, his twin's tongue lashed over my center. It was gentle and slow. It fucking stung, the pain and pleasure of it setting my nerves on fire. My head fell back on Raff's shoulder with my cry.

A string of dark laughter poured from him as I squirmed in his arms, Riff's tongue assaulting my core with a frantic pace. The wet appendage was large but surprisingly nimble as it purposefully danced around my throbbing clit, driving me into a lustful rage.

"St—stop teasing m—me, dammit!"

"Look who's the one giving orders now. She's so cute." Riff's gravelly baritone was just as much of a tease as the rest of him, with the way it curled inside me.

Frustration had my tail coiling around his horn, and with all my strength, I tugged his huge head up. He laughed, sounding impressed for a moment before giving me what I needed. The tip of his tongue found my opening and sunk inside.

"Oooh, fuck, *yes.*"

Riff's hum of approval had his tongue vibrating inside me. He was only a few inches in, if that, and yet it felt like I was splitting apart. When my legs started to tremble on the shelf of

Raff's arms, Riff reached up and wrapped his hands around my thighs. They were so huge his fingers swallowed me, his claws meeting all the way around.

He could easily crush me. Break my bones with a single squeeze and eat me whole.

That was the beautiful thing about being with these monsters, I realized. Knowing they could so easily break me and having them drown me in pleasure instead.

Riff's tongue pushed deeper inside, the stretching sensation making my eyes water. Without warning, his jaws clamped shut—his deadly teeth stopping just in time enough not to puncture me. I screamed and felt the tug on my aura, knowing he was having himself a nice little meal.

They were right. I was turned on when I was afraid. Obviously, it had to be a certain kind of fear. I'd been afraid for that helpless bunny shifter in the haunted house, but all I'd felt was anger.

These demons knew just how to pluck and pull at me to make me wet with fear.

"More, please, *more.*"

Riff's claws gouged deeper into my thighs, making little pinpoints of blood bead on my pale flesh. He sunk another inch inside me, lapping and sucking and feasting on me like I was his last meal.

Raff's tale uncoiled from my waist to wrap around my throat, making my moans come out strangled and ragged. The spade tip hooked into my mouth, forcing my jaw open, the slight degrading position only wringing more pleasure from me.

My orgasm mounted, the little ball of pleasure quickly turning into an inferno of searing heat that had my flesh burning. Perched in the cradle of this clown demon's gaping maw, with his brother's painted clown face looking down at me, should have been scary.

It was. But it was also beautiful.

I felt like a dark queen sitting on her throne made of fire and flesh and bone.

I came with another scream, my back arching off Raff's chest.

Riff's tongue slipped from me, ropes of saliva spilling out and soaking the bed. Raff lowered me to the damp sheets, his hand skimming over the marks left by his brother's claws. "I told you to be gentle."

"I was gentle. She's still breathing, isn't she?"

The next moment, I felt Riff's hand on my horn, forcing my head off the bed. I found his cock a kiss away from my lips. It was engorged and swollen with need. Thick pearls of pre-cum seeped from the slit, coating his Prince Albert piercing.

"Kiss me," Riff urged, nudging his cock at my lips. "Lick me clean as I have done for you."

Keeping my eyes fastened to his, I swirled my tongue over his head and lapped up the seed coating his silky flesh.

"You know…We showed our true forms to a lover once," Raff said as he arched over me and kissed my shoulder. "She screamed, and not in a fun way. You're the first to not only like us like this but also the first to ever ask for it."

The blue flames in Riff's eye sockets pulsed and flickered as I smirked against the head of his cock. "Sounds like you two have been shagging the wrong girls."

"We've been looking for a mate. With not much luck…" Raff swept a sweaty lock of my hair behind my ear. "Until now."

The twins shared a look over my head. I couldn't read their expressions—especially Riff's painted skull—but I felt what they did, as the strong emotions bled from their aura and mixed with the bedroom's heady, sex-scented air.

They were afraid this wouldn't be more than a one-night thing because if Alistair didn't let me into the troupe, that would be it. I wouldn't be in the demons' lives unless I decided to keep chasing them across the country, attending every show I could.

My bank account, my poor little car, and my heart wouldn't take that for very long.

I crawled off the bed and wiped my mouth with my hand. "Come on. I need to get ready. I have to nail this audition."

I have to.

21

Something Twisted

MEG

"Look at you. You look devastating." My eyes locked with Raff's in the reflection of the full-length mirror mounted beside the twins' closet, and I smiled at the admiration in his voice.

I did look awesome.

Black fishnets dotted with blue diamonds hugged my shapely legs, and thanks to the high-cut slits running up the nun's habit, you could see all of them. An oversized rosary hung around my neck, decorated with silver and blue beads and an upside-down cross. The best part of the getup was the headpiece, made to look like a nun's and a harlequin's cap. My feet were way too small for Riff's black shit-kickers, so I opted to wear my worn all-black Converse.

"You're more beautiful than Lilith Terself."

I blinked. "Isn't that one of Daemon's hounds?"

He nodded, laughing. "Yeah. But that's not who I'm referencing. He named the hound after Lilith, an ancient and powerful demoness said to have been Discord's greatest and oldest disciple. She literally worshiped the ground he walked on, and she was said to be more beautiful than any demoness before her. The first sex demon—" The incubus paused, tweaking a brow at me. "You don't know this? It's basically a Mother Goose story for demons."

A blush burned my cheeks. "No. I was raised by my dad, who knew my mom was a succubus and that she used to work at Sinner's Sideshow. But he didn't know much more than that. Everything else I know is from what I've found on the dark web, and I could never find much."

"Yeah. Our kind don't travel to the Upside often, and few of them are technologically inclined. The ones who are don't like leaving much of a digital footprint. Gotta lay low and all that."

"So what about this Lilith? Was she Discord's mate, then? A devil queen?"

"No. She was madly in love with him, but she only remained his loyal servant. The story goes that she was so beautiful, he didn't want to spoil her."

"So the first ever succubus remained a virgin?"

Raff shrugged. "At least for a few eons or something."

I turned to face him, chewing flirtatiously on my bottom lip. "So when you say I'm more beautiful than Lilith, you're saying

I'm hotter than the demon who was too hot for even the devil to touch?"

He ran a hand through his acid-green hair, which stuck out in every direction. *Damn.* He looked so mouth-watering in the trailer's red lighting. "Yeah. You're the prettiest clown nun I've ever laid my eyes on, and we'll just glaze over the fact that the only other one I've seen is my brother."

"Right. Wow, so this was Riff's costume." It was very clearly tailored for a woman, with the bodice nothing more than a tight corset. "I bet he looked good in it."

Raff shrugged. "We're incubi. We can pull off anything. You look good in his colors, you know."

"What?"

"The electric blue. The color of his hair. The color of his eyes when he's not wearing contacts. Also, his preferred accent color for all his costumes."

I looked back at my reflection in the mirror and smiled. I did look good in it. All sex demons had crazy colored hair as their natural hue—that I did know about concubi. And my rosy pink color went well with the blue.

I turned and licked my lip, my tongue feeling out the indentations my teeth left. "I look good in green, too."

A suggestive smirk curved his lips. "Guess you'll have to wear some soon."

"Just fuck already." I turned to see Riff stumbling down the hall with wet hair and nothing but a towel wrapped around his waist. A rush of heat dropped to my apex when he pulled the towel from his hips and rubbed it over his soaking hair.

I stared at his bare cock for a beat before tearing my gaze away.

"Would," Raff said as he reached around to pull his phone from his back pocket and shoved it in his brother's face, "but we only have ten more minutes. Come on, you paint her face. You're better at it than me."

Riff guided me to a vanity tucked around the corner. I sat down in the chair, eyeing myself in the lighted mirror before inspecting the huge collection of cosmetics. Most of it was theater paint, but there was a large selection of eyeliner and eyeshadow, too.

"You guys really like your paint, don't you?"

"Of course," Riff answered, and he moved to the table and hopped up so that he was sitting in front of me, blocking my view of the mirror. I bit my lip, trying not to look down at his crotch, which was inches from my face. Riff twisted around to grab a small pot of white face paint and popped the lid off with a flick of his finger. "Who doesn't want to change how the world perceives them?"

I peered up at him to see all his face paint was gone.

I'd seen so many versions of his face today. First, the mask in the haunt. Then, the paint, and next, the fire-filled skull head of his demon form. As much as I loved all of it, his bare human face was my favorite. No paint, no mask. Just his human face, with a broad jaw that had faint traces of blue stubble and his "Riff" tattoo over his one eyebrow.

"Sometimes I want to let the world know I'm going to rip them to shit if they fuck with me. Paint helps convey that."

"Saves people a few holes in their body," Raff added from behind as he collapsed onto the bed, the spring of the mattress groaning. My brain turned to jelly at the noise. "Paint's just a mask. We can be anything we want to be."

I worried my lip as I watched him dip two fingers into the pot of face paint. He was making a show out of it, going slow, swirling his fingers around the cream... "And what do you want me to be tonight?"

"Ours," he answered simply. Matter of fact.

I closed my eyes, letting him apply the cool paint to my face with his fingers.

Now more than ever, I needed an official place in this troupe.

Tension spread through the room. As the minutes slipped by, we all became anxiously quiet. This wasn't just an audition. My time in front of Alistair would dictate if this was going to be a one-night fling or if I was going to have something deeper with these two clowns.

I had only known them one night. One fucking night.

I was being naive and reckless because I loved them already.

Ever since Walker's went under and my dad passed, I'd sensed a powerful draw to Sinner's Sideshow. I didn't know why back then. I did now.

"I can't go back," I suddenly blurted.

Riff leaned back on the makeup vanity, two fingers covered in white paint frozen in midair. Raff twisted onto his side to stare at me from the bed. "Can't go back where?"

"Back to living like a human. Living in my car. Chasing this feeling that led me to Sinner's Sideshow was the only thing keeping me going for the last few years. Now that I'm here, I know I'm home."

"Meg..."

"I've met so many great people. Lollie is epic. I lost all my friends when Walker's Circus went bankrupt three years ago. I was so busy trying to take care of my dad that I just fell out of contact with them. When he died, enough time had passed to make it weird to contact them again. It would be nice to have a friend like Lollie again. I met her boyfriend, and I've yet to meet Mollie, but I'm sure she's great too. Even Creature. He smells like a mausoleum and gravy, but even he doesn't seem so bad. Then *you* guys. When I came here tonight, after two years of searching for this place, I'd come with a plan. Lay low. Try to get an audition with the ringmaster. Do my old act. Try my best, then figure out something else for my sad little human life if it doesn't work out. Everything has *not* gone according to plan. And now getting a job here feels like a life or death matter."

I didn't know where all this was coming from.

I'd been having the time of my life tonight, which had been perfect for distracting me from the mounting fear that I wouldn't make it into the circus while my love for it grew.

And I couldn't remember the last time I'd been this vulnerable with anyone."

"Hey. Don't be nervous. You are our harbinger."

"Of what?"

The twins looked at one another, then back to me with ear-to-ear grins. "Of whatever the fuck you want. You can have this whole circus in the palm of your hand. All you have to do is impress Alistair."

"How?"

"Think of Larry's act for a second. Sure, he's got a big dick, but just fucking an audience member isn't enough. It's about creating a dark fantasy. So, treat her like a hunk of meat, dress the ring up as a butcher shop, slap an apron on him, ass fuck her with a cleaver."

"You can still swallow that pretty sword of yours, set it on fire, all your usual tricks. But add a twist. Make it totally fucked, if you can."

Make it fucked...I was realizing my original idea to add some burlesque into my sword swallowing bit was likely too tame for Alistair's tastes.

"I think I have an idea, but I'm going to need your help. From both of you. It's a little twisted."

"Twisted? That's the magic word. We're in."

22

Discord's House of Worship

DAEMON

*S**he's late.***

My fists squeezed at my sides as I stood watch at the back entrance of the big top. Still no sign of them. That's what we get for leaving her with those fucking clowns. They were sex demons like her, so no shit, they were late. How long had it been since she'd seen someone of her kind? Maybe she'd never seen an incubus before. Naturally, she'd be curious.

Jealousy stabbed me in the gut like a hot knife. I wanted to be the one to sate her curiosity, to teach her about the Downside, maybe a few phrases of Infernal if she was interested, assuming she didn't know any. I'd teach her the pleasure of taking a mate.

Who was I kidding? The last time I'd tried to claim a lover as my true mate, I'd killed her.

My blood ran cold, and I forced my mind on other things. My gaze skimmed the muddy circus grounds, taking in all the workers as they scrambled to put back all the equipment they'd just taken down. Alistair had decided we'd stay for one more night in this town with one more show tomorrow before making the jump.

Staying in one spot for too long agitated me. It risked mortals taking notice, even with the powerful spell cloaking us from human eyes. If we stayed for too long, the land around us would start to wither and die from Alistair's erosive magic.

But it made sense to stay one more night. We had to make sure Megaera wouldn't follow us.

I was grateful to Alistair for agreeing to help me scare her off, though I doubt his decision to help me had anything to do with any care for me. I knew who Meg was. I didn't know exactly what had gone down between Alistair and Astrid twenty years ago.

He'd meant to kill her. He hadn't. I wasn't sure why he'd spared her. Back then, he wasn't exactly a paragon of mercy. All I knew was that he never wanted her to come back.

Having her daughter in the show ran the risk of Astrid popping back into our lives.

Three figures emerged from the dark, and my shoulders tensed when I registered Rafferty's arm thrown around Meg's shoulder. Rifton flanked her other side, with her hand in his and her guitar case slung across his back.

Those clowns worked fast.

"You're late," I spat, my arms folded over my chest, blocking their way into the tent. "You know how the ringmaster gets when he's made to wait. You're lucky if he doesn't crucify you for your insolence."

Any other monster here would cower at my tone, but the demons only laughed. "Don't threaten us with a good time, Daemon."

"Let us through, ass hat," Meg demanded with a cute little foot stomp. "And do you ever wear a shirt? It's been raining off and on all night."

"You're one to talk. Look at the shit you're wearing." I curled my lip at her sexy nun outfit, pretending it didn't make me painfully hard the second I saw it. They'd also painted her face like theirs, only instead of black diamonds over her eyes, they'd given her one blue and one green one. Their colors.

Over the corners of her mouth, they painted two little hearts topped with horns that hitched with her sickly sweet smile. "Hello? Anyone upstairs?"

When she reached up to rap on my head, I caught her by the wrist and dragged her up onto her tiptoes, our lips close enough to taste each other's ragged breath. The two clowns growled and started for me, but I pointed a threatening claw at them. "Stay the fuck back, or this gets ugly, imps."

I turned my attention back to Meg, expecting to find her either terrified or furious. Instead, I found her looking up at me with wide eyes and heated cheeks. That delicious scent was bleeding between her legs again.

"Listen to me, Megaera."

Megaera.

Her name was like honey and smoke in my mouth. Smooth, decadent. Addicting.

I wanted to have so much more than her name in my mouth.

"You have to leave. Give up your stupid dream of working here. This isn't a place for little half-blooded pups like you."

Her eyes narrowed, the flames behind them morphing into an inferno. "Take your hands off me now, otherwise you'll be jerking off with bloody stumps from here on out."

Raff bared his teeth. Riff laughed, his eyes cold as he looked me up and down. "She means it, too. And fair warning, I will jerk it while she does it. Hope you don't mind."

"This place will kill you. These clowns will kill you. Don't you get that?"

"They won't kill me if I'm their mate."

My heart froze over as fire swept through the rest of my body. I'd been afraid of that. "Do you know how monsters forge a mating bond, pup? They have to mate you in their true forms. They'll kill you."

She blinked, something akin to surprise passing over her face. She hadn't known that.

A beat later, her smile snapped back into place. "So what? Riff's already shown me his monster form, and it doesn't scare me. I'm a succubus. I was made for fucking monsters."

I jerked her closer, and my dick twitched when she winced. "You're only half-succubus, pup. And even if you were a full-blooded monster, you could still die."

"Why do you give a shit?"

I froze at her question. It's not like I could tell her the full truth—that the monster inside me wanted her so desperately it took all my strength to hold it back. If she stayed here, I wouldn't be able to keep it tethered forever, and once it broke free, it would destroy her.

"I'm trying to save you," I told her after a moment of uncomfortable silence. "You don't want to get tangled up with any of us. Especially Alistair."

"How about you just admit that you don't want me around because you hate the fact you want to fuck a half-blood?"

"I don't want to fuck you," I snarled low, hackles rising.

She laughed, the sound cloying and filled with needles. "You liar. I'm a sex demon, remember? Your desire for me has more stench than the lingering aromas from Larry's act."

I gnashed my teeth. "That's your charm in effect. You still don't have a full handle on your powers yet."

She shook her head, her manic smile looking right at home on her painted clown face. "I wouldn't use my charm if you were the last male on the Upside. And even if you were..." Her hand brushed against my erection. Her touch didn't linger. It was just to prove what was so painfully obvious.

I was hard as a rock.

"I wouldn't need to charm you," she whispered. "This is all you."

With that, she tore her arm free from my grip and stomped past me.

"There you are," Alistair drawled as I sat in an empty seat beside him. "I take it your efforts to persuade her to leave failed."

I grunted, and he laughed. "Well, you tried. Now we do it my way."

My chest tightened as I stole a sideways glance at the shade, who was positively beaming with dark excitement. He would succeed in terrifying her. That's what I'd wanted. I'd practically begged him for his help.

That didn't mean I was going to have fun watching him hurt her. He wouldn't physically touch her. But I'd been victim to Alistair's illusions many times before. She'd see and feel whatever he wanted her to. The nightmares would live with her forever.

"Besides," Alistair began, stretching out a gloved hand and motioning for his shadow—which sat in the chair on his other side—to take his cane, "don't you want to see what our little demon can do? She's known the circus all her life. She must be very talented."

As the lights in the house dimmed everywhere except the ring and Meg walked out, Alistair's smile turned wolfish. "Seems like the twins have taken a liking to her."

A liking? They more than liked her. They'd inducted her into their creepy little clown club. They'd painted her up like one of them. She was wearing their clothes. Carrying their scent. Riff had even shown his true self to her.

The beast inside me flexed, and I had to swallow back a growl. What did they do to her? She still had that undetectable aroma of a virgin succubus, but...they'd *touched* her. I didn't give a shit if she was a virgin or not. I'd made a big deal about it during my act, but that was just for show. What bothered me was the idea of her losing her V-card to anyone here.

Anyone with sense would want her as a mate. Which meant they'd have to claim her in their full monster form.

"She's beautiful, is she not?" Alistair observed, his jaw resting on the L his thumb and index finger created against his face. "Even more than her mother."

"Wouldn't know. I never met her."

"Consider yourself lucky. She was evil incarnate."

A smirk curved the corner of my mouth. "You would know."

We shared a look that filled me with a sense of calm. It didn't matter what Alistair was. It didn't bother me, never had. He was in my corner. That's all that mattered.

A spark of light drew our attention to the ring. Even Alistair's shadow appeared riveted by the start of Meg's performance. It began with the basics, typical circus shit and was still riveting to watch. She used practical effects as she swallowed her flamed sword with precision and skill. Her footwork, her breathing, her posture—it was all perfect. No magic, no gimmicks. It was the skill that came with years of dedicated practice.

She knew how to hold our attention in her grip and keep us in her command until she gave the word, like animals on a leash.

No one in the show was as good as me. Not even the twins and those bastards could do everything. Juggle, knife throw, fire eating, acrobatics, they even made dumbass slapstick gags look good.

All I did was make the audience my bitch. And Meg was giving me a run for my money with the effortless way she dominated the ring.

And she was just getting started.

"Look at you all. Creeps and cunts, monsters and maggots. All of you! This is Discord's dark house of worship, and it's a disgrace." She spat at her feet and threw her head back, her crazed laughter echoing through the house.

There weren't many people in the stands, just a handful of curious workers, Lollie and Sinclair among them, with Larry sitting a row in front of them, taking up three seats. We all went still, everyone looking at Alistair for his reaction.

He took his cane back from his shadow, planted it between his feet and leaned forward.

Well, fuck me. Alistair was absolutely riveted by this audacious little half-blood.

She continued, skipping around the ring. "We humans call him Lucifer. Beelzebub. The devil. He has many names, but there's one thing we mortals can agree on. He's to be purged from our world."

The succubus ran her tongue over the flat of her sword. I tried to push the obvious innuendo out of my head, but just then, her eyes locked with mine, and she licked her lips.

One of Alistair's hands left the grip of his cane to settle over my groin, giving my erection a squeeze. "I have a feeling our brazen little demoness is about to give us an interesting show, pet."

The shade was never wrong. Something truly fucked was about to go down. The foreboding sensation worked through me like acid.

I didn't want to watch, yet I couldn't look away.

Meg placed herself in a wide stance, mere feet in front of Alistair. One hand held her sword above her head while she made the sign of the cross over her chest. "I shall summon two of his minions and slay them all for the glory of my human god!"

A tendon twitched in my jaw. She was going to get those fucking imps involved.

Meg paused for the drama. I don't know how she did it, but the next moment, an explosion of smoke filled the ring. Murmurs broke over the crowd. I strained my eyes, trying to see through the screen of smoke.

Riff and Raff's crazed laughter rose over the smoke. Meg's sword flashed through the haze as it started to disperse. It caught on one of Raff's horns.

He rammed into her, sending her small body flying back into the dirt. He stood over her, his heavy boot resting between her spread legs, the steel toe nudging her center.

"Go ahead, slay us, sister. Prick us good and make us bleed. If you don't, we'll do the same to you."

Every muscle in my body strung tight as I realized exactly what kind of show they were about to put on.

"Put a stop to this now, Master."

The shade looked at me like I was crazy. "And why would I do that? The fun's just beginning."

The twins and Meg were looking at us. If they were really about to rape her, they wouldn't stop, and she wouldn't be waiting for Alistair's approval to continue.

He dipped his head in a nod, waving the free hand that wasn't on my cock. "Proceed."

23

Cum, Sweat and Damnation

ALISTAIR

I liked to consider myself a demon of class. I had taste. I loved music and literature. I collected books and fine clothes. But at the end of the day, I was still a demon. And what demon could resist a front-row seat to watching this beautiful little half-blood get ripped apart by two clowns?

It was all for show, anyway. They'd planned this. That was the beauty of Sinner's Sideshow. It was a place for all monsters to come and indulge their darker fantasies from the safety of their seat—so long as they hadn't purchased a death seat.

Raff pressed his boot against her center, making the most glorious shade of red spread across her cheeks.

Riff stepped around his brother to stand over her head, leering down at her with a wicked twinkle in his eyes. "Yeah, you fucking like that, don't you?"

An angry V formed between her brows. "Go to Hell!"

Her fingers curled around her sword, and she swiped up at him. Panic flashed across her face when she realized she'd miscalculated. Riff jumped back to avoid the blade, but he was too slow. Its serrated edge sliced into his arm. Blood poured from the wound, spilling onto her face.

It was rare for me to become aroused for a female, but there was something about her painted face, splattered with blood, that I found *inspirational.* My dead cock came to life, growing rigid in my slacks.

When my hand pulled from Daemon's cock to rub over my own, I felt his glare burning holes into the side of my face. "You are one twisted bastard."

I laughed, snapping at my shadow that was already out of its chair and getting on its knees before my hound. Just as I expected, he didn't object when my shadow freed him from his pants and stuffed him into its mouth.

I turned my attention back to the ring to find Riff lashing his arm with an unhinged laugh, watching his blood splatter over Meg's costume. Seeing that he wasn't at all perturbed, her apologetic expression was replaced with a mock scream.

"In the name of Jesus Christ, be gone, demons! Her voice came out shrill and desperate. She was a good actress.

Raff knelt to the ground and crawled over her body, caging her beneath him while Riff kicked her sword from her hand, sending it skidding away.

Raff took a handful of her habit and, with a jerk, ripped it open at the chest, bearing her breasts to the crowd. Her nipples hardened at the cool air and the little metal bars running through them glimmering in the stage lighting.

Daemon's breath hitched at the little demon's pierced nipples, his hands grasping at my shadow's horns.

Riff grinned at her as his brother continued to tear her costume down to her navel. He held his arm so his blood dripped onto the milk-pale flesh of her breasts. "Where is your god now, sister?"

Raff's hands palmed her tits, squeezing them together as he arched and pressed his face between them. When he came back up, her flesh was smeared with his face paint and Riff's blood.

She thrashed as Raff pried her legs apart and stuck his face between her thighs. "No! Stop! God save me!"

"Let's make a deal. If your god appears and commands us to stop, we will."

The green-haired incubus flipped her so she was on her hands and knees and pushed her habit over her hips, exposing her ass. He ripped her plain black panties off and tossed them to Riff, who knelt to his knees and stuffed them into her mouth.

She looked up at the blue-haired clown, who gave her a cruel smile. "We'll save your virginity for our lord and master. But that doesn't mean we can't ruin that sweet virgin ass of yours."

He held out his arm, the two sharing a silent conversation all in a look. Raff nodded in understanding and placed his mouth over his brother's wound. Riff's nostrils flared, and he drew in a breath through clenched teeth.

Raff pulled back, spread Meg's ass cheeks, and spit a mouthful of his twin's blood on her hole. With his index finger, he smeared the concoction of his saliva and his twin's life force, laughing as she struggled. His hand ripped the fly of his jeans open and fisted his cock.

Riff did the same, tore her panties from her mouth, and with a punch of his hips, filled it.

"Bite me, and you'll only make me more excited, sister," he cackled as he fucked her throat hard. Her eyes watered, creating track marks in her makeup. She was selling the fact that she was being raped, but there were clues that she was eating up every depraved second of this moment. When Raff lined himself up to penetrate her ass, she wiggled her hips and leaned back, eager for the invasion.

I glanced at Daemon, whose head had fallen onto the back of his seat, his knuckles white as he had a death grip on my shadow's horns, which sucked him off silently. I smiled at the sight of his dick, which was just visible through my shadow's smokey body. His cock was leaking pre-cum everywhere, and my shadow's pointed tongue lapped it up eagerly.

"Y–you're an infernal ba–bastard," my hound gritted to me as he watched the show. "I can't fucking watch this."

"Then leave."

As I predicted, he didn't budge from his seat. I expelled a smug *hmph* and turned back to the ring. "Bitch all you want, pet. I know you're enjoying every bit of this."

Her lips loosened from Riff's cock as Raff started to sink his girth into her darkest place. I closed my eyes, savoring the delicious little mewl she made as if it were a masterfully composed melody.

Death and darkness, she was beautiful. I'd been aroused by females before—it was rare, though it did happen. It never went further than that, but I could picture myself between the thighs of this one.

Especially knowing it would enrage Astrid should she ever find out.

Too bad I'd already promised Daemon that I'd help chase her away. If she stayed, someone would claim her as their mate. Whether that was the twins, Daemon, myself, or even all of the above, one of us would end up killing her.

And that would be a sad day I'd rather avoid altogether.

Raff fucked her ass with great care at first, then as he lost himself to the pleasure, he picked up the pace.

She was a noisy little thing. It had me wondering what commotion she'd make if Raff was in his true form. There was no way in my darkest depths that she'd survive the three flaming cock's of Daemon's true form.

Riff was the first to come undone. His brow pinched, white face paint flaking some. His head tilted back, and he let out a broken groan. He pumped one more time into her mouth before wrenching his hips back. Thick torrents of cum oozed from her lips and mixed with the blood-soaked dirt at his knees.

He then flipped onto his back and slid beneath her, placing his mouth on her clit with his twins' dick inches away. Suddenly, all the jokes about their twincest started to make sense.

She screamed, her fingers clawing the dirt, her sweat-soaked thighs trembling. Riff's hands came up to hold them steady, his claws slicing holes into her already torn stockings. She bent down, taking Riff's cock into her mouth as he suckled her clit, Raff pumping into her ass with no sign of slowing.

I glanced at Daemon to find him staring at me. The moment we locked eyes, his beautiful features twisted, and he came with a low growl. I dropped my attention to my shadow and watched as a torrent of cum filled his head.

A smile touched my lips, and I turned my attention back to the trio in time to see Raff expel himself inside Megaera. He pulled out of her ass with a huff, his mouth kicking into a smile as he watched his seed slick down her inner thighs.

Grabbing her by the hair, he plucked her off Riff's cock, pushed her to her back and kissed her.

The few of my employees in the stands were all touching themselves, some of them coming for the second or third time. I couldn't blame them.

These three were a sight to behold, a tangle of limbs covered in sweat, blood, and cum. Watching them had truly been a religious experience.

If the three of them had an act like this in the show, we'd sell out every night.

Pity.

The twins eventually—reluctantly—rose to their feet, peering down at their desecrated little nun. "May Discord take what's left of you, whore."

I chuckled. *If only.*

The twins faced the audience and took a bow. I clapped—I was the only one. Everyone else's hands were still busy. "Wonderful."

The twins beamed with pride as they helped Meg to her feet. She didn't bother covering up. In fact, the succubus seemed to love having everyone's eyes on her. She was probably feeding from everyone's lust, judging by the way her pink eyes glowed.

"Well?"

"What can I say?" I pushed to my feet. "I was positively *moved*. Aside from your generous body, you are a very talented sword swallower and fire eater. You will have a very bright career as an entertainer, I've no doubt. Sad to say, it won't be on my stage."

I braced for the storm. If she was anything like her mother, she'd have a temper fitting the fury bowels of the Downside. Sure enough, dark storm clouds roiled behind her glare. "Excuse me?"

My only response was a terse smile. I didn't like to repeat myself.

"I...I've been trying to find your show for years."

"Ah, yes. I don't make it easy for mortals to find my show. Sadly, that would apply to half-bloods. It's a wonder you tracked us down at all."

"It took years. Years of living in my car, barely making it. Showering at truck stops and gyms and living off convenience store food, and giving the occasional creep a blow job because I'm a fucking monster. All my mom ever left me was what I inherited through her blood. I love the circus, and this is the last one standing. Finally, I thought the blood in my veins could get me something, really, the only thing I care about."

She was trying to stir my sympathy, and curse her, it was almost working. My lips thinned, and I shook my head. "I'm sorry. The answer is no."

Bitter tears tracked through her makeup. "I won't take no for an answer. I'll follow you across the country. I'll attend every show. I'll annoy you until you either kill me or hire me."

I sighed.

She was stubborn like Astrid, too.

Without turning away from her, I instructed everyone to leave and get back to work. Those in the stands filtered out of the main entrance, the sounds of the motion-activated decorations filling the awkward silence.

When they were gone, my attention shifted to the twins. "Leave us."

They looked at one another, then to Meg. For the five years that the two young demons had worked for me, I'd never known them to be defiant. But there was no missing the churning gears behind their eyes. They didn't want to leave without her.

"It's okay," she said, lifting her chin in the air with a bright smile. "I can look out for myself. You've seen my sword skills."

They nodded, reluctantly tearing themselves away. Once they made their exit, I turned to Daemon, who'd stuffed himself back in his pants and was lounging back in his chair, looking just as cagey as ever.

"You too, pet."

His brows bent low on his face, the scowl sending a delicious shiver through me. I sent him a stern look and clicked my tongue in disapproval. "Now, pet. Remember…" I stuck out my bottom lip in a mock pout. "We're doing this my way. You promised."

"Fine," he snarled, the points of his canines gleaming. A wash of heat spread through me at the sight of them. "But don't get carried away, Alistair."

He stormed out, leaving the demoness all alone with me and my shadow.

She must have sensed the danger she was in, going by the look on her face. Still, she didn't back down or even step away as I approached her.

"I don't know what you're planning. But you can do anything to me if it means you'll give me the job. That's how badly I want this."

Oh. Sweet, angel. If she only knew what nightmares were in store for her.

"You're referring to sex, of course. Offering your body up to me as payment. It's a curious offer. But what if I wanted something else?"

"I don't have anything else except my shitty car, and unless you're an avid Volkswagen fan, I don't think you want that."

I took another step toward her. The air between us grew hot and began to buzz. "Did you know that succubus wings are a rare commodity among witches? The powder made from the ground-up bones is supposedly an aphrodisiac. What if I wanted your wings?"

She shifted uneasily but made no move to step away as I closed the last distance between us. "Not to sell to a witch, of course. I've no need for more money."

"What would you do with them?" she asked in barely a whisper.

A dashing smile split my lips. "I'd eat them myself, of course. You see, my cock, I stole it. From a mortal and a very bad one at that, so spare your pity. I have an awful time getting it up. If I were to eat your wings, I could top Daemon. It would be the first time in centuries."

I moved around her, turning to my shade state before reappearing in my corporeal form behind her. Winding a thick lock of her rosy hair around my finger, I held it to my nose and inhaled. She smelt of rose shampoo, of the twin's cum and sweat, and of damnation.

I smiled against the silky strands of her hair. "Perhaps I'll even use the magic of your wings to fuck you. The effects won't last long, so while I bury the dead cock of a murderer inside your tight virgin cunt, you'll be bleeding something awful from the two gaping holes in your back."

Just as I'd hoped, she whirled around to face me and stumbled backward, horror spreading across her face. But I was all shadows on the next beat of her heart and caught her from behind.

My arms closed around her waist, and I pulled her deep into my illusion. "I think it would go something like this..."

24

The Devil Inside

MEG

The world around me started to morph and change. I knew right away this was an illusion because I was in my demon form, my horns heavy on my brow, and I hadn't shifted. Whatever Alistair was about to show me, I braced for the worst.

He was trying to scare me off, and I was sure Daemon had put him up to it.

They wanted to play this game? Fine. I'd fucking play.

When my vision refocused, the scene took shape. I was on my back, naked, lying in an unfamiliar bed.

I wasn't alone.

Alistair hovered over me, his long, shadowy hair undone and draped around his bare shoulders. He was naked, a thin sheet draped over his hips, covering him from the waist down. His hands were planted on either side of my head, the veins in his arms bulging against death-pale skin. Upon closer inspection, I could make out the tiniest stitches, his dead body held together by magical threads. He shouldn't have been beautiful, but he was.

His hips moved in a slow, erotic motion, rocking against the cradle of my spread thighs.

Alistair was fucking me. No, he was making love to me.

This was just an illusion. It wasn't actually happening, but it felt real. The pleasure of the rolling warmth between my legs was incredible. The friction of his body inside mine was similar to what I'd felt with Raff when he'd fucked my ass, only without all the pressure.

The euphoria was almost enough to distract me from the blinding pain coming from my back.

Wait...

My blood froze in my veins as it occurred to me that I could feel my horns but not my wings. I tried to shift them and winced when a searing pain shot through my shoulder blades.

The mattress beneath me was cold and damp. Why was the bed wet?

I blinked up at Alistair, his face stark with something that melted the ice in my veins. Something warm and unexpected.

My heart caught in my chest when I registered his perfect lips, covered in blood—my blood.

That was why the bed was cold and wet. I was lying in a pool of my own blood.

I took a slow breath in, grounding myself. This wasn't real. He hadn't really used my wings as his own makeshift Viagra.

He was toying with me.

The most unsettling thing about this entire illusion was that I didn't hate it. Knowing it wasn't actually happening smoothed over the worst of my fear, leaving nothing but that familiar sensation fluttering low in my belly.

I couldn't read the shadow demon's emotions, but his face was vulnerable, and I could read it clearly for the first time. He hadn't expected me to enjoy myself. I think what surprised him more was that he hadn't expected to enjoy it either.

"Scream for me, little demon," he said in a low drawl, his voice as vicious as honey. "Make this dead body of mine sing."

I did scream, in pleasure. I arched my back off the bed and bucked up to meet his every thrust.

The shade faltered. Maybe it was the trick of the dim light—the only illumination coming from a single candle on the nightstand—but I swore I saw the ghost of a smile touch his bloody lips. "You shouldn't be enjoying this."

"Well I am. Don't you see? I'm perfect for your fucked up little circus."

"Not if you're dead." While he spoke, his hips kept pumping into me, his pace agonizingly slow. He meant for this to be torture, and it was, though not in the way he'd intended.

The building pressure deep within was slow and steady as he pinned me down, forcing me to take the friction at his own rhythm.

"Faster. Harder. P–please."

His phantom smile dissolved, and something dark carved his ghostly visage. "You're supposed to fear me."

I did fear him. In that strange little way that had me spreading my legs wider, allowing him deeper access to my body.

"You're going to have to try harder than that."

He took in a breath, even though I knew he didn't need to breathe. Then, his emerald eyes gleamed with amusement. "Oh, little demon, you better tread carefully." His eyes fluttered closed for a beat, and he shuddered as he kept fucking into me, the tender motions of his body a terrifying juxtaposition to his arsenic-dipped words. "It sounds like you're challenging me."

"I am challenging you. If that's what it's going to take to prove that I can survive your creepy circus. Bring it."

Whatever trace of vulnerability he allowed me to see was snatched away in an instant, and his indiscernible mask locked back into place. With a jerk of his hips, he wrenched out of me, the wet sound tangling with my cry at the loss of him.

"You will come to regret those words." His voice was hard steel, sheathed in velvet, and his viridian eyes glowed with malice.

He was the most beautiful nightmare I'd ever seen.

Taking me by the horns, he flipped me around and pushed my belly down into the wet bed. He crawled on top of me, and I thought he was going to take me from behind, so my heart skipped a beat when his knees clamped around my ribcage.

I bit back a yelp when the tip of his cock nudged against one of the gaping holes where my wings had been.

He was going to fuck one of the wounds. This wasn't my idea of a good time, but I didn't protest. My fingers twisted into the sheets, and I steeled myself for the moment of penetration.

This isn't real. None of this is real.

I kept repeating those words over and over, waiting for him to push inside. He never did. I twisted around to glance back at him over my shoulder. His head was bowed, his long hair concealing his face.

"I can't," he said. "Whether you believe it or not, I'm not a cruel lover. But you know who is?" He lifted his head, his eyes finding me through his shadowy screen of hair. "Daemon. He wants you. But I suspect you already know that."

My pulse drummed in my ears as I gave a slow nod.

"If he loses control of his urges, he'll try to claim you as a mate. Are you aware that in order to forge a true mating bond, he'll have to bed you in his true form? He's not like Riff and Raff when he's fully shifted. He's not himself. That form of his is responsible for countless deaths. I would know. I'm the one who tamed him. But there's still a wild part of him that will never be quelled. It's that part that will have to mate you to forge a bond. He killed the last female he tried to take for himself. Burned her alive. He'll do the same to you."

A fist-sized lump swelled in my throat. "It doesn't matter. I'd rather suck Discord's cock than become Daemon's mate."

Alistair released his hold over my horn as he turned to shadows and materialized so he was kneeling in front of me, fisting his hunger.

"Well, little demon? I'm right here." A sadistic smile fitting the devil himself curved his lips. "Get to sucking."

No.

It was impossible.

It couldn't be.

I wasn't sure what was harder to believe, that Alistair was Discord himself or that I'd had the devil between my legs...and I liked it.

My mind lurched into overdrive as my demon and human instincts went to war.

A fearful little voice in the back of my head screamed at me to get the fuck out of there. Where was I even? A small caravan filled with bits and bobs, the walls lined with ancient books and antiques. This had to be Alistair's trailer, though it looked more like an old-school circus caravan.

But I wasn't actually in his room, was I? This was all an illusion. He hadn't really made love to me. When my core throbbed with longing, I scolded myself. Why in the fuck was I disappointed? This meant my wings were safe and sound. And did I really want to lose my virginity to the devil?

No. Yes. Maybe. My succubus urges were always more potent and louder than my human survival instincts.

He'd gotten his wish. I was afraid of him, and that fear had my thighs slick with arousal.

Dark intrigue had my eyes drifting toward his cock, thick and eager for my attention. He'd said he wasn't used to becoming aroused naturally, and seeing his cock up close, I understood why.

It was like the rest of him. It was human, or at least it had been. The pale-as-death flesh had been stitched together with magical thread made of shimmering darkness. The stitching was tighter than it was on some parts of his face, but there were still stray tendrils of shadows leaking out from the occasional stretched seam.

It had felt fucking amazing.

And the sight of it had my mouth watering.

Fuck. Why was I attracted to this? He told me he'd stolen this skin from a dead man—a bad man. For all I knew, it was some sort of murderer or rapist.

The idea of taking this thing inside me should have repelled me.

All it did was tighten my intrigue. There was a macabre beauty to Alistair, a devilish allure. Which made sense now. He was literally the devil.

Lifting my gaze to his, my lips parted for his cock. His eyes shot wide as he realized I wasn't backing down. Then, that sly smile crept back into place.

"Be a good little fuck demon and open wide."

The second he pushed his length inside my mouth, I regretted it. This wasn't the silky, strangely cool flesh I'd felt between my legs moments ago.

It was burning. *I* was burning.

Flames lashed at my face as I felt my brows singe, and my lips blister.

I opened my eyes to see the same flaming hound from the dream I'd had in the cage. Only now, he had his tongue shoved down my throat, burning me up from the inside out.

It was Daemon. And I wasn't myself anymore. Going by the red shade of my skin, I was some other full-blooded demoness. And I was screaming as best I could with my burning vocal cords. He had me on my back, my legs spread, his three flaming cocks at the ready.

My thoughts felt strange and foreign as memories with Daemon that weren't mine surfaced.

I wanted to tell him to stop. I wanted to tell him that had been a mistake and that I shouldn't have pushed him into claiming me. I was wrong for thinking I'd survive him.

It was too late to go back now. Before me was a feral hound, ready to claim what was his. With a savage punch of his hips, sparks erupted. Blinding pain shot through me. His flames consumed me to the point where I couldn't tell where he started and I ended.

I felt nothing but agony until darkness consumed me, and all that met my ears was the whimpering of a heartbroken hellhound.

25
Corpse Carnival

MEG

I woke up to the sound of music. It was like the kind you might hear at a carnival, only this tune was off-kilter.

Creepy.

Sinking right into your marrow.

There was something deeply off about the place I'd woken up in.

I was outside, lying in a patch of dead grass. The sky above was blood red, and a dark mist covered the ground.

At least I had my wings now. I wrapped them around me more as a means to keep out the chill nipping at my flesh than out of modesty.

I pulled myself to my feet, noting how I was still completely naked, then surveyed my surroundings.

I was at the front gate of a carnival. The electronic buzz of someone winning a carnival game rang out over the commotion. A distant clown exploded in crazed laughter. The whir of shifty carnival rides clanked and clattered in the distance.

The main entrance was a smiling devil's head. With my heart in my throat, I wandered into its gaping mouth and passed through to the other side. What greeted me on the other end was something straight out of the Downside.

Hacked-up corpses lay on the ground, with guests stepping over them like they barely noticed. A clown with a rotting face—his peeling flesh spilling onto his neck ruffle—blew a balloon from a corpse's intestines and twisted it into the shape of an animal. With a tug, he snapped the intestines and handed off the balloon animal to a passing child—an imp at closer glance—with a grin.

All these people were dead, rotting, monsters and humans alike.

The prizes that hung from the game booths were maggot-filled limbs, severed heads with gaping eyes, and swollen-yellowed skin.

I had just walked through a row of games when a familiar voice called out, "Step up, creeps and cunts, dunk the corpse and win a prize!"

Alistair was dressed in slacks, a loose white, lantern-sleeve shirt that left much of his chest exposed, and suspenders. He stood behind a counter, with dolls fashioned to look like the Sinner's Sideshow performers dangling from above.

Beside the booth was a clear dunking tank filled with blood. On the shelf sat a charred corpse dressed up in an old-school, striped bathing suit.

A gasp locked in my throat when I realized the half-singed corpse was me.

"Would the lady like to try her hand at winning a prize?" Alistair smirked.

His shadow approached me, offering me three baseballs. I hesitated for a beat before taking them and whipped around to face Alistair behind the prize booth.

"Are we in the Downside?"

His emerald eyes glittered like jewels, rimmed by thick black lashes. He had his hair tied back into a ponytail. Fuck. He had no right to be so gorgeous.

"Is that what you think?" He smirked as he pretended to busy himself with straightening the row of boar-headed Larry dolls. "That Hell is just one schlocky, horror-fueled gore fest? Well, you wouldn't be alone in your thinking. Most humans have spread horrible rumors about my realm over the years. None of it's true."

He picked up a doll of a flaming hellhound and laughed. "Well, except for the fact that I keep the company of a three-headed hound. Though the three-headed part got a little lost in translation over the years."

"So this is just another illusion, then?"

"Yes. If you were in the Downside, you'd know it. I don't think it would be much to your taste. It's very dull. Quiet." A wistful sigh blew from his lips as he moved to the hellhound dolls and tugged on one's studded plush collar. "Especially since I tamed Daemon. He was one of the few monsters stirring chaos in my dark depths."

He made a sweeping gesture toward my burnt corpse in the dunking tank. "That's how you'll end up if you spend any extended length of time around him. He'll kill you just as he killed her."

My eyes narrowed on him. "I already told you. I'm not going to let him claim me."

"If he loses control over his true form, do you think he's going to ask for your permission? He'll burn you alive, girl. And he's not the least of your worries. The twins aren't as safe as you might think. They'll wear you, and by the time they're done with you, you'll be nothing but a puddle of blood and cream."

With a snort, I hurled one of the balls at the target and missed. I glanced back at him with a scowl. "So far, you're doing a shit job at getting me to change my mind."

The devil propped his elbows on the counter and rested his chin on his knuckles. "I'd call you fearless, but that isn't quite right, is it? You're different. A curiosity."

"Go on, say it. I'm a freak."

He dissolved in a whisp of smoke and reformed behind me, then took me by the wrist, and we threw the second ball together. Another miss.

"Yes. You are aroused by your own fear, aren't you? That makes you very much a freak."

I worried my bottom lip, turning my head to find him study-ing me through slitted eyes. "Don't you like that about me?"

A flicker of surprise seemed to pass behind his eyes before his signature smile snapped back into place. "Oh, I like it very much, little demon. I don't know how much you know of Dis-cord since you were raised by your human father, but I essen-tially feed on fear. Much like a sex demon feeds on lust. Though I need far more of it than you ever would care to consume. It's why your mother started Sinner's Sideshow in the first place. She was a loyal disciple of mine once. I allowed her to go to the Upside to harvest fear as an offering to me."

I wasn't sure why he was choosing to tell me about my mom. I had thought I hadn't wanted to know. But there was a dark bend to his tone that ignited that little flame of curiosity. "What happened to her?"

"She got reckless," he said simply. "She started killing hu-mans, innocent humans. Despite common opinion, I don't care for that kind of thing. I hunted her down with the intention of killing her so I could send her back to the Downside for good."

There were times I could read Alistair's expressions quite easily. Now was one of those times. He had a distant look, and his touch softened where he still held my wrist. "But..."

"But you didn't kill her."

"Not when I found her, no."

I swallowed thickly. I wasn't sure I wanted to know the end-ing to this story, but I couldn't deny myself the truth anymore.

I had to know what became of the woman who'd abandoned me.

"Why not?"

"She was pregnant."

A chill skipped down my back, and my skin turned ice cold. I folded my wings tighter around my shoulders and forced the next words from my mouth. "You allowed her to have the baby—allowed her to have me. Then you killed her."

He said nothing to confirm it. He didn't deny it either.

I wasn't sure what to say or how to react. I'd spent all my life believing she'd abandoned me and my dad. He'd loved her, and he'd been made to believe that she'd up and left.

My mother hadn't abandoned us at all. She'd been murdered.

I should have been enraged. I wanted to be pissed. But I couldn't seem to summon so much as a flicker of fury. Alistair's hand trailed from my wrist, skimming up my arm to curve over my shoulder, his slender finger tracing my jawline. His one hand was sweet and tender while the other slipped beneath my wing and cupped my breast.

"Tell me you hate me," he whispered into my ear. "Tell me that you never want to think about my show again, let alone enter into my employment."

I closed my eyes, reveling in his mesmerizing aura. The ringmaster of Sinner's Sideshow was not only the devil. He was my mother's murderer. If there had been any question that I wasn't a twisted masochist, there was no doubt about it now.

Because even knowing all that I did now, I still wanted a place in the devil's circus. More than that, I wanted him. I wanted him and his creeps.

My eyes shot open, and I hurled the last ball at the target. This one landed, and my burnt corpse plunged into the bloody pool with a splash. "If she killed innocent humans, then I guess she had it coming, didn't she?"

Alistair stared at me, appearing gobsmacked by my response. Just as I expected, he recovered a moment later with a dismissive laugh. "You are truly full of surprises, Megaera."

His shadow grunted, the hulking monster making a noise for the first time. He gestured to my choice of prizes on the counter. A Riff and Raff doll, complete with green and blue hair made out of yarn and their name tattoos over their brows, with Riff's on his left and Raff's on his right. Then there was the Daemon doll, who appeared in his flaming hellhound form with his spiked collar and a muzzle made out of felt. Lastly, there was an Alistair doll wearing his ringmaster outfit and his top hat. He had his cane sewn to one hand and a little mini-doll of his shadow sewn to his other.

"Choose a prize, darling." Alistair's voice was practically a purr in my ear. I agonized over it for a moment before realizing I couldn't choose.

I turned to him. "What if I want all four?"

The devil's lips pursed in thought. He knew I wasn't talking about the dolls. "Then I'd say you're a foolish little slut."

Before I could lob my rebuttal at him, he was gone. The carnival melted away, and a new scene formed. The first thing that met me was the pungent scent of rotting flesh. I was lying on a pile of corpses.

My hand slipped on a bloody face, and when my palm hit something that felt like a rubber ball, a squeak filled the air. Oh god. I was lying on a pile of clown corpses.

The twins were picking through the pile of bodies, searching the pockets of the dead. Riff held up a plastic flower and cackled when a squeeze to its base squirted his brother with a spray of blood.

I knew what was coming. I wasn't sure how, but I did. This wasn't the real Riff and Raff. Alistair was probably just using them in one last-ditch effort to make good on whatever deal he'd made with Daemon. I could have tried playing dead, but in truth, I wanted them to find me.

It wouldn't be rape if they had my consent from the start.

So, I found the clown nose and gave it another pinch. At its loud honk, the twins stopped rooting around and perked their heads up like raccoons on high alert. I sat up, flipping them both off while sticking my tongue out. Then, with a mad laugh, I scrambled away.

"Look what we have here. A live one," Raff said.

"A female, too. Oh, goodie."

I always wanted to be chased, though I didn't get very far. One of them caught me by the tail and gave it a jerk, pulling me back to them. Riff spun me around, his knee kicking my legs apart. Raff held me steady as his twin ripped his belt off and looped it around my neck—using it as a makeshift leash.

I moaned as the blue-haired incubus entered me with a punch of his hips. The pile of bloodied limbs was hard to get purchase on. I kept slipping. Raff held me up by the horns while Riff held my leash in one hand and the base of my tail with his other.

A series of obscene noises came tumbling from my lips as I made a very loud show that I was enjoying myself.

The bodies started to shift, and Alistair emerged from the pile, covered in blood. He peered down at me, his eyes bright with amusement. "It's going to take a lot more than this to make you crack, isn't it?"

"Y–y–yeah," I answered, my voice disrupted by the piston of Riff's hips. "A–and you're a busy guy. So why don't you just throw in the towel and offer me the goddamn j–job already?"

Almost to my disappointment, the scene changed again. We were standing back in the ring, and I was no longer naked. I was back in my torn nun costume. Back to reality.

"So? Does this mean I'm part of the show?"

Alistair's brows bent with his scowl. He dipped his chin, the brim of his hat casting his face in shadows. "Why do you want this so badly?"

"Because something deep inside me tells me that this is where I belong. And I don't think it has anything to do with my mother. I want to be here. Even if it kills me in the end. I don't care."

He whipped around and made his way for the tent's back exit with his shadow trailing behind him in a cloud of smoke. "Follow me."

26

Virgin on the Altar

ALISTAIR

As the oldest demon in all of existence, there wasn't much that surprised me anymore.

This little demon, however, threw me for a loop.

I'd shown her things that would have made any other creature wet themselves with fear.

Then again, she *had* wet herself in fear in a way I hadn't counted on.

This little half-blood actually got off on her own terror, and the most shocking part of it all was that I *liked* it. I more than liked it. She crawled under my skin and brought my dead body to life in ways no other female had before.

My liking for her was greater than my desire to keep my word to Daemon. We hadn't had a contract, so there was no magic in place binding me to honor our deal. He would resent me, though. Being what I was, I was no stranger to resentment.

Daemon's opinion of me, however, was one of the few I gave two harpy fucks about.

The thought of hurting my pet had my heart aching, but something told me that Megaera would be worth it.

He wouldn't be the only one. If I was going to go through with this, I'd have to ensure her safety. Meaning I'd have to take certain measures to prevent her from being claimed.

She wouldn't like it one bit. The darker part of my being didn't care. I was giving her what she'd so relentlessly begged for. And I was making an effort to make sure she didn't die and waste my time in the end.

I could have transported her straight to the altar tent. But I wanted to see the look in everyone's eyes as the little half-blood tailed after me through the camp, their fear for her so pungent it was like walking through a buffet. She'd been here for all of a night, and my monsters already cared for her.

They thought I might hurt her. Maybe I would, in the end. What I had in store for her wouldn't protect her forever. Hell.

Maybe even I would claim her at some point. And there'd be no surviving my true form.

Meg's worn-down shoes—which were barely fit to grace her feet—slapped against the rain-logged ground as she jogged behind me.

"Not everyone has creepy slender man legs. Slow down! Erm..." I paused, allowing her to catch up with me. "What should I call you? Discord? Sir? Ringmaster? My lord?" She wrinkled her nose at the last one, then her mouth kicked up. "Daddy?"

A small smile touched my lips as I turned my back to her and continued toward the altar tent. "Just Alistair is fine. For now."

When we approached the tent, Meg stopped just short of the entrance. I turned around slowly to face her, my brows tweaking. "Something wrong?"

"What is this place? It has a weird energy." She shivered. "It's giving me the chills."

"Perhaps what's giving you the chills is the fact that your breasts are still exposed."

Her eyes dropped to the front of her torn nun costume, the ripped garment exposing her from her clavicle all the way down to her navel. If she was embarrassed, she didn't show it, although there was no reason for her to be abashed after the show she'd put on with the twins.

The entrance to the tent opened, and one of the sideshow grunts slipped out, dipping his head to me in respect before wandering toward the trailer lot. Before the tent's flap closed shut, Meg caught a look at the pews inside, filled with a handful of monsters, their heads bowed in prayer.

"Wait." Meg took a step back. "Is that a church? Maybe I should go find a shirt."

I laughed, and even my shadow quaked with a silent chuckle at the demoness' unintended joke. "It's a church of Satan. You'll find you're dressed appropriately."

"A church of Satan. As in Discord. As in *you?*"

"Well, it's certainly not a church of Latter-day Saints, my dear. Of course, it's a church of Discord. Who else?"

"Does anyone here know who you really are? That the devil they worship is right under their noses?"

"Daemon is the only one who knows. And if I bring you on, you will be the second."

Her eyes lit up with something that had my chest...*stirring.* It was strange how this girl had me feeling as though I was a flesh and blood man with a working heart. She had an odd way of striking my interest in things I'd never cared for in all the years I'd been alive.

Like her body.

I'd never cared for the female form before, but I couldn't stop looking at her, stripping her bare with my eyes, flesh and all, down to her pretty little skeleton.

She'd been so beautiful in the ring, trembling as she took what the twins gave her like the good little cock hungry slut she was.

I recalled the moment in my illusion, on the mountain of corpses, when Riff wrapped his belt around her pretty throat like a leash. Her eyes had rolled into her head, and her scent had gotten so strong it washed out the pungent stretch of decay.

I'd never been dominate in bed before, but the thought of having my newest pet crawling on her knees toward me with a collar around her throat had my cock hardening.

I put Daemon's collar on him long ago. It wasn't just a pretty part of his costume. It was the closest I could get to making him mine since he refused to forge a true mating bond.

I'd collar Megaera, too. Although hers wouldn't hang around her neck...

My shadow propped the entrance for us, and I ushered her inside.

The tent was simple, with just a few pews and a single electrical cord connected to a neon light fixture made to look like an upside-down cross. Its purple light illuminated the room in a soft, sensual glow.

At the front of the tent sat a large obsidian altar with a simple polished obelisk at the top, looming over a flat table-like surface where Astrid had once made sacrifices to me years before. Now, it was just used as a place of prayer, as well as a quiet place for lovers. My attention went to the back pew where Sinclair the vampire was draped over one of the gorgon sisters. Her legs were wrapped around his hips as he rocked against her.

He stopped, his red eyes going wide, when he realized he had company. Lollie thrashed in frustration and reached to swipe her tangle of serpents from her eyes. "Why in the fuck are you stopping—" Her face paled when she followed her boyfriend's line of sight. "S–sir!"

Sinclair scrambled off Lollie, and she sat up, hurriedly fastening her clothes back in place. I dismissed them both, and they scurried for the exit.

Lollie stopped as she passed Meg, her hair hissing with their mistress' excitement. "*Girl.* Holy freaking fuck feast! That show you put on with the wonder clowns was insanity. You have half the troupe screwing each other's brains out right now. Everyone's so horny."

Meg let out a soft laugh. "Um, thanks."

"Sir, you have to put her in the twin's act." Lollie gushed, turning to me. My brows kicked up in surprise. She rarely summoned the courage to speak to me directly.

"Thank you, Lollie. I'm considering it. You may go now."

The gorgon hurried out into the night, the few people inside who'd been absorbed in prayer picking up and trailing quickly after them.

Meg walked through the tent, eyeing the altar. "This thing is creepy. It looks like something that was used for virgins back in the day."

A dark smile stretched my face. "What do you mean, back in the day?"

She spun around, and a scream locked in her throat when she came face to face with my shadow, whose hands were already on her. He was a huge beast and towered over Meg by several feet, but he was just a small representation of my true form.

He pushed her down onto the altar, and to my surprise, she didn't fight it. In fact, excitement danced behind her pink eyes. I approached the altar, shooing my shadow away. He dissolved into a glimmery mist, then reformed back at the tent's mouth to stand watch.

"If you're going to shove a girl down, you should do it with your own two hands. Don't have your muscle do it for you."

"My muscle *is* me. Just in a different form, is all."

She blinked up at me, and I could practically feel the heat of her question burning in her mouth. I silenced her with a wave of my hand before she could ask it. "This isn't about me right now. Spread your legs."

I could sense her blood spreading straight to her pussy, heating at my command. She did as I instructed, her thighs parting.

If I had a functioning heart, it would be racing at the way she peered up at me through her rough locks of pink hair. When I lowered myself to my knees between her spread legs, her pulse jumped, and her breath hitched in her chest.

I peeled off my gloves, set them aside on the altar's base, and smoothed my palms over her thighs. Goosebumps broke out over her moon-pale flesh in the wake of my touch.

"Is this your first time touching a woman?"

I smiled at her without looking up from my task of gathering the hem of her skirt over her hips. She still wore fishnet legs, though the twins had torn a large hole at her apex. She was crusted in cum, and her labia was swollen with need. "Am I that obvious?"

She shook her head. "It's just something I heard."

"You'll find most things you've heard about me are complete bullshit, darling." Her scent was intoxicating, pulling me closer. Succubus charm had never worked on me before, though I was sure she wasn't using magic on me. This was nothing but a natural attraction.

I stroked my fingers through her glistening folds, noting how thick her arousal was. A breathy moan curled up from her throat when I pushed two fingers into her cunt.

"Are you going to fuck me?" Her words dripped with hunger.

When I found what I was searching for, I pulled out of her and licked my fingers clean. *Curious.* She tasted like sugar and sin. "Not tonight. I was simply ensuring your virginity. I'm not like Daemon. I don't have the nose of a hellhound, and I'm not a sex demon who can glean such things from your aura."

"What does it matter if I'm a virgin?"

The only reason I cared if her hymen was intact was because it was going to make my means of protecting her from Daemon that much easier. She'd never agree to this otherwise.

"I'm offering you the job, but on one condition."

"What is it?" She peered up at me with hope and defiance and all the beautiful things that had me wondering if I would allow myself the pleasure of her body one of these nights, knowing Daemon would be furious.

I sent her a devilish smile, my lips curling against my fingers as I licked the last of her from my dead flesh. "You sell me your virginity."

27

Deal With the Devil

MEG

I wasn't sure what was crazier, that the devil wanted my virginity or that I was without a doubt going to give it to him.

"I already told you I'd do just about anything for this job."

The truth was, I wouldn't want to fuck him if he was like most ringmasters I'd seen before, old, balding. But the man on his knees before me was devilishly handsome. His macabre beauty did things to me no corpse should.

The truth was I wanted to fuck the devil. And it went deeper than carnal lust. That moment in the illusion—the one where he'd made love to me—he'd meant to terrorize me. Instead, I felt something he hadn't intended. Something more.

Something I didn't understand yet.

"You can have me. Just give me the job." My desperation leached into my tone, and I squirmed on the altar. I was probably the most demanding virgin who'd ever laid here.

Dark lines carved Alistair's face. "This is more than a job, Megaera. I give my monsters the bliss that is ignorance. Other than Daemon, they don't know I'm their lord and master. They just think I'm a powerful disciple of Discord, like your mother. But you see, I own them."

I searched his face, looking for any hint that he was joking. The expression on his face was stark, serious, as cold as the dead flesh he wore. He was being serious.

"If you take this arrangement with me…" He held up an index finger, and his nail grew into a jagged claw. He brought its razor tip to my thigh and started to carve into my flesh. I gasped but didn't flinch as he drew the word "mine" on my skin in the most elegant script I'd ever seen. "I'll own you too. But don't worry."

The shade leaned forward and brushed his lips against my flesh, where the wound had already faded. "I treat all my pets well."

He extended his hand to me, and I took it, allowing him to pull me up into a sitting position. "So, is your answer still a yes?"

I nodded at the same beat. I didn't have to think about it. I'd wanted this for so long. Now, it was within reach.

"Very well," he crooned, his cool breath washing over my skin like a caress—touching me in places I'd give anything to have him touch.

After the illusion we'd shared in his bed, I couldn't stop imagining what it would be like to have him inside me in real life. With a hard swallow, I reached to smooth my hem back over my knees, but Alistair snapped a hand out and caught my upper thigh, preventing me from covering myself.

I blinked up at him, stunned by the sudden dominance. "I'm not done with this part of you yet. Keep yourself open for me."

Fucking Christ. Was he trying to torture me? I guess, where the devil was concerned, this kind of torture wasn't so bad. I bobbed my chin in understanding and drew the fabric back over my hips.

"Good girl. Now, kiss me." His voice came out strained, almost desperate. It didn't feel like a demand. Alistair was begging me to kiss him. "Give me your mouth, little demon."

My heart clenched at the devil's request. How could I deny him when he was on his knees before his own altar, begging for my mouth?

I leaned forward and brought my lips to the devil's.

His flesh was cool and softer than I expected. My pulse thrummed so hard I could feel it in my ears. His kiss was gentle, almost loving. He rose from the ground and pushed me down against the altar, his body draped over mine.

His tongue pushed into my mouth, and I jumped when I felt a sharp prick. He broke away, leaning back to produce a piece of parchment out of thin air. I'd seen this in cartoons before, where Satan would produce a flaming contract to sign their life away. Only there was no smoldering paper consumed in fire. It was made of shadows and dark magic.

"What did you do?" I touched my lips to find them soaked in blood.

"Blood is a binding ink, pet. Kiss on the line here, and our deal will be done. You will have a home and secure employment. You will be provided with everything you need."

Tense silence folded around us as I leaned forward, hesitating for just a moment. I wanted this to the point of pain, so why was there a foreboding sensation hooking in my belly? Tamping down on my nerves, I pushed the feeling away and pressed my lips to the magical contract.

The bloody imprint of my kiss glowed, and then the contract vanished with a swipe of Alistair's hand. "Perfect. Now you're *mine*."

Before I could say anything, a light lit up the darkened tent, cutting through the murk. I couldn't see anything. There was a warm tingle, like fizzing bubbles against my skin. When the light cleared, and I blinked away the spots in my vision, I looked down.

And my blood froze.

There was a contraption clamped over my pelvis.

It looked like metal panties, with the front portion shaped like a giant heart-shaped locket and chains of glimmering light dropped around my hips, connecting to the back portion.

"What the Hell is this?"

Alistair rose to his feet, a look I couldn't parse on his face. "That, my dear, is a chastity belt. I don't care about preserving your maidenhood, but I can't have you forging a mating bond with any of my monsters. As a half-blood, I doubt you'd survive their true forms. Perhaps Riff and Raff's. Not Daemon's." Alistair's eyes gleamed. "And certainly not mine."

"You had me sell you my virginity just so you could slap this shit on me?" My face burned red hot with rage. "You tricked me."

"Foolish girl," he tutted. "You made a deal with the devil. What did you expect?"

"I expected you to give me freedom over my own vagina. You can't keep me celibate. I'm a succubus. Now that my powers have awakened, I need to feed."

"Then feed. You can still use that pretty mouth of yours. A cock would be right at home between those tits. And if you want, you can still fuck. You can lie with anyone you wish, so long as they remain in their human or half-human form. But it should be under my supervision to ensure your chosen lover doesn't fully shift."

"This is bullshit. I should have a say over who touches my body and when."

"That's so adorable coming from the one who just sold her body to the devil himself. You belong to me now, Megaera." The shade's eyes darkened. "What's done with your body is my business."

If he was anyone else, I would punch him in the throat. Or if I had my sword on me, maybe I'd just stab the fucker.

"Aw, don't give me that face, pet," he mused. "This is what you wanted. You could show a little gratitude. I'm betraying my hound's desires so I can give you yours."

I rapped my knuckles against the belt. "This? I didn't want this."

"I don't get pleasure from collaring you in such a way. This is to keep you safe. To keep you alive."

"Why do you care about keeping me alive? So I'll sell tickets?"

"I already told you I have no need for more money." A frown split his face. "You bring something to life inside me. I want to keep it breathing, whatever it is. In exchange for granting me that, you have a home here with me. I will protect you by whatever means necessary. Even if it means you'll resent me. I'm no stranger to resentment."

I opened my mouth to speak, but a whip crack lashed through the air, jerking our attention in the direction of the deafening sound. Alistair's shadow moaned as the whip wrapped around his throat. It crumpled to its knees with a guttural moan, then dissolved on the next breath and reformed behind its master.

Daemon appeared on the next rapid pound of my heart. Shirtless, as always, looking stupidly fuckable with the way the neon light washed over his tattooed body.

Daemon's golden eyes sparked with fire when he saw me on the altar, my nun's habit pushed up over my hips with a shiny new piece of hardware locked tight around my pelvis. "What the fuck did you do to her, Alistair?"

"I made her mine in a way that will prevent you from making her yours."

28
Beware of Dog

DAEMON

A growl tore from my throat as I stormed into the tent. Any other monster would have backed off, but Alistair held his ground with that frown plastered on his face like he was sad over the weather rather than having ripped my fucking heart out.

"You betrayed me."

Disapproval twisted the shade's features. "Don't cause a scene, Daemon. Not in front of the latest addition to our troupe."

My attention flicked to Meg, where she sat with her legs spread on the altar, her nipple piercings catching the tent's purple lighting.

Alistair had put some kind of contraption around her lower body, complete with a magical lock. Like some kind of— My blood went cold, then hot again as realization worked through my veins.

It was a chastity belt.

I had begged this motherfucker to spare this woman from my twisted nature. So what did he do? He put a fucking chastity belt on her.

I slowly turned my glower back on him. The fire behind my eyes was so out of control that I could see their reflection blazing back at me in his emerald orbs. "If you didn't want me to cause a scene, you shouldn't have stabbed me in the back."

"You're being a touch dramatic, Pet. Calm down before you lose control of your true nature. We wouldn't want things to get heated."

"Fuck you," I spat, the glob of saliva flying right through him as he dematerialized and formed a beat later. He appeared cool and collected, but I knew him well enough to know I was getting under that cold skin of his.

Good. He wasn't going to get away with this. He wasn't going to bend me over a barrel and fuck me like this without me shoving a dose of his own medicine down his throat.

"What I promised was to try and scare her away. I don't break my word, and even if I did, there was no contract."

I stared at the shade in disbelief. "I didn't think I needed one. In all the years I've known you, you've never done this to me. You use that silver tongue on other monsters. Not me."

"I'm doing this for you, pet. You want her badly. You want to rut her and claim her as your bonded mate, and while I can't condone that, since you'll surely kill her, I can keep her close for you. She can warm our bed. If you behave yourself, I'll even let you break in her virgin cunt. Under my supervision, of course, to ensure you don't shift."

Alistair smiled down at Meg, who appeared paralyzed by our exchange. She was probably in shock as it was finally occurring to her that she'd just become this shade's personal possession.

But Alistair wasn't looking at her in a way he's ever looked at a female before... No, that was impossible. He'd never expressed interest in women before.

"Did you collar her for me, Alistair?" I took a step closer to him, eating up the little space left between us. "Or did you collar her for *you?*"

I wasn't ever afraid of the devil. Ever. But now, seeing that sinister smile snap into place on his stolen face, I felt it. For the first time ever, I was scared of Discord and what he might do to my true mate.

"Can't she be a treat for the both of us? Something to share? Imagine all the fun we can have."

"You're just doing this to torture me."

Hurt filtered behind the shadow demon's eyes. "I never want to hurt you."

I strode closer, teeth bared. "Then tell me why you're doing this to me."

He said nothing, standing there as still as a statue. I waited for several more seconds before my patience snapped like a brittle rubber band. I grabbed him by the throat and shoved him down onto the altar.

He didn't fight back. He could destroy me with a snap of his fingers if he wanted. Instead, he allowed me to push him down onto the altar. She scooted back, and Alistair fell into the cradle of her legs.

I hated to admit it, but he looked good between her legs. My cock thickened in my pants at the sight of him framed between her thighs. Which only stoked the fumes of my ire. I didn't want to enjoy seeing him lying next to her.

But I did. I liked it so much that the hellbeast within me stirred.

My hand tightened around his throat. "Fucking tell me why you're doing this to me."

"Because I want her too."

My muscles started to strain and bunch as I held my fury in while it clawed at my insides for freedom. "For what? For your show?"

"For my show. For my bed." Alistair's frown flipped into a manic smile. "For whatever the fuck I want, hound."

I gnashed my teeth, and my hand around his neck tightened. Since the skin wasn't his own and he couldn't heal properly, it would leave a permanent necklace of bruises. "You haven't wanted to touch a woman in the thousands of years I've known you. Why now? Why *her?* Your species doesn't even long for true mates. Your monstrous urges don't demand you to bond with her."

"Maybe not," he said, his voice so even that it only pissed me off more. "But I feel something for her. And it's enough to not let her go."

I fell grave still, glaring at the man with more fury than I'd ever felt before. "If you've ever cared for me, you'll release her."

"Darling, I more than care for you. You were the only flame in the darkest depths of Hell. My light in the dark. But I can't let her go. She's mine now. She's *ours*."

"Ours," I spat with a laugh that had the devil flinching. "She'll never truly be ours, Master. If we try to claim her, we'll kill her. And I'm not one for torturing myself by having a lover I can't forge a true mating bond with."

I knew my mistake the second the words had left my mouth.

It was too late to take them back.

Dark, storm-like shadows rolled in behind the devil's quiet glare. "Have I not been begging you to mark me for years? Or am I not a lover to you? Am I just the master you fuck because it's your job? Maybe now you will know the agony you put me through."

My chest heaved, anger rising inside me like a tide and threatening to drown me. "Is that what this is? My punishment for not claiming you as my bonded mate?"

He didn't answer me. He only stared up coldly at me from where I held him on the altar. Meg remained still, not daring to move.

"Since you love making deals so much, how about this one, *Master?*" My voice dripped with acid as I hunched down, my face an inch away from Alistair's. "Let her go, and I'll give you what you want. I'll give you my mark."

The devil had been after my mark for years, eons. For almost as long as I'd known him. I denied him because after I killed my last mate, I vowed I'd never try to bond with another again. He'd survive me. But that didn't matter. Or, at least it hadn't then.

So now that I was finally giving in, I wasn't sure what reaction I expected. I hadn't counted on him laughing in my face.

Hysterical laughter rolled from him, his unhinged grin stretching from ear to ear. "Oh! Goodie! Finally, I get to be mated to the man I love, not because he loves me back, but for some half-blood, he's known for a day. The answer is no, hound. Besides, the deal is done. She signed a contract. There's no breaking it now. Even if I wanted to."

With my hand still clamped tight around the demon's jugular, my glare shifted to Meg. "You what?"

Her throat twitched with a swallow. "He gave me the job. I... All he wanted in return was my virginity. I thought he wanted to fuck me. I didn't think he would do this."

Her fingers curled around one of the chains draped over her hip, and she gave it a futile tug. "I..." Her voice cracked, and her words died off. I didn't have to be a sex demon to detect the storm of emotions whirling inside her.

"Do you know what you've done, pup? You signed your life away to the fucking devil."

Her eyes narrowed into slits, and she bared her dainty little fangs at me. "Why do you care what happens to me? I'm not your mate who you burned to a crisp when you tried to claim her."

Rage consumed me. I couldn't look at him, so I just continued to glare at Meg as I felt the fire inside me start to eat me alive. The memory of when I'd murdered my mate years ago was branded into my brain. It was a source of pain, a weak point for me. Her screams would live inside me forever.

"You told her?"

"Technically, I showed her. I put her in your mate's body, and she lived through the last few seconds of your former lover's life."

I couldn't hold back any longer. Something inside me snapped apart. With a growl, I felt the flames inside me take over. It was coming. The shift. And there would be no shifting back until Alistair beat the flames down.

Who knew what or who I would destroy before he did.

29

Into the Hound's Flames

MEG

Daemon's aura hemorrhaged misery and heartbreak one moment, and the next, it was an explosion of pure rage. Alistair had shattered his heart into pieces.

Until now, I didn't think the hellhound had a heart to break. It was becoming clear to me that the devil and his flaming hound were way more than fuck buddies. Their relationship had complexities to it I probably would never understand. But I wanted to try.

Being caught between them had been a rush.

Sure, the whole chastity belt thing put a major wrench in any plans to crawl into the bed of these two. But Alistair had the key. There had to be ways to convince him to take this shit off.

Right now, there was no time to think about my latest accessory.

Daemon was transforming into a fiery hound right before my eyes. His body swelled, and flames pulsed from him. He looked just like he had in the illusion with a hound's head, a man's torso, and hindquarters caught somewhere between. The fire making up his body caught on the tent, and the entire thing went up in flames in a blink.

Alistair's shadow appeared from nowhere and pulled me inside the comfort of its cool body, protecting me from the embers and flaming pieces of debris raining down on us.

Alistair morphed into smoke with only his eyes and the vague outline of his body visible through the growing fire. "Get her out of here. Keep her far away from Daemon until I get him to shift back."

I should have wanted to get the hell out of there. Everything was going up in smoke and burning right in front of my eyes. My gaze dropped to the tattoo of the flaming circus tent on my thigh. I'd gotten it when Walker's had gone under to remind myself that nothing good lasted forever.

I didn't think my new circus was going to literally go up in flames pretty much the moment I joined it. And this time, I wasn't going to stand by and watch it turn to ash.

"Let me stay. I can help."

I pressed my face against the shadow, yelling so I could be heard over the roar of Daemon's fire. Alistair sent me a sad smile that lanced right through my heart.

"I'm sorry I dragged you into this. I was weak. Selfish. He has reason to be furious with me. The best thing you can do is let me quell his flames. I've done it so many times before."

Before I could protest, he pressed a kiss to his shadow's lips, which were so close to my own that I could feel their subtle chill.

Then, the shadow turned and carried me out into the night. I tried to open my mouth and protest, but tendrils of dark magic crawled inside my mouth. Even if I could speak, I doubt Alistair's shadow would obey me.

Unless...

I'd never charmed a shadow before. If Alistair hadn't told me the shadow was basically an extension of himself and not a product of magic, I wouldn't even consider it. My charm effects didn't work on Alistair directly, but maybe they would work on a lesser version of him.

I exhaled, focused as best I could in all the commotion. The circus workers were all running toward the tent to witness the chaos. The flames danced high in the sky, and circus workers streaked past without one glance thrown our way.

I took handfuls of my breasts and pinched my nipples between my fingers while allowing my pheromones to bleed from me without holding anything back. The shadow stopped in its tracks, and it omitted a deep moan that shook me to my core. I watched in fascination as it reached between its legs and started to stroke itself.

Watching from inside the shadow was odd, but I didn't hate it. The angle made it feel like I was touching myself—you know, if I was a man made of shadows and dark magic. I wanted to stay and watch it come. Would I feel it? Would I be able to see its seed spurt out?

My questions had to be saved for another time. While the shadow was distracted, I pried myself from its insides and stumbled backward onto the grass.

Another shadow fell over me, but relief washed through me when I realized there were two shadows. "Riff! Raff!"

"What in Discord's black hell is happening?" Raff asked, his attention flitting from Alistair's masturbating shadow to the flaming tent in the distance.

"You guys have to help me."

"What's happened, harbinger?" the blue-haired demon asked. His "Riff" tattoo crinkled as his brow furrowed when he caught the dull glowing light from under my costume. With the toe of his boot, he pushed up the fabric to reveal the chastity belt. "What in the... What are you wearing?"

"She reeks of the boss' magic," Raff muttered, his tone deepening. "Must have locked her pussy up to keep her safe from Daemon's hellbeast."

"Looks like he lost control," Riff's twin answered, turning his attention to the massive fire.

"We have to help them."

Riff frowned down at me while Raff remained transfixed by the flaring flames. "If Alistair's with him, it's best we leave him to his work. He's the only one that can calm Daemon down."

Raff nervously scrubbed the back of his skull, making his acid-green hair stick out. "Let's just hope no one dies this time around."

I was on my feet, sprinting back toward the chapel tent before I could change my mind. The twins shouted after me, but I was already gone. The chains of the belt clanked as I ran, my mind racing a hundred miles a second.

I should have been running in the opposite direction. Far away from Sinner's Sideshow, its dark master and all his creeps. But it was too late to turn back. No matter how insane shit got, this still felt like home.

If it was going to burn down, this time, I'd burn right along with it.

I bolted past the crowd as they stood by, watching everything go up in smoke. No one was bothering with trying to put it out. Why would they? It wasn't a match that had started this. It was a gigantic, three dicked flaming dog-man.

Lollie's voice screamed for me to stop—at least, I think it was her—but I didn't listen. I ran right into the flaming tent, squinting through the screen of smoke to find Alistair in his incorporeal form, holding Daemon's whip and lashing it at the hound in the corner, his hackles raised.

In the time that I'd been gone, Alistair had managed to put a muzzle that seemed to be the same magic as my chastity belt on the hound. Its golden eyes found me through the haze, its feral growl turning low and whining.

Alistair whipped around. My skin prickled with dread as I registered raw panic in the devil's eyes. "Why are you here? Get out before he—"

It was too late.

Daemon leapt over his master and landed between us, his weight making the ground quake. The hound prowled toward me, his hackles still raised. The heat from his flames was so intense that the spikes on his collar glowed like freshly forged metal.

In a last-ditch effort not to get my head ripped off, I released my pheromones into the acrid air. The hound stiffened. His nostrils twitched. Before I had time to react, he lunged forward, his snout pushing against my chest and knocking me on my ass.

I braced for the pain.

It never came. It didn't even hurt.

Daemon omitted a growling sound that sunk straight through my core, setting my insides on fire. His claws snapped at my dress, ripping it off my body. It burned up in seconds. But I didn't even feel the heat on my skin.

Was it because I was shifted? No. Wings and horns didn't change the fact that I wasn't immune to fire. Right?

Daemon nudged at my pelvis, his muzzle clanking loudly against my chastity belt. My heart clenched when his huge, molten eyes locked with mine. Then I felt them. His emotions were turbulent and caustic. But he didn't want to hurt me.

He wanted to make me his.

His giant canines gnawed on the chains of my belt and pulled on them hard enough to send me skidding across the ground. His hands—which were shaped like that of a man's—caged me in, and from my position, I could see where he'd gotten the reputation of a three headed hound.

He growled as he tried to break through the belt. He wasn't trying to hurt me, but one of his incisors gouged into my flesh, and the metallic scent of blood laced the air.

A whip appeared from the dark smoke and cracked across the hound's back. His head jerked up, but one of my chains got caught on his teeth, and he sent me flying a few feet into the air. My pathetic little wings flapped as if they could hold me up for even a second. I squeezed my eyes shut and braced myself for the ground. Instead, strong arms wrapped around me and pulled me against a hard chest.

I opened my eyes, expecting to see Alistair's shadow, so my heart skipped a beat when I saw Alistair himself instead, holding me close against him. He had to shift into his human form to catch me.

While I seemed to be fire-resistant, Alistair's human skin wasn't. The flames devoured him, eating away his flesh and leaving nothing but the darkness within.

"Damn." His sigh tickled my ear. "I really liked that skin, too."

"I'm sorry."

"If I tell you to leave this time, will you listen?"

I nodded, allowing his shadow to appear and scoop me up in its arms. He got up, took a step toward Daemon then looked back at me with a vulnerable expression that had my entire body pulsing.

Even with his peeling face consumed in embers, I wanted to kiss him.

"I meant what I said, Megaera. You're mine now. I do what it takes to protect my favorite pets." The shade licked his charred lips as his gaze dropped to my chastity belt. "Even if it means muzzling the both of you."

30

One Month Later

MEG

I woke up to the sound of tapping. My eyes blinked open to find Riff and Raff in my bed. Riff was crouched between my legs with Raff spread out beside me, his head propped on his hand.

Riff had managed to slip my sleep shorts down to my ankles without waking me and was now fiddling with my chastity belt, trying to break it open for what had to be the hundredth time.

"Looks like sleeping beauty has awakened," Raff purred when I stirred to life. "Maybe a kiss will break the curse."

I gave him a sleepy smile and kissed him, then fell back into my pillow with a groan. "If that was the case, this stupid metal diaper would have disappeared weeks ago."

Riff gave a one-shoulder shrug and fell into a relaxed position between my legs, winding the chains over my hip mindlessly around his finger. "At least it's a sexy metal diaper."

I groaned again in my pillow, and the mattress shook with Raff's laugh. "Nah. It's more like a sexy metal bikini. Slave Leia style. Now there's an idea for an act."

"Maybe after a season of our current one. Dressing up as catholic exorcists and terrorizing our virgin succubus. I'm not going to get tired of that for a while."

I rolled over and peered at my incubi through my tangle of pink hair. "How did you guys even get in here, anyway? I locked the door."

"Aw, but you didn't lock the bathroom window. You really gotta start locking that shit, babe. Wouldn't want the local riff-raff breaking in, watching you sleep."

"Can you blame us? Your RV is way nicer than ours. Plus, ours doesn't have a sexy succubus in it who looks like an angel in her sleep."

"And sounds like a whore."

"What do you mean I sound like a whore?"

"You moan in your sleep, babe. Especially last night." Riff's eyes flashed through his blue locks. I loved both of them like this. Bare-faced, wearing nothing but black joggers. I loved them when the paint went on, too, and we could let loose in front of monsters who paid for the privilege of watching our crazy.

"Did you dream about us?" He stuck his tongue out, prodding the corner of his mouth as it stretched into a playful grin, and his fingers tapped the stylized metal heart clamped over my center. "Maybe where we finally sunk into this tight little pussy of yours?"

They were obsessed with fucking me in the one place they hadn't. We were all obsessed. We were sex demons, for fuck's sake. "God. Fuck Alistair."

"Careful. Speak of the devil, and he shall appear."

I looked at Raff, wondering if he realized the irony of his words. No, he wouldn't. Nobody knew who Alistair really was except for Daemon and me.

I wanted to talk about what had happened with the hellhound the night I'd signed Alistair's contract. I'd tested out my resistance to fire after that night and got burnt for the trouble. It was only Daemon's flames I was immune to for whatever reason. And every time I found the opportunity to talk to him, he'd find a way to excuse himself.

I almost missed his animosity for me. His cold shoulder hurt more.

He was snubbing me because I'd taken a deal with Alistair, knowing he was Discord. I got why. But his sudden disinterest in me was more painful than if I'd actually gotten burned by his flames.

It's not like I wasn't paying for my recklessness.

This chastity belt was a complete bitch. Being around Riff and Raff all the time was awesome, but we were also sex demons. Not being able to be touched by them was fucking torture.

At least when I bathed with the thing, the magic would dissolve, and I could rub one out for sanity's sake. But as soon as anyone else came close, it would solidify again.

How had the twins held out this long without touching me? It had been almost twelve hours. That had to be a record. Being what we were, our bodies were constantly pumping out powerful pheromones, making the very air we breathed an aphrodisiac.

"I'm hungry."

Raff's brows shot up. "For food? Or for us?"

"Both. Just put something in my mouth."

Riff cackled as he rose off the bed and sauntered off to the kitchen with a feline flick of his tail. "I'll let you have this one, bro. Since I had more time inside her in the ring last night."

Raff rolled onto me, his hot eyes burning into mine. He wasn't wearing contacts, and as much as I loved the acid-clown type style the twins had going on, I adored his green eyes. They matched his hair color, and Riff's were cerulean blue.

His claw raked down my sternum, and I squirmed beneath him. "Don't tear this shirt. It's my favorite."

He took in the big-breasted ghost on my shirt, scowling at it like it had personally insulted his mother. Raff had a thing for tearing me out of my clothes. Pushing the shirt over my head, he tossed it aside. His hands dropped to his fly, and in a blink, he had himself out.

I grinned at the clown Shibari tattoo, but the smile was wiped off my face when he placed his dick between my breasts and spit on them before pushing them together. He fucked my tits hard, making the bed shake enough for Riff to comment on it from the kitchen. He spent himself with a grunt, his face twisted with ecstasy. Then torrents of hot cum spurt onto my breasts and face.

"Be a good little slut and open up," he panted as he continued to drip. My lips parted, and he held his tip over my mouth, dribbling thick ropes of seed onto my tongue. "Fuck. You look so good covered in my cum, little harbinger."

I smiled up at him, happy and frustrated all at once. I couldn't orgasm unless it was by my own hand, thanks to this stupid magical contraption. I grabbed my ghost boobs shirt and ran it over my face. When I looked back up, I found Raff on the edge of the bed, watching me quietly and Riff approaching from the kitchen with a plate of eggs and toast.

"Guys. I can't take much more of this. I need this shit off."

"Does that mean you're ready for the plan?"

The "plan" wasn't much of a plan. We'd discussed it before, but I'd chickened out. Now, weeks later, I was going stir-crazy, and the "plan" wasn't sounding so crazy anymore.

I took the plate, set it on my lap and took a bite from the toast. "So what? I'm just supposed to show up to Alistair's caravan and seduce him?"

"You're the one who gets wet around him every time he so much as looks at you, babe," Riff said with a half-cocked smirk. "Would it really be so terrible? He's gonna have to take the thing off to fuck you."

It wouldn't be so terrible. I'd fantasized about it constantly for a month.

I'd been traveling with the circus for four weeks, with a show almost every night. Every night he'd watched me with the twins, fucking me with his eyes.

I wasn't nervous about offering myself to Alistair. I was nervous about running into Daemon. He didn't sleep with the ringmaster every night. He had his own trailer and slipped into the boss' caravan less often ever since I signed Alistair's contract. I wanted to talk to Daemon, but not with Alistair there. It would be too weird. Too tense.

I had to wait for a night when Daemon didn't spend the night with Alistair.

After a stretch of silence, I smiled over my toast at the twins. "I'm going to do it."

31
Out of the Doghouse

ALISTAIR

I was feeling more feral than usual tonight.

I'd seen Daemon's show countless times, and tonight, his sweat-slicked body held me in dark rapture. He hadn't touched me in over a month. Not since I made Megaera one of us.

The hellhound could barely look at me now.

I couldn't blame him. When was the last time he'd asked me for anything? I couldn't remember—that's how long it had been. So when he'd practically begged me to send Megaera away, of course, I agreed. It was supposed to be easy. I could have simply magicked her away. Instead, I couldn't resist toying with her.

That was my mistake.

Now, I wanted her in ways I'd never wanted a woman before. All those years ago, I'd gone out of my way to save her from her psychotic mother and this entire circus, and now I was dragging her back because she made my dick hard.

So, of course, Daemon hated me. I deserved the torture of watching him on stage and not being able to touch him after the fact. He still slept with me in my caravan on occasion, but he'd immediately shift into his lesser hound form and fall asleep at the foot of the bed.

I deserved the torture.

The problem was it only heightened my lust for Megaera.

Daemon's act had wrapped, and now she was on stage, dressed as a harlequin with her wings spread, cackling madly as she skipped around the ring with Riff and Raff—dressed up as catholic exorcists—trying to capture her.

They did.

"Bless me, Father, for I'm about to sin!" She let out a mad laugh as she spread her legs and wiggled her hips.

"The bitch is charming us," one of the twins cackled. Then they pretended to put a chastity belt on her, which was already there, of course, but with her clothes concealing it, it appeared as though they'd only just put it on as they tore her skirt away. Next, they proceeded to give into her charm, and she fucked them in every way the belt would allow.

By the time the act was over, she was left wearing nothing but the belt, black thigh-high boots, and the twin's cum. Then, while still dripping with demon seed, she'd swallow her sword.

Tonight, she had the crowd eating out of her palm. She stood on the armrests of a werewolf's chair, pointing the sword at his throat before shoving it down her own to Doja Cat's "*Boss Bitch*" with her tail swishing to the beat.

We'd had a packed house every night for the past month. Every monster in the Upside flocked to see her. She was a natural, pulling everyone into her thrall with ease.

Including me.

It wasn't succubus magic. I truly, naturally, desired her. She brought a dark hunger to life inside me that no one had before. Not even Daemon.

A hunger that wouldn't be content to simply watch her forever.

If I were to share her with Daemon, I could keep his hunger in check. But what of my own? As a half-blood, she didn't have a full monster form, so her mortal flesh would tear if I tried feeding her mine.

No. Mating her as my true self wasn't an option. I'd be stuck with pleasuring her with my shadow or fucking her with the dead cock of the last worthless human I harvested. Watching Daemon fuck her would likely be the most satisfying for me. I'd have to watch him closely, though.

A month ago, he'd lost control and tried to claim her. He was more gentle with her than I thought. It was a miracle she hadn't been burned. Perhaps she had some kind of fire resistance to certain Underside species. Sex demons sometimes had certain immunities that allowed them to bed even the most dangerous of creatures. I hadn't expected her to have anything like that since she was a half-blood with no true monster form so that eased my concerns. Not enough to remove the belt. He'd still ruin her if he tried to fit even one of his three cocks inside her.

Especially if he knotted her.

She was so small. The size difference would be too much for her body to handle.

By the time the demonic trio act wrapped up, I could barely think straight. The supplier of my latest skin was more endowed than the last.

My cock was so hard, the dark magic filling it demanded to be satiated.

The magic that comprised my being was a sinister, chaotic energy. It didn't like the rules I forced on myself, and if I didn't do something to alleviate the pressure, I ran the risk of losing control of my true form.

I would do whatever it took to prevent that.

When the show ended, guests started to filter out back through the haunt. I slipped out the back with the flow of workers and caught a glimpse of Daemon's ink-swathed back, his torso slicked in sweat from his act.

I started to follow him, but a voice from behind stopped me, slicing through the cloud of lust strangling my mind.

"Uh, Sir?" I turned to see my boar-headed fomorian standing over me, his hands pulling nervously at his apron.

"What is it?" I asked with a polite, albeit stiff, smile.

"What did you think of tonight's show? The fellow tonight was nice. I know my Butcher act doesn't pull in tickets like the concubi…"

The fomorian was the most intimidating of all my circus creeps, with his tusks and the scars covering his beefy physique. He was also the most quiet, insecure member of my troupe. I blamed that on his old clan. He'd been the smallest giant among them and had been bullied relentlessly because of it. His sweet disposition hadn't helped his standing in the clan either. Larry had become more confident through the years, but occasionally, his old insecurities would flare up.

I didn't fully face him, my lips slanting into a frown. I didn't have time for this. "Is that why you chose a male volunteer tonight? You thought it might please me more?"

The giant didn't say anything, but he didn't have to. His body language confirmed my suspicions.

"The Butcher is a staple in my show," I told him, "and it always will be. No matter what act precedes or follows yours. And you're not to select your partners based on what you believe my preferences to be. Is that understood?"

The giant nodded, a look of relief passing behind his eyes. "Yes, Sir. Thank you, Sir."

I turned to leave, but Larry stopped me again. "Uh, there is something else, Sir. There's a woman from the audience who wishes to speak to you. Says she's a fan."

My frown deepened. "Then give her a t-shirt from the merch table and send her on her way."

"But, Sir, she—"

Before Larry could say a word more, I dissolved into shadows and coiled through the thick of the crowd in search of my hellhound. I found him beside one of the bonfires, helping dispose of the bodies from the death row seats.

I reformed and leaned on my cane, watching the way his muscles flexed in his back as he hauled a body up from the ground and tossed it into the fire in a burst of embers and smoke. I didn't miss the way he flinched at the fire.

"Daemon. I need to speak with you."

The small group of workers gathered around the fire all paused, looking at me, then at Daemon.

The hellhound's shoulders tensed at my voice. He didn't want to speak to me, but he knew better than to refuse me in front of everyone.

"Fine," he growled after a tense beat. He stormed past me, charging right through my shadow. There was a collective gasp from the onlookers, but I didn't show any reaction, even though I had to hold back a smile.

"Back to work," I instructed them before turning and following him behind the office trailer parked beside the haunted house. "I don't know how it's possible, but you're even more alluring when you're furious with me. Something about the way your muscles bulge."

He whirled around, his fists clenched at his sides. "Fuck you, Alistair."

"Please do."

Red flecks of fury danced in his golden eyes. His rage was palpable, rolling off him with all the heat of a wildfire. "This is serious. I'm so pissed at you that I've wanted to kill you more than once in the past month."

I snorted. "It wouldn't be the first time, pet."

"No. But it is the first time that I feel justified in my hatred. This isn't because I'm a fucking 'hot head,' either, as the humans say. I didn't want her here, didn't want her around me. I have a deep, unshakable need to claim her as my mate. And I never can. So you go and clamp your creepy little magic around her pussy, and you think that solves my problem?"

I raised a brow. "Doesn't it? That night in the chapel when you lost control, the belt prevented you from mounting her."

"Fine. That's true. But it's *torture*." His voice suddenly lost its edge as it softened. "I can't stand not touching her."

"Then touch her. The belt doesn't stop you from that. It most certainly doesn't prevent you from talking to her. I understand you avoiding me, but giving her the cold shoulder is just cruel."

"Don't speak to me of cruelty, Discord."

"I'm sorry."

Daemon's eyes widened at my words. It was the first time I'd said them to anyone. "What did you say?"

"I said I'm sorry," I repeated, my tone causing Daemon's skin to pebble. "Do you want me to say it again?"

I stepped toward him until our chests were nearly touching. The heat rolled off of him to seep into the cool tendrils of my shadows. "I'm so very sorry. I was selfish. I was weak. Because I did plan to honor your request, and I couldn't."

He glared at me through the darkness. The clouds covering the moon were thick, making the night darker than usual, but I was darkness itself, so I could see him perfectly.

"Explain," he ground out between clenched teeth.

"I created an illusion where I had her in my bed." I closed my eyes, summoning that moment like I had a hundred times before. "It was meant to terrorize her."

"Tell me about it," Daemon growled. The rumble had my cock thickening. Or maybe it was the memory of her—or both.

I told Daemon about the illusions in great detail, emphasizing the one in the caravan where I'd eaten her wings and made love to her with the erection they'd given me. How her lashes fluttered when I'd pushed inside her. How her lips had parted on a breathy moan when she saw her blood on my lips.

"I didn't intend for the moment to be so intimate. I didn't want it to mean anything. But there was something in the way she looked at me." I let out a sigh and shook my head. "I don't know what I saw in her eyes. Whatever it was, I..."

I didn't dare say the words.

How could the devil love anything? I didn't have a heart. But I did know this feeling. I'd felt it before with Daemon. "I want to keep her close. She's something new for me to give a damn about other than this circus and the boring, never-changing realm below it. I want her for me. For us."

Daemon leaned forward, his breath fanning over my lips as his face took on a pained expression. "Us? And what am I supposed to do with that, Alistair?"

"You're supposed to say thank you, Master, and eat what I put in front of you." I hooked my finger under his collar and tugged, dragging his lips to mine.

He sighed against my lips, the oxygen emptying from his lungs. "That's what I'm afraid of. That we'll devour her until there's nothing left."

"Have I not taught you restraint over the years? Obedience? Control? So you had a slip-up. I was there to pull you back. I will always be there to pull you back."

Daemon leveled me with a glare. "Yeah, and who's going to be the one shortening your leash if you're the one to lose control?"

I didn't respond to his question right away. I'd been struggling with the answer to that question for weeks.

"I don't know yet," I finally admitted after a long moment. "Until I figure that out, I'll keep my distance."

He searched my eyes for several long minutes that seemed to last an eternity. Debating. Weighing the weight of my words, no doubt. Finally, he leaned forward, and his lips skimmed mine in a soft kiss.

My eyes rounded, caught off guard by his sudden gentleness. Even when he wasn't angry with me, he wasn't usually this tender. "You forgive me?" I asked.

"Damn you," he murmured, his teeth suddenly nipping at my lips. I gasped as warmth washed over my dead flesh in waves.

My brow rested against his, and I smirked against his lips. "I'll take that as a yes."

"So this is why you sent me away?" a female cooed from nearby. "You'd rather fuck a dog than the demoness created for your pleasure?"

If I had a heart, it would have frozen in my chest at the chill in the newcomer's voice.

Impossible.

Why is she *here?*

There was no way in my darkest depths that she'd be stupid enough to show her face here. But I didn't have to turn around to confirm the identity of the newcomer.

Daemon's heart beat so fast, I could feel it thumping against my chest. "Master. Is that...?"

I turned to face the demoness with a poison-dipped smile, bowing my lips. "Why are you here, Astrid?"

32

Stone Cold Succubus

ALISTAIR

"**Y**our god asked you a question, succubus," Daemon snapped. He stepped closer to her, pausing just a few feet short of the demon. He murmured something in Infernal tongue—a spell I taught him long ago—and his tattoos glowed molten yellow, illuminating the dark.

Astrid looked the same as she had the last time I'd seen her twenty years ago. She was beautiful, always had been. Yet, every time I looked at her, a coldness swept under my skin, filling my body with ice.

She was a cold, heartless bitch.

Obnoxious, too, what with her relentless pursuit of me.

Mcgacra didn't look much like her mother. Astrid was tall and lithe, while Meg was short with soft, mouth-watering curves. Astrid's hair was a dusky shade of purple, with matching eyes—all concubi had irises to match their hair. Plus, Astrid always seemed to have a permanent tan, whereas her daughter was almost as pale as Sinclair.

The only shift in Astrid's appearance was that she'd been heavily pregnant the last time I saw her.

"My god prefers a mongrel's company over mine, so excuse me if my piety is running thin lately."

Daemon's eyes narrowed and dropped to the obsidian obelisk she wore around her neck. "Yet you're wearing a pendant of Discord?" He gave a mirthless laugh, his eyes glowing the same golden hue as his tattoos. "You're just as hard up for him as ever."

"Fuck you, you worthless shifter. You're just a stray he picked up because he was bored. I was made for him."

It wasn't true. She was the first demoness to ever form from my darkness, but so had a lot of other things. She hadn't been created for my pleasure. Over the eons, I'd come to believe her sole purpose was to annoy me.

"I told you never to come back here."

She laughed, turning to inspect the circus grounds. "It's my circus, My Lord."

I cringed. I hated it when she called me that. "It *was* yours. But you never really cared about it, did you?"

She turned back to me, her perfectly formed lavender brows hiking up. "I cared about it for what it was: a means to harvest fear from the lesser creatures of this trash realm in your glorious name. It was never about the clowns and the peanuts, My Lord. It was about keeping you fed."

"And you got sloppy. You started killing humans and compromising the security of the monsters here on the Upside."

She laughed again as if I'd told a joke. "I never got why you gave two gorgon fucks about them. They're cockroaches compared to the monsters of your realm. All of them. The circus was just a way of harvesting fear in style."

Her smirk turned smug when distant screams echoed from the haunted house. "I've noticed you haven't changed much about Sinner's Sideshow since I left it. Other than killing my entire troupe."

"I wanted a fresh start to the operation. You put a sour taste in my mouth for disclosing my identity to my disciples. They become annoying when they know who I really am."

The succubus gave a little huff, her attention snapping in Daemon's direction. "This one knows who you are."

"He's special."

"Not special enough to mark you, apparently."

I resisted the urge to react. She'd hit a soft spot, and she knew it. "Why have you come back? Answer the fucking question. You know I have almost as much impatience for repeating myself as I do for you, Lilith."

Her hand closed around her pendant, and for the first time tonight, she donned an expression that didn't turn my stomach. "It's been a long time since you've called me that, Discord."

I turned my nose up, looking down at her with cool indifference. I didn't share her sentimentality.

She propped a hand on her hip—something Meg did a lot. "I want to see my daughter."

"You watched the show?"

The succubus' gaze hardened. "Yes. I told your pig-headed giant that I wanted to meet you after the show, but you were too busy tongue fucking your mongrel, I suppose."

"If you saw the show, then you saw Meg. Mission accomplished. Now get out." My terse smile dropped, and my voice was full of warning. My patience was thinning with every second this woman remained in my orbit.

"You know that's not what I mean when I say I want to see my daughter."

"I'll kill you before I let you speak to her."

"My Lord. You know you can't kill me. It's in our contract."

Fuck. I was afraid she'd bring that up. Then again, how could she not? Of course, she was shoving that in my face.

The contract was the only reason she was still breathing.

Daemon's infernal glare burned into the side of my face. I hadn't told him about the contract.

"I have ways of sending you to the Underside forever."

"You know I'm immune to most of your magic, My Lord. I was created from your darkness to be your partner, your right hand. Even when you don't want me to be. Don't worry. This feud of ours will soon pass. It's just sad you've made it come to this."

A chill worked through me. "And what is 'this?'"

"Me, using my daughter as leverage against you."

"Still the same coldhearted bitch, I see. See how your twisted obsession with me has warped you over time? She's your daughter."

"Don't forget why I had her in the first place, Discord."

As if I could ever forget.

"You ran away because you knew I was going to punish you for murdering all those poor innocents. You broke my one rule. Never harm an innocent. Monsters who want to die? Sure. But never innocent humans. You claimed to shed their blood for me, but it wasn't for me, Lilith. You're just a bloodthirsty bitch."

"And you're the fucking devil!" Her cadence turned shrill. "You're supposed to take offerings given to you with a 'thank you, may I have another, my love?' But no. You have to be all righteous. I tried to fix it. I thought you would want my offering."

I scrubbed a hand over my face, a sigh winding out through my spread fingers. "Oh, Astrid. You could have raised Meg alongside that human man you charmed into breeding you. You could have had a happy life after I made you sign that contract not to harm her. You could have pretended to be normal."

In all honesty, I was glad the succubus left after I swore to let her live so long as she didn't harm the baby. Megaera had to grow up without a mother, but not having one at all had to be better than enduring this twisted harpy.

"I had her for you, My Lord. She's your offering. And look, she's found her way to you. How perfect." Lilith pressed her claw-tipped fingers to her mouth, giggling. "You like pretending you're good. You should put that act in your show for how phony it is. You're a sick fuck. After all my years of servitude, you refused to touch me. I thought it was because you weren't interested. But now you have my daughter, and you're forcing her to remain celibate? You like females. You just prefer to watch them suffer."

Daemon pulled his whip out, giving it a threatening crack. "Get to your point, succubus, or I'll flay it out of you."

The demoness' eyes gleamed. "Down, boy." She looked at me, running her forked tongue over her lips. "I guess you have a bit of a masochistic streak in you, Discord. I can do that for you, you know."

Astrid always was insistent. Just like her daughter. However, I found Megaera's persistence far less irritating.

"What do you want?"

"You. I've always wanted you. And I'm not talking about just any old fuck. I want you to claim me as your mate. I also want my circus back. I was created to serve you, so I should be the one collecting your offerings. Not you. That kind of work is well below your station, My Lord."

"And if I refuse?"

"Then I give Megaera a very *detailed* account of what you've done over the years. Sure, she might accept you now, but that's because you're but a shadow of your former self. Once she learns about all your former exploits, she'll hate you."

An uncomfortable tightening spread through me. Lilith's threats always were potent, and this time, she'd come prepared. Good thing I was the inventor of the poker face. "What do I care if the girl hates me? She's bound to me through an Infernal contract."

"You can't bluff me, My Lord. As the only succubus who's ever been able to feel your emotions, you're falling for her." Lilith's voice was bitter with envy.

"Then you also taste my hatred for you. Why would you want to be mated to a demon who will forever resent you."

"I was made in your image," she said darkly. "I am no stranger to resentment."

She pulled her amulet from her neck and strode toward me. When Daemon stepped in front of her with a growl, she slapped the necklace in his hand. "Fine. You give it to him, mongrel."

Her muted violet eyes found me over Daemon's shoulder. "This obsidian has absorbed my energy all these years that I've worn it. That should be enough for you to find me. You have three days to properly fuck and mark me like you should have done years ago, or I will be back. And I will *decimate* any future you have with my daughter."

She snapped her fingers, her long horns sprouting from her skull and her wings pushing out from her back. I'd forgotten how huge her wings were. They spread out to their full span, and in a blink, she launched herself into the night sky.

Daemon stared up at the sky for a beat before passing an annoyed look at me. "Thank fuck we're hauling to the next town tomorrow. Her desperation will stink up this place for a while."

With a sigh, I turned and made my way into the office trailer. The antique fairy light on my desk flickered to life the moment I entered. I sat down at my desk and thumbed through financial ledgers, pretending to give them my attention.

Daemon entered the trailer, his arm stretched over his head as he leaned into the doorframe. "So just to make sure I'm following. Twenty years ago, you came to the Upside. I remember because you left me behind. You never left me behind. It was to take care of Astrid, who'd gone rogue in collecting offerings for you. You left out the little part about her being Lilith, by the way."

"It wasn't important. None of the stories are true. I never touched her because she's a fucking ice harpy. Not because she's 'too beautiful.'" I hissed in displeasure, aggressively flipping a page in my ledger. "Who came up with that shit anyway?"

"So she runs off, hides out in another circus, and charms some poor human fuck. Then, what? Gets pregnant with the intention of sacrificing it to you?"

"She's known me the longest out of any soul, living or dead. Yet she doesn't know me at all."

Daemon pushed off the door frame and strode toward my desk, his smoldering tattoos bathing the space in an amber glow.

"So you strike a deal with her. You let her live, and she leaves the baby unharmed."

"And now that she knows I've grown fond of her daughter, Lilith has leverage to get what she's been after all these years."

"So what's the plan?"

I shut my ledger and leaned back in my chair. "Killing her would be the easiest course of action. But my Infernal contract with her prevents me from doing anything of the sort."

Magic had rules that even I had to abide by. But that didn't mean there weren't loopholes. And I certainly wasn't above using them.

"I think I know where this is going. You want me to kill her."

I stretched out my hands, looking around the room. "Who else? Not my shadow. It counts as an extension of myself."

Daemon nodded. "I have a condition, Alistair."

I arched a brow. "A condition? We don't normally have those between us."

"Yeah, well, you owe me."

A sinful smirk played across my face as I ran the edge of my polished shoe up his calf. "You want a payment in flesh, naturally?"

The shifter swallowed, making his leather collar twitch. "Yes. But you don't pay me with your body. Not this time. You pay me with your virgin succubus'. Though you're going to have to change her stage name once I'm done with her."

Satisfaction wound through me. I hoped he was going to say that. "Fine. Kill Astrid for me. Do this, and I'll give you the key to her daughter's chastity belt."

He stared down at Astrid's amulet in his open palm. Judging by the expression on his face, a million emotions were blasting through his mind. It was as if he hadn't expected me to agree.

A war waged inside him. The hungry hellhound had made the deal, but the softer side of him was having second thoughts.

"What if I hurt her?"

"You won't. You only lose control when you're angry. If you keep your calm, you won't shift. That being said, I insist you have someone else there. Just in case. The twins—"

"Those imps aren't going to babysit me," he snarled.

"Fine. Then I will. Or my shadow, if you prefer the illusion of privacy."

He debated for a moment, then nodded. "We have a deal. And this time, I want a fucking contract."

33

The Ringmaster's Caravan

MEG

My fist hovered over the door of Alistair's caravan, nerves freezing me before I could knock. What if Daemon was with him?

No, I'd seen him walk alone, well, not alone, but he'd only had his dog with him.

My human flight instincts started to take over. What if he rejected me? What if there was no chemistry between us, and I'd only been romanticizing that night in the illusion?

No. There was a lot of mystery surrounding Alistair, but I was sure that moment we'd shared hadn't been a figment of my imagination.

The devil had made me feel something other than fear.

Ugh. If I was going to do this, I really needed to ignore the fact that I was about to booty call Satan.

What I'd felt with him in his illusion wasn't the type of emotion that could be replicated with magic. Whatever it was, it had been real. Very freaking real.

Me showing up in the middle of the night at Alistair's doorstep wasn't just a desperate attempt to get the chastity belt off. I wanted to experience that feeling again. With him.

Steeling my nerves, I grabbed the old-fashioned brass handle of the antique caravan and pushed inside.

The smell of old books was the first thing to hit me. My eyes flitted around, taking in the small space. This was the room where he'd made love to me in the illusion. Everything was generous and every bit the kind of place a traveling wizard would live. It was small, but shelves were built into the walls, lined with all sorts of books and trinkets. A single lamp suspended from the ceiling, the tiny flame painting the room in strips of gold and shadows.

Alistair knelt on his bed with his legs folded beneath him. He was wearing form-fitting high-waisted pants and an old-fashioned lantern-sleeve shirt with a low neckline that exposed much of his chest. He'd improved his tailoring skills since he'd made his last skin suit because this new one had much finer stitching. He looked completely human, save for his glowing green eyes and the thick cloud of magic clinging to his aura.

In one hand, he held a book—an old one judging by the yellowing pages—and with his other, he was petting his dog, who lay curled by his side.

The shade looked up from his book as I entered and closed the door behind me with a soft click. A frown tugged at his mouth, but it didn't reach his eyes, which sparkled with amusement.

"You have a lot of nerve, bursting into your master's quarters without an invitation," he said, his attention returning to his book.

I planted a hand on my hip. "Oh. So it's 'master' now? I thought 'just Alistair' was what I was supposed to call you."

"It is. But when you come to my caravan in the dead of night, reeking of lust and carnal intent, you'll refer to me as the former."

Heat crept up my spine. "I kind of took you as a bottom."

"Well, not when it comes to you."

I stepped up to one of his bookshelves and perused the titles. I turned my back to him but could feel his eyes glued to me. "So you're a switch, then?"

"I haven't had much opportunity to explore it much, but I believe so." His silken timbre caused me to shiver.

I was out of my depth here. How was a twenty-year-old half-demon supposed to seduce an ancient and malevolent—allegedly—shadow monster? If I was going to get in my head about this, I might as well walk out and save myself the embarrassment.

Books. I knew books. Books were sexy.

"Tell me about your collection." I glanced back at him while gesturing to a random shelf, barely looking.

He tweaked a brow. "The demon fetuses or my antique collection of German grimoires?"

My attention shot back to the shelf, my jaw falling open. How had I missed the creepy jars filled with half-formed demons? Some of them had two heads, while others had multiple limbs. I even spotted one with three tails and three sets of wings. "Where did you get these?"

"I inherited those from your mother, actually. They came with the rest of the circus."

"Oh." I wasn't sure how to even begin unpacking that, so I decided to push it to the back of my mind for now. I pivoted to fully face him. "This is the room from the illusion."

"It is."

"You were trying to scare me, right?"

"No, I always try to seduce my lovers by consuming a body part of theirs first," he said, his tone dripping with sarcasm.

"I ask because it was so..." My blush deepened. I'd come here thinking I was going to be all seductive and sultry, but Alistair's attention made me shaky. It had the same effect as an adrenaline shot to the heart.

He swept his hand through his hair, trying in vain to tame the shadow tendrils, which seemed to have a mind of their own. "It was intimate. I wanted you to feel like I was making love to you. There's an art to making people feel fear. Gore and guts are fine and well for unnerving most people. I knew you were different."

I swallowed. "Different, how?"

"You've been through a lot in your life. Lots of loss. If I was going to scare you, I wanted to show you your future here if you stayed. What's more terrifying than the devil himself falling in love with you?"

"You're not like any Satan, Devil, or Beelzebub I've ever heard of."

He gave me a melancholy smile that made him look so handsome in the dim flamelight. "Those stories didn't start from nothing. Though, I'm not what I used to be."

I moved toward him, my hands fiddling the hem of my skirt. "What changed?"

"Daemon, mostly."

"You love him."

The silence that unfolded was excruciating as Alistair appeared bewildered by my statement at first, then his expression softened with his quiet smile. "I suppose I do, yes."

The hound lifted its head, giving a soft whine and Alistair gave it an affectionate pet between the ears.

"Does he sleep with you every night? The dog, not Daemon," I added with a nervous laugh.

Alistair's eyes glittered with mirth like I'd said something especially hilarious. "Most nights."

He was a monster. But damn, was he a pretty one. He really smiled—not with one of those fake smiles he wore in the ring—his eyes brightening like polished emeralds in the sun.

I was attracted to him, but not in the same way I was attracted to Riff, Raff, and Daemon. Alistair mesmerized me. I hadn't realized I was reaching out to touch him until my fingers were already on him, tracing the subtle divot between his pectorals. "I like this skin."

"It's the skin of a murderer, Megaera."

"It would be a deal breaker if it wasn't." I laughed awkwardly. "It's nicer than the other one. Do you specifically target beautiful criminals?"

"I try to make use of those who were otherwise worthless in their living state. I have a vast collection but I only wear the ones that appeal to me."

My thighs clenched as warmth swept through my core. Fucking Hell. *Really?* I really was meant for this circus because I was, without a doubt, an absolute freak.

His lips twitched. *He knew.*

"You're adorable when you're nervous. You can suck cock and eat fire oozing with demon cum while hundreds of strangers watch without so much as a bat of your beautiful eyes. But in a private, and dare I say romantic setting, minus your mother's pickled demon specimens, you choke."

"I'm not choking."

He closed his book and set it on his bedside table. He seemed to size me up for a few moments before he leaned back onto his elbows, his gaze silently daring me. "Prove it."

I sucked in a breath, then tentatively lowered myself onto the bed.

"You're so confident in the ring. Yet you're shaking now."

"You make me fucking nervous."

His gaze seemed to soften. "I won't hurt you."

He remained perfectly still as he watched me climb into his lap and clamp my thighs around his hips. I steadied my palms against his chest and the moment my skin touched his, the shaking stopped.

"We can explore it, you know."

The shade stared up at me, his brows bending with confusion. "Explore what, little demon?"

"You said you hadn't had a chance to explore this new side of your sexuality. That you haven't tried being more dominant in bed. You can explore that with me. I wouldn't mind." I swallowed. "I'd like it."

My fingers slipped down his chest, feeling out the contours of his torso. When I moved to unbutton his pants, his hand snatched my wrist.

I gaped at him in surprise. "I want to fuck you."

The next moment of silence crawled by on its hands and knees. This beautiful bastard loved twisting me into knots.

"No," he finally said with a shake of his head, dashing all my hopes in a single syllable.

My heart sank. "Why not?"

"There are a lot of reasons."

"Give me one."

He took me by the hips and gently lifted me off him, dropping me onto the bed next to him. "I'm the devil, little one. I'll admit, I want you. But it will be some time before I allow myself to touch you. You're too young. Too innocent still."

I blinked, flabbergasted that was one of his reasons. "Innocent? I'm romantically involved with two unhinged, demonic clown twins who bang me on a regular basis in front of strangers every night."

"You are too inexperienced. Maybe when you've been—"

"Are you serious?" I spat, the slits of my eyes glowing with my sudden spark of anger. "You don't want to fuck me because I'm too vanilla for you?"

"That's not what I said." His voice came out as steel wrapped in velvet. "I don't want you to lose your virginity to me. You deserve more than to have the cock of a murderer inside you for your first time."

"Oh..."

A sharp, uncomfortable pain pulled under my stomach, burrowing into my bones. Holy shit. And who said romance was dead?

"That doesn't bother me."

"It should. Everything that I am, everything that I was, should bother you. You don't want to rush into being my lover. As much as I want you, I won't allow myself to touch you. Not yet."

Liquid fire tore through my veins. "Don't tell me what I want. You might have wormed your way into telling me what I can do with my vagina, but you can't tell me what I want. I want you."

"What if I wanted my shadow to bend you over my desk while I watch? What if I decided for our next show to bend you over and take you while the entire troupe watched?"

"You can fuck me in your true form for all I care. Whatever it is, I want it."

His smile went from vulnerable and gentle to cruel in an instant. "And what if I wanted my dog to fuck you?"

Horror wound through my gut. I instinctively leaned away from him on the bed. "What? That's *disgusting*. I'm not—"

The dog jumped over me, shifting into a man in midair, and everything that happened next was over in a single heartbeat. He landed on top of me, pinning my arms above my head. He was muscular and covered in dark ink.

It was Daemon. *Of course.* For the first time, I noticed the ring in his ear. Although, it wasn't really the first time. I'd previously seen it on his hound form and thought it was weird for the dog to be wearing human jewelry. I felt stupid having not made the connection earlier. If Alistair wasn't a dead zone for my succubus magic I would have been able pick up on Daemon's emotions even in his lesser hound form.

Still. There'd been some pretty obvious clues.

Alister let out a mischievous chuckle as he reached for his book and settled into his nest of pillows. "Want to rethink your answer, darling?"

"I'm not going to fuck your king bitch. He just so happens to hate me."

"I don't hate you, little pup. You annoy me because you're a total brat. But that doesn't mean I wouldn't bring you the heads of your enemies should you provide me a list of your greatest foes. Doesn't mean I won't protect you with my life."

An unholy sound clawed up from my throat when his hand loosely curled around my throat. "And it definitely doesn't mean that I don't want to rail your brains out."

Gods. *I wish.*

The way this man ignited my blood had me wet with need. And the idea of Alistair watching us? Hell yes.

I arched my back off the bed, my hips writhing against Daemon's. The need for relief was driving me to the brink of madness. My hands wrapped around Daemon's wrist in a desperate attempt to pull him closer. "A–Alistair. Please."

Here was his naked hellhound shifter, caging me against the bed with his master lounging right beside us, so close I could feel his subtle heat licking against my skin. And Alistair pretended to read. Like we both couldn't feel his eyes devouring every inch of our flesh or see the way he broke into goosebumps at the slightest brush of our bodies.

He flipped a page. "This is the part where you should tell her, pet."

I gaped up at Daemon, whose dark hair spilled over his molten glare. "Tell me what?"

Keeping one hand on my throat, he brandished a key seemingly from nowhere. It wasn't just any key. It glowed with the same kind of dull light as my chastity belt.

It was the key to the belt.

"Where did you get that?" I wheezed in disbelief.

"You're not the only one making deals with the devil, pup. If you only knew what I had to agree to in order to get this." His smile was a slow crawl across his face. "You'd hate me."

"I already hate you."

"Liar."

I was lying. I'd stopped hating him after the night in the chapel tent. He'd asked Alistair to scare me off, not because he hated the idea of a half-blood in the troupe, but because he wanted to keep me safe. From him. The thing was, after he'd shifted into a hellhound, I was sure he wouldn't hurt me.

"You've been avoiding me," I said, allowing the hurt to filter into my voice.

"I didn't want to hurt you."

His hand eased what little pressure he'd been applying to my throat, allowing me to take a breath. "I would love it if everyone stopped being so obsessed with my vagina's theoretic fragileness. It's really starting to get annoying. Let's make a game plan to be more gentle with Meg only when someone snaps her spine in two while giving her dick, 'kay? Until then, everyone needs to shut the fuck up."

My nerves launched into overdrive when I noticed the primal part of him banking in his eyes. I didn't try to pull away. I trusted he'd keep it at bay. Even if he didn't, I wasn't afraid of it anymore.

"Your mouth has pissed me off since the moment you opened it. I've been dreaming of the night when I get to fill it with something other than your bratty little comments," he rumbled.

He was so close and his growl was so deep it started in his throat and ended in mine.

"So here's what we're going to do. I'm going to unlock this belt. Then you're going to run, and I'm going to hunt you. If I catch you, I'm going to be the reason why you're gonna have to change your stage name."

34

The Hunt

MEG

The moment the hellhound eased off me, I scrambled off the bed and flung myself out of the caravan. Behind me, I could hear Alistair chuckling to Daemon. "Make her scream. I want the whole camp to hear."

I ran through the camp as fast as my feet could carry me, even though I wanted to be caught. Jesus. I *wanted* Daemon to catch me and make good on his promise.

The chains of the chastity belt thrashed against my hip, their metal weighing me down. The camp was empty. With morning just around the corner, everyone had gone to sleep. I sprinted across the deserted campgrounds, zigzagging between tents and crates.

I wanted him to catch me, but that didn't mean I wasn't going to make him work for it.

My legs pumped hard, my muscles starting to ache, but I didn't slow down. Didn't look back. I felt his presence behind me, gaining ground. The air around me grew hotter as he closed in, making every frantic breath I drew burn.

When I arrived at the center of several tents, I looked around, my attention pinging to each one. Where was I supposed to go? I couldn't keep running forever. He'd catch me out in the open.

I slipped into the nearest tent. It was another one designated for storage, filled with stacks of barrels, crates, and various stage props.

My heart slammed against my ribs when my attention landed on a cage in the back. It was just like the one Daemon had tossed me into the first night we'd met. This one had to be a spare because his pack was nowhere in sight.

"Well, isn't this just fucking perfect."

I whirled around to find him standing in the mouth of the tent, his bare chest heaving and his eyes wild. It was dark, but the faint light coming from outside outlined his muscular body in a thin thread of silver.

"Don't touch me," I panted. I took several steps back until my back hit a wall of crates.

Trapped.

"If that's what you want, I won't. But you have to use your words. Tell me you don't want this. I'll even leave you with the key."

"You're lying," I choked out. "You wouldn't. Not without getting your payment for whatever dirty work you agreed to do for your master."

He prowled toward me, eating up the space left between us. "He's *our* master now, pup, like it or not. And try me. Tell me to fuck off, and I will. You'll get your belt removed either way, and the twins can be the ones to pluck your little cherry. They can argue among themselves about who gets to do it first. Or maybe they'll just take you at the same time."

That bastard. I wanted this so badly. I wanted him, and he wasn't going to allow me to pretend that I didn't.

"If I stay, what are you going to do to me?"

"I'm going to do what I said I would when we first met. I'm going to teach you some obedience so you can be the perfect little pet for your new master."

He took a final step that closed the last few inches of space between us. He reached up, the back of his knuckles stroking the edge of my jaw. At his touch, fire lashed through my core. I squirmed, and he laughed. The sound was as deep and dark as Hell. "You are going to be so fun to tame, little pup."

"I'm not some dog you can teach tricks to, asshat."

"We'll see about that." He held up the key, which swayed to and fro on the chain pinched between his fingers. "You want this, right?"

"R–right," I said, my breath catching.

"Then *beg*."

I opened my mouth to protest—or comply, I hadn't decided yet—when my gaze caught a dark shape skirting around the tent's inner perimeter.

"Alistair's shadow…"

Daemon didn't bother turning around. He wasn't surprised in the least. "It's here to watch me and make sure I don't shift. Alistair can see through its eyes." He pushed me up against the crates, his thick cock jabbing at the metal edge of my belt. "Don't you want him to see what a good little pet you can be for the both of us?"

Discord's depths. "Yes," I bit out.

"What was that?" The shifter tilted his head. "Speak up, girl."

My cheeks flared hot with indignation, all their warmth quickly falling to my apex. The slight degradation was working me up into tight knots, driving my succubus thirst wild.

Something inside me snapped.

"Yes. I want it off. Please. *Please.*"

Daemon leaned back, and his eyes glowed with satisfaction. "That's a good girl. Now take off your clothes. All of them."

I stood there for a beat, realizing this was going to go no further until I obeyed him. So I did as he instructed, removing my shirt and bra first, then my pants and finally my shoes. Leaving me in nothing but the chastity belt.

His eyes roved down the length of my body. His cock twitched. He leaned toward me, his mouth finding the column of my throat, and planted a sweet kiss to my jugular. "You're so damn beautiful, Megaera."

The emotional bend in his tone caught me off guard.

This whole thing had started to feel like just another part of his act. Sexy, sure. But part of me couldn't help thinking he was putting on a show for Alistair as our master watched through the eyes of his shadow.

Then, the gentle graze of Daemon's lips against my throat and the adoration in his tone had me relaxing against him. His hand dropped between my legs where the heart-shaped padlock hugged my apex.

The key *chinked* against the metal as he fitted it inside the hole. Our eyes met as the mechanism clicked. Then, the belt faded away along with the key.

Leaving me bare.

His hands skimmed my body, taking their time as they mapped out my curves. His lips pressed more kisses to my throat, my shoulder, my hair. I reached up, my fingers digging into his shoulder blades as I breathed in his musky scent.

At my touch, his tattoos started to burn hot, like crackling embers beneath his skin. I resisted the urge to pull away, and sure enough, there was no pain. "You're, erm, glowing. Do you ever do this for your show? Seems like something your fans would love to drool over."

He pulled away, blinking at me in surprise. His serious expression snapped back into place a breath later. "No. It's something I only do when I'm feeling protective over a mate."

"But I'm not your mate."

"No, but you should be." The expression on his face had me getting wetter. My thighs clenched, sticking together with the arousal trickling down my thighs.

His attention flicked down my legs. A dark smile stained his lips. "Alistair has tortured you long enough. Your virgin hole is ready for a fat cock, isn't it?"

I nodded, heat slamming through my core. The hellhound's voice was riddled with hunger, and his golden eyes were stark with impatience. By the bulging veins in his arms and the straining cords in his neck, he was doing everything in his power to draw this out nice and slow for me.

He picked me up, alarm thrumming through my body as it dawned on me that he was carrying me toward the cage. The last time he'd put me in one of those, it hadn't been such a great time.

"Wait..."

To my surprise, he stopped.

"I don't want you to throw me in there and leave me."

Sadness and regret bled from his aura, making my heart ache. "I'm sorry for doing that to you. I thought manhandling you and making you hate me would be the best way to protect you. If you didn't want anything to do with me, I wouldn't have the chance to hurt you like I did with the last woman I fell for."

The last woman he fell for. Was he saying what I think he was saying?

"I'm going to get into the cage with you, alright?"

I swallowed and nodded. "Alright."

The shadow moved to the cage and opened the door for us. Daemon set me down carefully. A clean blanket already lay inside, padding the bottom. He crawled on top of me, his eyes burning through the dark. Alistair's shadow closed the cage with a creak but didn't lock it. It stood guard at the door, watching us all the while.

My mind briefly wandered back to the caravan. What was Alistair doing? I pictured him still sprawled across his bed with his open book forgotten on the side of his bed and his hand on his cock, watching us intently through his shadow's eyes.

And what were the twins up to? Tomorrow, they'd ask me to recount every detail of this night to them. Then they'd get excited, and I could finally fuck them.

I clung to Daemon, savoring his warmth. They'd all become so important to me in such a short time. From the moment I'd learned about Sinner's Sideshow, I'd felt a pull to it.

Now I knew why.

A gasp wrenched from my throat when Daemon's hand sunk into my hair and angled my head back. "Are you thinking about other men while you're with me, pup?"

I blinked up at him, the pain in my scalp making my eyes water while the pleasure of it made my pussy throb. I flashed him a toothy grin. "Maybe."

His lips spread into a smile of his own. "You're playing with fire. But you seem to fair well against my flames, don't you? Too bad I'd split you open if I shifted into my true form. Otherwise,

I'd take you right here and now. That way, when you fuck Alistair or those maniacal little imps, they'll see my mark and know that you also belong to me."

"Also? Wow. So I guess the big bad hellhound knows how to share, after all. Somebody's been watching their *Sesame Street*."

No sooner than the words left me was his mouth on mine, devouring my gasps. The kiss was rough and bruising. His teeth cut into my lips, and his tongue ran over my flesh to lap up the blood. He released a guttural groan into my mouth as my flavor hit his tongue.

Raw lust and desperation rolled off of him in powerful waves, making my head spin. His fingers found my center, rubbing firm and eager strokes over my seam and spreading my juices.

"Fuck, you're so wet," he groaned. "You have no idea how hard it's been watching you with the twins and not being able to join in. The shade has been torturing us all."

A cavernous chuckle echoed from the shadow and fell silent again.

My hips lifted from the cage floor, eagerly searching for my friction. With every passing second, my hunger spiked. I needed an orgasm, and I needed one fast if I was going to keep myself from absolutely tearing into this man.

Maybe I would, anyway.

I shifted with a scream—I couldn't help it. My horns pushed out from my brow, my wings spreading out at my sides in all their stubby glory, and my nails extended into sharp claws. I sunk them into his back, racking ribbons of red down his flesh.

When he growled, I thought it was from the pain but registered the way his gaze was glued to my wings. "They're fucking beautiful."

My self-consciousness about my tiny wings immediately disintegrated with his words. I smiled up at him through my mess of pink hair. "Make me come. Please."

The corner of his mouth kicked up into a grin. "Fine. Because you were a good girl for me and asked nicely."

His thumb found my clit and began rubbing circles around it, teasing the edges before finding the exact spot that had me seeing stars. When I thought it couldn't get any better, he sunk two fingers inside me.

My body couldn't get enough of him. My hips kicked and bucked, and my pussy grew slicker with every thrust he made inside me. Sensing my need, his speed picked up. Then—*Jesus Christ*—he curled his fingers and hit a spot inside me that had me shaking with mind-numbing bliss.

Fuck!

The orgasm tore through me, ripping my nerves to shreds. I thrashed and moaned beneath him, feeling the blanket go wet beneath me. His eyes widened, and he stilled. He looked down and slowly started to laugh.

I blinked. "Why are you laughing? Did I do something wrong? I'm not good at this, you know."

"No, Meg. You're perfect. You got a little excited and squirted for me. It doesn't always happen. But when it does—" He swore in Infernal. "It strokes my ego."

"I don't care what you stroke. Just do it inside me."

He was laughing again, this time the sound coming out darker. "*Fuck.* You're such a good little slut for me. Are you ready for my cock?"

I looked down at the piece he fisted, getting a good look at it for the first time.

It was *huge*. And ribbed, with a complex network of bulging veins wrapped around its girth. It wasn't longer than the twins, but it was thicker and definitely more textured. Drool gathered at the corners of my mouth. "I'm ready."

He paused for a second, thought churning behind his eyes, then he sat back on his heels and started to unbuckle his collar.

I rose up on my elbows, watching him through the dark. "What are you doing?"

"I can't claim you, at least not until we can figure out a way to safely do it. For now, you'll wear this. I've been wearing it for years. Every monster who works here or who's ever seen our show knows it's mine."

He arched over me and fastened the spiked leather strap around my neck. The leather was worn and had absorbed his scent. I wasn't sure what to say. I'd expected rough animal sex. This was better.

"Thank you."

"Look at that. All I have to do is slap my collar on you and call you a good girl, and you're all smiles, sugar and dripping pussy."

He hooked his finger into the loop and dragged my lips to his in a feral kiss that shook me to my core.

"Daemon," I whimpered into him as he shifted. His one arm swooped around my back and pulled us into a sitting position, with me straddling his lap. I moved my hips, lining us up. Our eyes locked as he slowly began to lower me onto his cock.

"So good," I warbled, my head tilted toward the heavens. "Ooh. *Yes.*"

His fingers curled tighter around the loop of his collar, applying the perfect amount of pressure to my throat. "That's a good girl. Take what I give you."

I slid down until I was fully seated on him. His hand slipped from the collar to band around my middle, holding me flush against him. The warmth of his tattoos bled into my skin and sunk down to where we were joined.

"Fuck, this is good," I groaned, my brows pinching together in ecstasy. I drew on his lust, gorging myself silly on his emotions and his cock at the same time. For the first time ever, I knew what it was like to feel full.

"Are you ready for me to fuck you now?"

I bit my lip, nodding frantically.

He started out slow but quickly built up to a frantic rhythm that had the cage shaking. His hands curled around the base of my wings, making me writhe on his cock. The noises coming from my mouth were obscene, embarrassing animal noises, but I didn't care. All that mattered was the promising ball of pleasure that grew with every thrust he made inside me.

"Come for me, baby."

The second the last word left his mouth, I came with a scream. He made me come not once but twice more before his movements became fragmented. He punched his hips up while pushing me down on his cock and finally expelling himself with the most erotic noise I'd ever heard fall from a man's lips.

A hot wash of cum filled me, its molten heat spreading through me, my muscles unwinding in the wake of the deepest satisfaction I'd ever felt. "*Fuuuuck.*"

Without pulling himself out, Daemon gently lowered me onto my back. His hands rested on either side of my head, peering down at me with a thunderstruck expression. His gaze roved down my body, which glistened under a thin sheen of sweat. When his eyes landed on the place where we were still connected, a delirious grin spread across his lips. "I'd hoped you'd bleed."

At that, my lungs slammed together, and I gasped for air. Peering down between us, I saw the dark stain of blood smearing the base of his cock. It was one of the hottest things I'd ever seen.

"You really are perfectly twisted, you know that?" he asked me in a whisper. "We're never going to let you go now that you're ours, Meg. We'll do whatever it takes to keep you safe."

Whatever it takes. For some reason, those words sent a chill through me, but I didn't question it. The moment was too perfect to disturb.

I fell still beneath him, and our chests knocked together as we gulped down air. I basked in the afterglow, enjoying the weight of his muscles on top of me. But then, a new pressure began building between my legs.

"What's happening?"

"I..." His hand wedged between us, and I gasped when his finger slipped inside me alongside his cock. He swore in Infernal. "This never happened with Alistair."

"What hasn't happened?"

"I think I'm knotting you."

A fresh wave of heat swirled through me. "Knotting? But isn't that for—"

"Breeding. Yes. Which was why it never happened with Alistair." His expression turned stony. I couldn't decipher it, but there was no hiding the raw hunger in his voice.

My breath stuttered. "I'm a succubus. I can't breed unless I want to."

A tendon ticked in the hellhound's jaw. "Yeah, try telling that to my dick."

"What do we do?"

He pressed into me, rolling his hips ever so slightly. I gasped at the sensation of him throbbing inside me, wedged in so tight that the intense pleasure of it was almost too much.

Almost.

"We stay here." His hushed whisper had the hair on my nape standing.

"Stay here? Like this? For how long?"

"Until the swelling goes down."

"It will be light out soon. What if people see us?" I didn't normally have any issues with being watched. But in a cage, with Daemon, literally stuck on him with his collar around my neck? The entire scene was obscene.

"What *if* people see us? You tell me," he challenged.

"I look like...like..."

"Like a bitch in heat?"

"You've got a lot of nerve."

"That's cute coming from the little half-blood, one-third my body weight, wrapped tight around my cock." His hand found my throat and gave it a gentle squeeze, the added pressure wringing more pleasure from me.

"I fucking hate you." The words came out on a swollen and strangled moan.

He chuckled softly. "Keep telling me that. One of these days, I might actually believe you."

We fell into silence for several minutes. Or maybe hours, time seemed to lose its meaning. Finally, I spoke up. "Daemon?"

The shifter's face was buried into the crook of my neck, his "hmm?" coming out muffled.

"Do you care about me?" I already knew the answer to the question. I needed to hear it from him anyway.

"I more than care about you. I'd commit murder for you."

Coming from Daemon, that was probably about as close to I love you as I would get.

An hour later, he was able to extract himself from my swollen lips with an embarrassing sound that had him growling softly.

Then he scooped me up in his arms and carried me outside. The sun was just starting to come up, the sky a pretty hue of dark blue with streaks of bubble gum pink.

At first, I thought he'd taken me to my trailer, but once we were inside and his masculine aroma invaded my senses, I realized he'd taken us to his.

He laid me in the bed and wiped me down with a cloth he got from the bathroom. Once he finished cleaning me, he tossed the rag aside and climbed into his bed next to me, tucking me against the cradle of his hard body.

My eyes shuttered the second my head hit the pillow. I wasn't sure how long we slept when I felt the bed shift. I flipped on my side to see him sitting on the edge of the mattress in fresh black pants and a black t-shirt. He hunched, muscles shifting as he laced up his boots.

"Where are you going?"

He stood up. A chain was wrapped around his knuckles with an obsidian pendant catching in the dim light.

"I'll be back," he grunted. "There's something I have to do."

"Is it dirty work for Alistair? Off to kill another bad guy?" I asked through a sleepy grin.

Daemon bent down, brushing a kiss to my temple. When he pulled away, he smiled, but even in the dark, I could see that it didn't reach his eyes. "Yeah, pup. That's exactly right."

THE END OF BOOK 1

Find out what happens next to Meg and her circus creeps in

Carnival Creeps: Sinner's Sideshow Book 2

About the Author

Aiden Pierce is a writer of dark paranormal romance and erotic horror. Her love stories are on the spooky side and usually end up with the monster or the villain getting the girl.

She lives in the Pacific Northwest with her husband and their three fur babies. When she's not daydreaming about the characters that live in her head, she can be found curled up on the couch with a black coffee and a dark romance novel.

www.ingramcontent.com/pod-product-compliance
Lightning Source LLC
Chambersburg PA
CBHW071729150726
47998CB00005B/1569